# WHEN THE CURTAIN FALLS

In 1952, two young lovers, Fawn Burrows and Walter Brown, meet backstage in a beautiful West End theatre during a production of *When the Curtain Falls*. Between clandestine meetings and stolen moments, they must hide their love from the one person who will stop at nothing to keep Fawn for himself. But tragedy and heartache are waiting in the wings for all the players ... Almost seventy years later, a new production arrives at the theatre, bringing with it Oscar Bright and Olive Green and their budding romance. But no sooner has the new cast settled into their dressing rooms than strange things begin to happen. Ghosts of productions past haunt the theatre, or so the story goes. Can Oscar and Olive get to the truth of the matter before tragedy strikes once more?

# SPECIAL MESSAGE TO READERS

## THE ULVERSCROFT FOUNDATION
**(registered UK charity number 264873)**
was established in 1972 to provide funds for
research, diagnosis and treatment of eye diseases.
Examples of major projects funded by
the Ulverscroft Foundation are:-

- The Children's Eye Unit at Moorfields Eye Hospital, London
- The Ulverscroft Children's Eye Unit at Great Ormond Street Hospital for Sick Children
- Funding research into eye diseases and treatment at the Department of Ophthalmology, University of Leicester
- The Ulverscroft Vision Research Group, Institute of Child Health
- Twin operating theatres at the Western Ophthalmic Hospital, London
- The Chair of Ophthalmology at the Royal Australian College of Ophthalmologists

You can help further the work of the Foundation
by making a donation or leaving a legacy.
Every contribution is gratefully received. If you
would like to help support the Foundation or
require further information, please contact:

## THE ULVERSCROFT FOUNDATION
**The Green, Bradgate Road, Anstey
Leicester LE7 7FU, England
Tel: (0116) 236 4325**

**website: www.foundation.ulverscroft.com**

# WHEN THE CURTAIN FALLS

## CARRIE HOPE FLETCHER

LARGE
PRINT

First published in Great Britain 2018
by
Sphere
an imprint of Little, Brown Book Group

First Isis Edition
published 2019
by arrangement with
Little, Brown Book Group

A catalogue record for this book is available
from the British Library.

ISBN 978–1–78541–764–1 (hb)
ISBN 978–1–78541–770–2 (pb)

Published by
F. A. Thorpe (Publishing)
Anstey, Leicestershire

Set by Words & Graphics Ltd.
Anstey, Leicestershire
Printed and bound in Great Britain by
T. J. International Ltd., Padstow, Cornwall

This book is printed on acid-free paper

This book is dedicated to all the ghosts haunting the UK's theatres. May the actors of today do you proud.

xxx

# Prologue

A certain kind of magic is born when the curtain rises. Intoxicated by the smell of the greasepaint and powered by the glow of the footlights, lovers successfully elope, villains get their just deserts and people die in epic stunts and yet live to tell the tale. Thousands pay to sit and be fooled by illusions and still jump to their feet to applaud despite their gullibility. It's an inexplicable, delicious, addictive power that keeps people entranced and coming back for more, again and again. However, for one theatre on one special night of the year, it's when the curtain falls that a whole different kind of magic takes to the stage. Mice scurry through the gaps in the walls, mirror lights flicker in the small hours of the morning and ghosts roam the wings in search of props from productions long past. When the curtain falls in the Southern Cross Theatre, the lonely stage door man wanders the halls checking each door is firmly bolted. All, that is, except one. He turns the key of dressing room four and swings the door open to find the lights still on and a faint scent of jasmine in the air. A high-backed green velvet armchair faces the mirrors, hiding the woman in the reflection from view. The man

1

doffs his cap to the red-headed lady and her green eyes sparkle at him.

"You're here," she says.

"Not disturbing you, am I?" he says with a wry smile.

"Never," says her reflection. "I'm always glad of the company. It's rare one finds it these days. Come and sit with me a while, won't you?"

"Always." He walks to the green armchair and swivels it around, only to find it empty, just as it is every year, on this day, when he comes to dressing room four. He sits down and faces the mirror where he watches the woman pull her pink silk dressing gown tighter around her shoulders.

"You look beautiful." He smiles, stroking his chin, trying to hide the wrinkles beneath his palm.

"Stop hiding," she says, reaching out a hand. "I know what you look like and you know that I like it. Seeing you is such a rarity. I can't bear it when you hide yourself away. It's almost unfair." Her eyes glisten in the yellow light, and he is afraid her tears will spill over.

"Sorry." He pulls his hands away and places them on the dressing table, his fingers splayed apart. "I know, I know." Every day of his life builds up to seeing her on this night each year and every year he feels like he lets her down. He's grown older, his skin has wrinkled further, his hair has greyed and yet she's stayed vibrant and sparkling, full of life and full of love for him.

"Please don't hide," she begs, her fingers pressing up against the glass.

"I won't ever hide from you. Never," he promises, pressing the tips of his fingers against hers, tricking

2

himself into believing that he can feel the warmth of her skin.

"It's almost time." Her voice catches in her throat.

"Already?" He checks his watch. 11:45p.m. Fifteen minutes.

She nods sadly and stands, her limbs carrying her to the reflection of the door. Her body moves slowly, as if through treacle, every muscle fighting against a force she can't control, a force that is carrying her away from him.

"I'm sorry," he sobs, a tear trickling down his weathered cheek.

"Don't be. All I ask is that you come earlier next year. Just a few more minutes, that's all I need."

"I hate letting you go," he whispers.

"Our time gets so much shorter and shorter and . . ."

"And what?"

"I feel like I'm losing you." She clutches the door frame, fighting the invisible tide that's crashing against her and forcing her back.

"You will never lose me. Not ever."

His gaze follows her reflection as she is pulled from the doorway. He gets to his feet and stumbles forward on his aching knees. Mirrors of all different shapes and sizes have been hung in an uneven line along the corridor walls. He catches a glimpse of her hair in one, the hem of her dressing gown in another and then her pleading eyes in the last one. Where he hasn't been able to hang mirrors, he's lined them up on the floor and propped them up against the walls so he can follow her stumbling legs. Some years she takes different routes through the corridors, past different dressing rooms and through different wings, desperately trying to cling to the theatre and the man she loved but ultimately, she is always pulled back to the same fateful place: centre stage. He chases her reflection, sometimes losing her and racing backwards, retracing his steps; it has become harder and harder every year as he struggles to keep up with her body elegantly bending and bowing away from him. It is a dance he had never learnt the right steps to and certainly one he never enjoys.

She calls his name and her voice echoes through the corridor as he turns the corner to see her silver shoe stepping through the golden frame of a mirror and delicately touching the floor. Despite the solid click of her heel against the stone as she pushes her way out of the frame, he can see the end of the corridor through her body. She is transparent and hazy but her green eyes still dazzle him to his very soul and his lips tremble at the sight of her, now in costume, ready for the stage. The train of her burgundy evening gown sweeps along the floor behind her as she is pulled from him once more, her beautifully coiffed blonde-wigged head twisting reluctantly away. People often speak of "the magic of the theatre" but they usually mean what happens on stage during a show. They don't know about the *real* magic that lingers within the theatre walls, left behind by every actor who treads the boards. And they don't know about the magic that takes hold of her every year, whipping her old pink dressing gown into burgundy silk and spinning her red hair into gold. The old man hobbles after her but with less desperation than before. Now that she is in costume, nothing can stop her and all he can do is watch from the wings just as he has done every year before. She pulls open the double stage doors and a silence falls over the theatre. Mice stop their scurrying and lights cease their humming. His breath catches as he watches her delicately sidestep props and set pieces, even though were she to come into contact with anything, she would float right through. She turns to face the stage and slowly the warm glow of the lights fades up and he can see the outline of her lovely face. It's all so achingly familiar — the way her cheeks flush at the thought of stepping out in front of an audience, the way she still touches the bridge of her nose even though she isn't wearing her glasses and the way her eyes swim when she turns to him and whispers, "I'm so sorry."

"It's me who couldn't save you." He stumbles forwards, steadying himself against the black painted walls, but her smile stills him.

"Oh, but you did, my love."

She takes a deep breath and makes her entrance onto the stage. He doesn't want to watch but the force that had dragged her to this place now has a hold on him too. It gently pulls his body to the spot she had just left. He dodges the props with much less grace but eventually he is manoeuvred into the same position that he takes up every year. Her dress ripples around her young, curved frame and her transparent skin still glows in the light but quickly that light turns blue and cold and the floor becomes slick with a thin layer of dry ice.

"*You were never supposed to find out this way,*" she says, her voice sultry and low, no longer her own.

"*You didn't do well to hide it,*" snarls a snide voice from the shadows. A figure steps into the blue light, tweed clad around his slight frame and smoke billowing from the cigar in his right hand. His thick, waxed moustache twitches against his powdered cheeks as his pale blue eyes drink in her beauty.

"*Leave her be, goddamn it.*" Another man appears in a tuxedo, his hair slicked back, jaw chiselled, but his eyes are hollow and don't appear to focus on her or the man in tweed. He isn't as present as she is, just a recalled memory, destined to rewind and repeat, year after year. He's on his knees, his lip bleeding. She runs to him and tries to help him up, but his body is heavy.

"*Please. Go back inside. Go home. Go anywhere but here.*" She looks behind her and lets her eyes settle on the figure watching them from the wings.

The woman he'd met in the dressing room only moments ago has been replaced by the woman from years before and he wishes that he'd seen back then the signs that something had been so utterly wrong. She, so usually full of light and hope, so young and oblivious, looked like a woman who was carrying the weight of the world on her shoulders. He could see it all so clearly now in this cruel memory; in the way she held herself and in the dullness in her eyes. If only he had noticed all those years ago, he may have been able to stop her, but his twenty-two-year-old self had been so blinded by love and the eagerness to escape to a new life with her. This night was meant to have been a night

6

of triumph. A night of life for their love and a night of death for all that stood in their way.

"*Yes, Larson. Do as she says.*" The man in tweed smiles, taking a long drag on his cigar, the smoke billowing from his lips as he speaks. Larson stays put.

"*Please, Lars. Not here.*"

"*She's not yours,*" Larson hisses through gritted teeth and from the wings he mouths the line along with him.

"*Actually, Lars . . . I am.*" She holds up her left hand and reveals a large engagement ring that sends slivers of light dancing on the black stage floor. The ghosts of the audience gasp and a few let out audible sobs.

"*Eliza . . . no,*" Larson whispers. "*NO!*" Larson pulls out a gun from his inside jacket pocket and aims it at the man in tweed. She jumps back, out of the way.

"*Oh, Larson.*" The man in tweed sighs and taps his cigar, ash falling to the floor. "*When will you learn? It doesn't matter how well you scrub up or how many lavish parties you sneak yourself into. It doesn't matter how many of London's finest you rub shoulders with or even how many wealthy women's beds you wheedle your way into. You will never be good enough.*"

"*Please don't listen to him, Lars. Just go back inside.*" She is Eliza now, immersed in her role. She puts her hands on Larson's arm and tries to lower the gun but Larson's hold is strong and steady.

"*Do you love him?*" Larson asks, not daring to glance away from the other man. Eliza looks at Larson, her eyes filling up but her face unchanging. "*Do you?*" he demands again.

"I fear you'll kill him either way."

"Eliza," he breathes. "If you tell me yes, how could you think that I would kill the man you love and put you through that misery? No, Eliza. Should you say yes, I will turn this gun on myself and the bullet will be destined for me."

More sobs erupt from the auditorium.

"Must we have all this drama? It's terribly dull," says the man, waving his hand, the smoke from his cigar billowing into the air, "We all know you don't have the gall to shoot a rabbit, let alone a man. Just put the gun down, Larson."

"Do . . . you . . . love . . . him?"

"I . . ." She hesitates and, back in the wings, Walter feels every nerve ending fizz. That wasn't her line then and it isn't her line now. He had wondered then if maybe she'd forgotten but she had never forgotten a line in her entire professional life. Was this the moment when she had second thoughts about their plan? He had wondered all those years ago what could possibly have stopped her from saying the line, but had he known, he wonders if he would have had the courage to stop it anyway. And now, utterly powerless, he is forced to watch once more.

"I . . ." A tear rolls down her flushed cheek. Her chest rises and pushes against the fabric of her dress. "I . . . do not," she says and what happens next is a blur.

The trigger is pulled, the sound of a gunshot rings out, the lights go out and the gasping audience is plunged into darkness. All of this is as it should have been.

8

"*Bring up the lights! The lights!*" shouts the man playing Larson. There is panic in his voice. Real panic.

Slowly the lights fade up to reveal her body, centre stage. Her limbs are grotesquely twisted underneath her from where she has fallen and blood is starting to pool and trickle onto the stage. The audience erupts into screams and people start to push their way out of the aisles, desperation and fear driving them forward. The crew and actors flood the stage but no one goes to her.

"Get out of here, boy."

He feels hot, wet breath on the nape of his neck and can smell the cigar smoke but when he turns his head all he sees is the darkness of the wing. Yet, he still hears a voice say . . .

"Run."

He looks back to the stage and he knows exactly why no one had rushed to her aid that night. He knows why there was a perfect circle of people around her and not one of them dared to close the distance. It wasn't fear or the amount of blood pouring from her. It wasn't the shock and horror of it all, it was the simple awful truth that there was no helping her. It was too late. He crouches in the wing, his tears falling onto the dusty floor, and he can see that the light and delicious vulnerability that used to live in her eyes, the light that she so happily shared when someone happened to glance her way, was gone.

His muscles relax and she and all of the other ghosts shimmer and fade and the stage is empty and cold once more. His eyes sting and he wills himself to stop crying.

He trudges back through the wing, his step heavy, and sighs at the thought of putting all the mirrors away. He has time though, so he walks past the mirrors, leaving them against the walls, useless to him now, and goes to his desk in his small room just inside the stage door. Newspaper cuttings cover every wall. Each one contains news and reviews of various productions of *When The Curtain Falls*, collected over the years, and clippings of the headshots of its ever-changing cast. He opens the laptop sitting on his desk and it springs into life and by the time he has managed to sink into the armchair, several emails have already pinged into his inbox. He scrolls through them, but one in particular catches his eye. It's from the production company that owns the Southern Cross Theatre and the subject line reads *Next In — CURTAIN FALLS*. His old heart drums against his ribs with more force than he thought it still had and his veins fill with fire. He opens the email with shaking fingers.

Dear Walter,
I am very pleased to announce that once *Gone With The Wind* closes, April brings with it a brand new revival of *When The Curtain Falls*, exactly 66 years on, almost to the date. An obscure choice, perhaps, but we've discovered this play has a cult following, largely due to an accident that occurred during its last production which also happened to be at the Southern Cross Theatre. We think the combination of this connection and our new star-studded cast will pull in the punters!

The show also has a wonderful plot that we think audiences today will still connect with and enjoy. The show starts with a pair of young teens who we can tell are destined to spend their lives together. However, she is from money and sadly, he is not and while she is sent away to school in the USA, the boy, determined to win the girl and seeing no other way of earning the riches that may also earn his way into her life, becomes somewhat of a con artist. When the couple meet again as adults, he has far more money than he'd ever dreamed of having, gained by clever but questionable means and he isn't exactly who he says he is and whilst he is now a man of importance, is it worth the price he'll pay to get the girl?

We hope you will welcome our new family with open arms, as you always do. Attached is a cast list to help you get acquainted with them all. They start rehearsals in East London at the end of January and will be rehearsing in the theatre from February 12th, ready to open on April 1st.

Sad to say goodbye to such a successful run of *Gone With The Wind* but we're all very excited here in the office about this new production and hope you are too.

Kind Regards,
Susie Quentin
Toastie Productions Ltd


He sits back in his chair, his breaths coming fast and quick. It's only when his gaze settles on the pair of eyes looking out at him from the photo on his desk that he calms down.

"Oh, darling. I wonder what you'll make of this." He picks up the frame and looks at the glint of mischief in her eyes. "You've caused havoc for the shows you do like and pure hell for the ones you don't. What will you do when you're watching someone else play Eliza? Not to mention when they survive each performance?" His desk lamp flickers. "Come now. You have to play nice. When The Curtain Falls is a good show. All casts are family but this one more so because this is your show. OK?" His desk lamp flickers again. "Oh, sweetheart." He clicks on the attachment in the email and scrolls down to find the face of the actress who is destined to play Eliza.

"Olive Green." The lamp turns off with a loud clunk. "I have a feeling you may be sorry you ever said yes."

TOASTIE PRODUCTIONS PRESENTS A
PRODUCTION BY C. H. FLETCHER

OLIVE GREEN and
OSCAR BRIGHT in

# WHEN the
# CURTAIN
# FALLS

Directed by
MICHAEL HUGHES

---

# THE SOUTHERN
# CROSS THEATRE

SHAFTESBURY AVENUE, LONDON

OPENS 1 APRIL 2018

# CHAPTER
# ONE

## Enjoy

Where the lights were the dimmest and the carpets were the dampest. That's usually where you would find Oscar Bright. He'd turn down the brightness setting on his phone and yet would still shield it with his hand just in case anyone might see his face as they passed the quick-change room in which he was hiding.

"Well, this is . . . classy," Olive whispered with a smile as she slunk in through the doorway after glancing back, making sure no one had followed. She closed the door behind her.

"Shhh . . ." said Oscar, rushing to her and wrapping his arms around her waist, holding her as close to him as he could manage.

"I'm being quiet!" she laughed into his shoulder. "Is this really the best place we could have met?" Her green eyes squinted at the peeling wallpaper and the props and odd bits of costume strewn across the chairs that lined the walls, bits of gaffer tape with names written on them stuck above them. Then she looked at him, taking him in properly even though she'd seen him the day before. His short black hair had clearly had nothing more than his fingers run through it that morning and the bags under his eyes were fuller than usual but even so, the blue of his irises shone down at her and his big toothy smile made her stomach lurch. As he sighed, happy to be close to her again, she caught the faint whiff of beer on his breath.

"Were you out again last night?" she asked, stroking his cheek.

He ignored her question and gestured around him. "This is best I could do at short notice." He shrugged, the movement bringing her closer to his face. "I wanted to see you before everyone else got here." He squeezed her tighter.

"Before anyone was around to see us, more like," she sighed.

"Hey, now. You know it's not like that." Oscar rocked her from side to side.

"Then why are we hiding? Why are we always finding the dingiest corners to be together in if it 'isn't like that'?" Olive turned her face away but still stayed close to him. Oscar snaked his fingers under her blonde, sun-kissed hair and stroked the back of her neck with his thumb.

"Okay, okay. It kind of is like that but you know it's not because I'm hiding *you*. *We're* hiding. *Together.*"

She raised her eyebrows, her lips pursed.

"I know this isn't ideal," he went on and kissed the top of her head. "But it's all I can really give right now."

"I'm not asking for a grand announcement. I don't want fancy hotels, flash cars and cocktails on tap, Oz. That's not me, you know that. I'm just asking for . . ." The word *you* got caught on her tongue and it melted

16

before she could say it. "I'm just asking for a little more of your time. I'm asking not to be made to feel like you're embarrassed of . . . whatever this is." She checked her phone. 8:55. "I'm asking to not have to meet you at the crack of dawn before rehearsals start and I'm asking if we can meet somewhere that doesn't smell like dead mouse."

Oscar pulled away and lifted her chin with a finger. "Is that what that is?"

"Yes, Oz. That is the unmistakable smell of rotting rodent somewhere in the walls of this room." They both took a moment to take in the room and all its (former) glory. Although the door was closed and neither of them said it out loud, they shared the feeling that they weren't entirely alone, but they both put it down to the adrenaline of hiding and the fear of being caught.

"Wonderful. You don't get many of them on set."

"The mice in the walls are harmless. It's the rats in the cast you usually need to worry about." She pulled her face away from his touch and he noticed that the look in her eyes had grown a little colder, sadder.

"Don't do that." Oscar shook her lightly. He had seen her roll her eyes a thousand times. Heard her say things specifically designed to push him away. Watched her harden and put up walls within seconds. Whilst he knew it was all to protect herself, he already felt tired at having to fight against the barriers she built up between them.

"What?" she said, fiddling with the sleeve of his T-shirt, nibbling the inside of her lip.

"Maybe we should just forget this." Oscar loosened his arms around her and stepped back, but Olive stepped forward, caught his hands and put them back on her waist. "Olive," he groaned. "I'm not what you need."

"Of course you're not," she admitted. "But you are what I want. It just sometimes feels like . . . I'm not what *you* want." *Although I'm probably what you need*, she thought. "I never feel like I'm good enough."

Olive had been warned about Oscar when she'd found out she would be working with him. He was new to the theatrical circles she'd been part of for most of her life, but he'd starred in one of the biggest soaps on television and while he wasn't quite a household name, he was certainly becoming more recognisable. His picture had appeared in various magazines, a different girl on his arm in each of them. Apparently, he'd broken up with each and every single one of them in quick succession because, according to the magazines, he'd deemed them all "not good enough" for him. The latest dumpee had been his on-screen girlfriend, an actress called Zadie Lanette, and now her side of the story was splashed across every tabloid that would pay her enough. As soon as Olive had met Oscar she knew she was in trouble. It wasn't just his ridiculous good looks or his excessive charm. It was how much he made her laugh and how at ease she felt when she knew he was just in the wings.

"What do you mean?" Oscar asked.

Olive looked down at her baggy grey dress and the chunky black boots that she wore nearly every day, even in the height of summer. She wasn't wearing any makeup and her hair still had hairspray in it from rehearsals the day before. "I'm not exactly magazine material. I'm not the sort of girl you'd usually go for."

"Magazines . . .? Olive, what are you talking about? I don't care about that. I'm here, aren't I? I'm here telling you that I like you. Doesn't that mean anything?"

"Of course it does!" she said, looking up into his face. His eyebrows pulled together in a frown and she felt her chest tighten. She went back to fiddling with his sleeve or she'd never get out what she wanted to say. "It means a lot," she whispered. "You just need to know that sometimes . . . I'm going to feel like I don't match up to your expectations."

"I have no expectations. Besides . . . *you* don't feel good enough, Miss Star-Of-The-West-End-Stage? People practically bow to you as you walk past. This is very much your territory. I'm the one who's way out of their depth here."

"Being good at my job doesn't have any bearing on how I feel about this, us, you," Olive said quietly.

"And how *do* you feel about me?" Oscar's lips twitched into a subtle smile, any trace of concern forgotten and replaced with mischief.

"I feel annoyed by you," she said, swallowing what she actually wanted to say. "I've made it clear how I feel. It's you that insists we meet in secret."

"You know I like you but . . . It wasn't all that long ago that I broke up with Zadie. Very publicly, too. Being seen out and about with you could be disastrous for everyone. I can't do that to you."

"Or her . . ." Olive muttered.

"Or *you*. Don't believe everything you read in those magazines, Olive." Oscar brushed his hair back with both of his hands and his chest heaved underneath Olive's fingertips as he let out a heavy sigh.

"I'm aware of the situation, Oz. It's just . . . frustrating."

"Then, like I said, maybe we should stop. The last thing I want to do is hurt you. Or make you feel like you're getting anything less than you deserve." Oscar tried to pull away again, but Olive held his strong arms in her slim fingers and he stopped resisting.

"Then don't hurt me," she said.

"Is it that simple?" Oscar took her face in his hands and the eyes he saw staring back already looked fragile. "I'd rather have this than nothing at all. I don't think I could see you every day knowing what we once had and not having it any more." Oscar moved a strand of her hair away from her eyes and held her cheek in his palm.

"As long as this is what you want?" Olive asked. She didn't realise she'd been holding her breath until he said, "Of course it is."

He kissed her then and Olive hated herself for feeling lucky. Of all the things she thought she could feel when someone's lips were pressed against hers, she suspected lucky was probably one of the worst. Inwardly, she berated herself as Oscar's teeth gently pulled at her bottom lip and she let her body lean against him for fear of her legs giving way beneath her. She wasn't starstruck by Oscar, and nor did the novelty of having a fling with a celebrity appeal to her. She hadn't put him on a pedestal and nor did she think he was a perfect god-like creature incapable of making mistakes. Olive had simply fallen for a good-looking man who was kind, funny and, self-admittedly, a little lost.

Olive had never been lucky in love. She'd had a handful of romances with fellow actors, but they'd all eventually ended due to commitment issues or worse, affairs with chorus girls in dingy corners of theatres much like the one she was now standing in herself. The chances of this time being any different were slim (she knew that, but he just felt so *good*) and so waiting for something to go wrong made Olive defensive and doubt if spending time with Oscar was worth it at all. Olive gently pushed herself away from his embrace when she felt the familiar urge to be closer to him start to pulse through her body.

"Everything okay?" he whispered, a strand of black hair falling over his left eye, and Olive hated how he could make unkempt look so suave.

"Yeah. Just . . . *enjoying* you." She smiled, her slightly crooked front teeth showing, and Oscar smiled back.

"I'm enjoying you too." Oscar rubbed his nose against hers and held her tighter.

Olive Green was what people described as a "gem". She was always where you needed her to be and perfectly on time. A million secrets from a million different corners of the West End buzzed around her head and when they were inevitably discovered, as is the nature of the loose-lipped theatre industry, you could guarantee it was not Olive's lips that had come loose. Olive was the person you asked when you wanted something done. When it came to staying late after rehearsals to discuss a scene further, of course Olive would stay. In fact, when it came to pretty much anything, Olive would very rarely be able to say no. Whether it was a need to be liked, a fear of being disliked or just a love of helping people out when they needed her, Olive ran herself ragged for everyone, and yet always found herself alone at the end of the day.

When she'd first burst, fresh out of drama school, straight into a leading role as her peers and tutors had expected, she'd been unnervingly trusting. Behind the West End's curtains were, of course, some of the world's most beautiful humans, inside and out. However, lurking in plain sight were those who favoured fame, power and money over a love of telling stories and who would do almost anything to reach their end goal. It quickly became apparent that Olive wasn't good at spotting the bad apples and would always be willing to help out those who would never return the favour.

After the end of year party for the cast of *Oklahoma!*, which Olive had organised whilst also performing eight shows a week *and* rehearsing for her next acting job during the day, she'd finally broken down and found a corner of the club to have a little cry. It was there that the oldest and most sober cast member had found her, weeping.

"Don't set yourself on fire to keep others warm, dearie," she'd said, and it was advice Olive had carried with her ever since, although she still had trouble following it. She looked at Oscar and she could already feel the flames around her feet from where she'd willingly thrown down a match because she thought she'd seen him shiver. Olive, who had already been badly burned herself, wasn't very good at guarding her heart, although she certainly wasn't naive. She was merely good at throwing caution to the wind and listening to her heart rather than her head, even when she knew there was a rather large possibility of getting hurt. Olive chased the feeling of being romanced and loved, and even if she only felt it for a day, she thought it was worth the scars she'd be left with. Despite her devil-may-care attitude, Olive always *hoped* things would work out for the best in each of her romantic endeavours. Actors seemed to be an untrustworthy kind and although she knew it was her choice of man and her choice to open herself up to potential hurt, it didn't make the hurt any less painful when she caught that man kissing someone else in the darkened corners of the theatre or heard from her cast mates that he'd been seen outside of the theatre seemingly loved-up with someone else. Olive had started to wonder whether it was her but when she had those thoughts she reminded herself that no one was forced to cheat or treat people without respect. Sadly, Olive just hadn't been lucky and she hoped with all her heart that this time, maybe this time, she would be.

"Eggs Florentine?" asked the waitress.

"That's me." Olive half raised her hand. The Southern Cross had a little café front of house in which Olive and Oscar often had breakfast and lunch (and sometimes even dinner). The theatre was the one place they felt it was justified they could be seen together without raising suspicion. They were playing opposite each other as onstage lovers, so why wouldn't they spend time together when offstage?

"And the Full English is yours, I assume?" the waitress said with a giggle.

"Yes, thanks," said Oscar, smiling at Olive, but Olive could only look at the waitress. She had tousled brown curls held loosely by pins at the back of her head, and a full face of simple, understated yet flawless make-up. The smell of her floral perfume wafted over the table as she walked away with a wink in Oscar's direction. He didn't notice.

"What?" Oscar asked, seeing Olive grasp her fork a little too tightly.

"Hmm? Nothing! Nothing," she said, cutting into the poached egg, the runny yolk oozing over the spinach.

"I hate it when you do that," he said, lightly grazing the tip of his shoe against her leg.

"I'm not doing anything! Honestly, it's nothing. I just . . ." Olive dipped the prongs of her fork in the bright orange goo and drizzled it in patterns around the edge of her white plate.

"You just . . .?" He pressed her leg again a little harder.

"I just sometimes wonder if you'd rather be sat here with someone else," she said into her lap, fiddling with the crumpled hem of her dress.

"Who?" Oscar looked around the almost empty café. An elderly man sat in the corner reading a newspaper and wiping tomato ketchup from the corner of his mouth on the sleeve of his coat. "Him?"

"The waitress." Olive nodded towards the bar where the brunette was twirling a loose strand of hair around her finger and flicking her eyes in Oscar's direction.

"Annie?" he whispered, pointing so that Annie couldn't see.

"You know her name?" Olive's heart sank.

"Only because she told me when I bought a coffee the first day we got here!"

"I'm sure she did."

"What's that supposed to mean?" Oscar said, a little stung.

"Why me?" she blurted out and then wanted to kick herself for sounding so needy. "I mean . . . I know that sounds like I'm fishing. I'm not fishing, I swear, I just . . . you're *Oscar Bright*." Olive splayed her fingers to the sides of her face and wiggled them like jazz hands. "And you're sat here with . . . Olive Green." She stuck out her tongue like she'd tasted something foul.

"No. I'm Oscar Bright." He gestured to himself in his scruffy tracksuit which he'd already managed to spill baked beans down. "And I'm sat here with *Olive Green*." He smiled at her and reached across the table for her hand. It was the most affection he'd ever shown her in public and whether he'd forgotten himself or whether he was deliberately making it known to those in the vicinity that they may be more than just friends, Olive didn't care and then she instantly gave herself a stern talking to. *Stop feeling grateful that he's showing you the affection you already deserve*, she thought. *He's got you wrapped around his little finger and you're thanking him for letting you be there?* She wriggled her hand out of his grasp and put it back in her lap, giving him an apologetic smile so not to appear too cold.

"I'm here with you, because I enjoy you," Oscar clarified. "Because I love your company and there's no one else at this present time that I would rather be here with."

*At this present time.*

"Okay." She nodded.

"I don't know what more I can say to convince you." Oscar sighed, sticking his fork into a sausage. "Besides, there might be someone you've got your eye on. How am I to know? And that would be fine, by the way."

"It would be *fine*?" Olive's heart sank further.

"Yeah . . . I mean . . . if you decided you'd prefer to . . . spend your time with someone else. That would be fine." He cut the sausage with a little more intensity than he expected, and the knife squeaked against the plate.

"Well, there isn't. Anyone else, I mean."

"No?" he said, not looking up from the now-massacred sausage.

"No, of course not. Is there someone else you'd rather spend your time with?"

"I've already told you there isn't. That's where this all started." He stuck a large chunk of meat into his mouth with such vigour that he almost choked on it.

"I know. I've just . . . I don't know. We've all got demons, I guess." She picked up her knife and fork again. "Sorry," she said it so quickly it was almost as if she hadn't said it at all. She gathered food onto her fork but noticed a lack of movement from the other side of the table. She glanced up. Oscar was holding his knife and fork aloft, on either side of his head like horns. When he saw her looking, he furrowed his brow, crossed his eyes and stuck out his bottom teeth. Despite herself, Olive laughed.

"Is that supposed to be one of my demons?"

"One of them? How many you got in there?" He stretched out his arm and tapped the side of her head.

"Too many," she said with a small smile.

"We all do," he muttered.

"Huh? What was that?"

"Good food?" he asked.

"*Really* good." She was pretty sure he'd said something else, but she'd let it go. For now. She wiped away a bit of yolk that had dribbled over her bottom lip. "We should come here more often."

"As often as you like." He smiled, stroking her leg again.

If only Olive knew just how Oscar felt. It was rare these days that anyone wanted to know who Oscar really was. Everyone thought they already knew him once they'd read the magazines and watched his countless interviews and what they saw, they loved.

Being papped at glamorous parties, premieres and press nights drew a certain type of woman his way. So when they discovered he only attended those parties for twenty minutes before going home to his little one-bedroom flat in Bow, and he only attended the premieres of the things he really wanted to see rather than going to everything for the exposure, the word "disappointed" didn't cut it for the high maintenance girls he had a habit of attracting. Oscar thought it was fine to wear designer gear, to eat out in central London every night and to want to be in every magazine Tesco had to offer but often when the girls he dated found out that wasn't who Oscar really was, they'd only stay with him for their image, making him feel miserable until he eventually ended things . . . and then they'd sell their exclusive story about how he'd broken their hearts. Oscar was beginning to wonder if every relationship would be the same.

Then he met Olive. Olive who cared about what he thought and made him feel like a person rather than a prop in a TV show. He could talk about how he actually felt, not how he was supposed to feel. He could say what he actually thought instead of having to carefully craft answers, and instead of striking poses for cameras and donning his designer clothes, Olive happily accepted him with his uncombed hair, his creased tracksuit bottoms and his T-shirt that was full of holes. He could be silly, and she didn't bat an eyelid. In fact, it made her laugh which made him want to behave that way even more, just so he could see her smile again. They'd go out after rehearsals and it would be Olive who suggested going somewhere quiet because she knew he hated feeling like he was being watched. He'd known her for just over a month and he felt more at home in her company than most of the people he'd surrounded himself with for years. However, as Oscar's TV star had risen he'd been trained to only ever give away a little of himself. As soon as you part with too much of yourself, you lose ownership of your own privacy and he was fighting against giving himself entirely to Olive. Nagging voices in his head told him not to trust her too much and they spoke of all the things that could go wrong if he did. Oscar Bright, star of stage and screen, was too good to be true — but Oscar Bright who lived in Bow and went to bed each night desperately alone didn't feel like he could ever live up to who the magazines said he was.

A wave of Olive's hair fell over her face and the end caught in her egg yolk. Oscar's heart swelled at the sight and Olive glanced up, obviously hoping his eyes were elsewhere. He coughed and averted his gaze just in time, but his heart remained happy. The waitress had reappeared, for no rhyme or reason, and asked, "Enjoying?" To which Oscar looked at Olive and said, "Yes. Very much so."

# CHAPTER
# TWO

## Unlocking The Gate

Oscar was one of those rare individuals who had found celebrity at a young age. Or rather, celebrity had found him. His career began as a child actor in a soap opera but as he'd grown, so had his part. And whilst he'd enjoyed his time on the set of *Love Lane*, he had spent ten years in the show, and now felt it was time to move on to new, more exciting projects. Work had poured in. Personal appearances, commercials, paid endorsements and even turning on the Regent Street Christmas lights, but nothing that flared his passion for acting. Every new offer seemed trivial and meaningless. Nothing he could really sink his teeth into as an actor.

"Panto? . . . Really?" Oscar sighed down the phone.

"Rickmansworth would love to have you!" Cassandra, his overenthusiastic agent, shouted excitedly. "They're doing Cinderella this Christmas!"

"I really don't want to be Prince Charming," he groaned.

"Well, that's good! That's good!" He could practically hear her nodding down the phone.

"What? Why?" he asked.

"They're offering you Buttons!"

BEEEEEP. Oscar had terminated their phone call and, later that week, their contract over a very expensive lunch. It didn't take him long to find new representation and his new agent seemed far more tuned in on Oscar's potential as an actor, as opposed to the cash he could make them solely through personal appearances. So when an audition for the role of Larson Hardy in *When The Curtain Falls* had arisen, Oscar was the first name to be put forward. An actor of his celebrity being attached to such an obscure show could only be good for business, but what was even better was that he'd nailed his audition. Oscar was perfect for the role.

What he hadn't counted on was meeting Olive.

"This is Olive Green. Your co-star. She'll be playing Eliza Small opposite you," Michael Hughes, their director, had said on the first day of rehearsals. The room was noisy and packed, bustling with the cast and other creative types. Awkward hellos between actors who didn't know each other at all or only half knew each other through friends or worse, knew of each other via other actors they'd slept with.

"Hi," Olive beamed, taking the hand Oscar was holding out for her to shake, stepping forward to kiss his cheek and accidentally treading on his toe. "Oh God! So sorry! Big feet."

"It's fine! It's fine!" Oscar laughed. "Careful though! I reckon those boots could take someone down."

"Well, they have done before. What's to stop me again?" She pulled her blonde hair back behind her ear and Oscar smiled without really knowing why. What she'd said hadn't even been all that funny, but it was as though someone had pulled a cord inside of him causing his heart to light up like a bulb, the fluorescent beams with nowhere else to go, shining out of his face.

It was then he realised that no one had said anything for several seconds.

"Yes, well ... I hope you two enjoy working together," Michael said, ending the moment between them and turning to address some other members of the cast.

Oscar turned quickly on the heels of his brown shoes, taking a seat on one of the chairs placed at the front of the room, which suddenly felt a few degrees warmer than it had before. As the rehearsal progressed, he found that he was unable to stop looking at his co-star during their read through, even during the scenes neither of them were in when he had no excuse to be looking her way. He even missed a cue for one of his lines, his script left forgotten in his lap, the page unturned. Occasionally, she'd catch him staring at her, and she seemed to find it hard to pull her own eyes away.

The world of theatre had acted like a flame to the flash paper that was their friendship. After mere weeks of rehearsals, Olive and Oscar were growing increasingly fond of each other and certain people around them had started to notice.

"Okay, okay, if you had to sleep with someone in the cast, who would it be?" asked Tamara Drake, a spindly creature whose smiles were saved only for those with the potential to further her career.

"Must we always play these games?" Oscar sighed.

Jane, a smaller, slender girl whose name was as plain as her face, giggled.

"If you *had* to," Tamara pressed, and flashed her teeth at Oscar. He brushed back his floppy fringe with one swift movement, his bicep tensing. Jane almost choked on her bottled water.

"What, I'm being held at gunpoint?" Oscar asked.

"Who would hold you at gunpoint and demand that you had sex with someone?" said Howard, a broad man who squeezed his way into the circle and awkwardly crossed his muscular legs, knocking over someone's can of Pepsi in the process.

"For someone who's playing a cunning villain, you're sooo clumsy, Howard," Jane sighed, sliding someone else's bag out of the way of the approaching pool of Pepsi.

"I'm not clumsy," Howard answered, mopping up the puddle with the towel he'd brought to the incredibly hot rehearsal room for when things got a bit sweaty.

"Well, you're large then," Jane continued, clearly enjoying teasing her fellow cast mate.

"You're not large, everyone else is simply too small," Olive said, smiling at Howard whilst sliding herself away from the spillage.

"*Anyway* . . ." Tamara said, repositioning herself. "A man is holding you at gunpoint and demanding you sleep with someone."

"Slightly odd demand for a criminal to make, isn't it?" said Doug, split-leaping across the room into the centre of the assembled group, his thin blond hair bouncing about his face.

"Sit down, Doug, you're making me dizzy!" laughed Olive, reaching for his hand. Doug took it, but instead of sitting down next to Olive, he pulled her to her feet, held her close to him and started to waltz.

The pair turned together in the centre of the circle the cast had created, before Doug spun Olive past Oscar and out into the empty room behind the group. His white tank top showed off his strong, muscular arms and had Olive not had eyes for Oscar, being literally swept off her feet like this might have otherwise made her swoon. However, having been friends with him since drama school, Olive considered Doug to be the brother she'd never had.

"I can see you looking at him," Doug whispered in her ear as he held her close and rocked her back and forth as they slowly turned in a tight circle.

"Who?" Olive whispered back, feebly, and she felt Doug sigh against her. "Everyone looks at Oscar," she continued, thankful that her head was resting against his shoulder and he couldn't see her blushing face. She glanced towards the group, but Oscar wasn't looking their way.

"Not the way you do," Doug said. "You look at him as though you don't expect or want anything from him."

"That's because I don't."

"Exactly. Do you realise how rare that must be for him?"

"I guess . . ."

"You also don't look at him like you want to eat him alive." He pulled back, so he could gesture behind him. Olive waited until they'd turned so that she was facing the group and saw that Tamara was baring her teeth again with a little more tenacity.

"You've got a chance, y'know," Doug said, resting his head against her hair.

"I'm not sure I want it. It feels a bit . . . cliché."

"What do you mean?" Doug tried to pull away to see her face, but she held him tightly in place.

"He's the man everyone falls for. I mean . . . has anyone actually ever told him 'no'?"

Doug laughed. "Probably not. I know it's infuriating but the thing is . . . he seems like a good guy. I think he's oblivious to his own . . . overall attractiveness. Which annoyingly makes him more attractive." Olive felt Doug shake his head.

"Do you think so?"

"Do I think he's attractive? Honey, I'm straight and even I want a slice of that pie."

Olive tutted in Doug's ear. "I mean do you think he's oblivious to just how good-looking he is?" She glanced over at the group again. Tamara had now taken Olive's empty spot on the floor next to Oscar and was laughing too hard at something he said. She used this as an excuse to touch his bicep, leaving her hand there and rubbing her thumb in circles across his skin. Olive, suddenly wishing she hadn't vacated her seat to dance with Doug, also realised she'd been staring for too long, which was only confirmed by Tamara whipping her head around and making direct eye contact with

**35**

her. Olive shut her eyes and buried her head back in the curve of Doug's neck.

"You know he's noticed you too?" Doug whispered.

"I should hope so! I play his lover," she laughed.

"You know what I mean. He looks at you the same way."

"I know, I know. I just feel a bit silly, like we're back in school. And I don't want to be lumped in with the hordes of other girls that throw themselves at him daily."

"You mean like Jane and Tamara?" Doug whispered, cupping his hand against her ear. Olive gasped dramatically and batted him back with her palm, still slowly turning about the room.

"Well . . . you said it. Not me!" She felt a little weight lift from her soul knowing that it wasn't just her who thought the other women's behaviour a little forthright. Whilst she felt childish, Jane and Tamara had made themselves look it and she vowed never to stoop as low to fight for Oscar's affections. "I think I'd rather sit this one out," she sighed.

"Well, that's your call but just so you know, he doesn't look at them like he looks at you." Doug kissed her cheek with a smack. "And every time I've turned you away from the group, he's glanced over here to check we're not snogging. So, that's something, eh?" Again, she batted him away playfully, feeling her cheeks flush once more but a sense of triumph fill her heart.

"Okay, gang! Back in!" called Michael, with his mouth still full of sandwich. With only a hint of reluctance, the cast got to their feet. All except Tamara.

**36**

"Oscar!" she called from the floor, holding out her arms and wiggling her long, delicate fingers. Oscar took them and gently pulled her up. "You're coming for a drink tonight, aren't you?" she said, placing her hands on his chest.

"I think so," he answered, stepping backwards and almost bumping into Olive who had wandered over to get her script even though she already knew all her lines off by heart. "Depends if this one is." He draped his arm around Olive's shoulders.

"Me?" Olive smiled.

"Her?" Tamara said, her sweet character momentarily slipping. "You're more than welcome, Olive. I just don't know if it's your thing."

"Where are you going?" Olive pulled her cardigan sleeves over her hands.

"The Hideout." Tamara shimmied, leaning in towards Oscar.

"The Hideout?" Oscar stepped back again. "Oh, well then, I'm definitely not going. That place is constantly crawling with paparazzi."

"I know. Why do you think we like it there?" Jane added as she passed them.

"I'm not really big on clubs." Olive's palms started to clam up.

"No, I didn't think you would be," Tamara said with a glance down at her boots. "I don't suppose much dancing gets done in *those*." She laughed.

"I dunno!" said Oscar. "I reckon she's got some secret moves." He did a "raising the roof" gesture with his upturned palms.

"Oh, they're not secret. Pole dancing's my thing, actually." Olive nodded.

"Yeah?" Oscar smirked.

"Yup." Her expression only wavered a fraction as she bent down to collect her script. She brushed her hair back from her face to let Oscar catch a glimpse of her smirk.

"Well, maybe we *should* go tonight, then? You can show off your moves." He folded his arms.

"And you can just . . . show off?" she smiled, and Oscar gasped, holding a hand against his heart.

"Ouch! Hurtful, *hurtful* words, Miss Green."

"So, you *are* coming?" Tamara asked, taking Oscar's hand and clutching it between her perfectly manicured nails.

"Is it happening?" Oscar looked at Olive, raising his eyebrows.

"Well . . ."

Oscar pouted at her.

"Oh, all right. We're in," Olive surrendered, and Oscar wrenched his hand free from Tamara's talons and held it out to high five with Olive.

"I just hope you're ready for this." Olive bit her bottom lip mock-seductively, and started to body ripple over-enthusiastically.

"There are those moves I was talking about!" Oscar stuck out his bum and started to shake it, Beyoncé style, mimicking her face of concentration. Olive laughed but it died in her throat when she caught Tamara rolling her eyes over Oscar's shoulder.

"Enough of that, you two!" Michael said, giving them the side eye but smiling all the same.

"Is it true this theatre has a mouse problem?" asked Jane, and although she had obviously changed the subject, Olive was grateful that the heat was off her.

"All theatres have mice," Michael replied without looking up, flipping through his script to find the right page.

"It's the ghosts you've got to worry about," said Doug, wiggling his fingers around Jane's head in an attempt to spook her, but she simply batted him away.

"Ghosts?" Oscar raised an eyebrow.

"Nearly every theatre in the West End has a ghost," Olive said, dragging a chair into place as part of their makeshift rehearsal set.

"Some have more than others," Howard added, hauling a table on its mark.

"The older ones, for sure!" Doug continued, sitting himself onto Howard's table.

"And this is just an accepted thing. That ghosts exist and the West End is infested with them?"

"Absolutely."

"Of course."

"Didn't you know?" They all nattered back, except Tamara.

"Of course they don't exist," she said.

"Thank you, Tamara!" Oscar shouted, folding his arms and sitting down in Olive's chair, enjoying her little exaggerated huff behind him. "See. The voices of reason." Oscar looked at Olive and gestured to himself and Tamara.

"Erm . . ." Doug raised his hand. "I'm calling bullshit," he said with a glint in his eye.

"What?" said Tamara, sitting on the floor and stretching out her legs into second position, her flexibility on show.

"When we were in *West Side Story* at the Festival theatre in Edinburgh last year I don't think I've ever seen anyone move as fast as you did when you ran into our dressing room, crying because you thought you'd seen the Great Lafayette."

"No, I didn't," Tamara snapped.

"Yes," Doug laughed. "You did!"

"Who?" asked Oscar.

"Lafayette." Olive turned to Oscar. "He was a magician that died in a fire when one of his tricks went wrong on stage. His ghost has been known to haunt the left wing ever since."

"Just the left wing?" Oscar folded his arms.

"Yup," said Doug.

"Right . . ."

"No, the left," Doug smirked.

"Something the matter?" Olive leant around from behind Oscar to get a look at his cynical face, her cheeks rosy, and her eyes sparkling with humour.

"No, no. Nothing at all. Everyone in this room believes in a ghost that only haunts one half of a theatre. Everything's . . . normal," he chuckled.

"Look, be as sceptical as you like, but sometimes spooky things happen that no one can explain," Olive said, plonking herself down on the floor beside him. She glanced over at Michael, who was still sipping his takeaway coffee and flipping through his notes and script pages. She estimated they had at least another four to six minutes before he realised he'd let them all slip into chatter again.

"I'm not sceptical. I'm right! Ghosts don't exist."

"Look, we're not judging you, Oscar. We all thought that too before we stepped inside a draughty, creaky, dark and spooky theatre where the rules of time and space don't apply."

"The rules of time and space . . . did everyone smoke something during the lunch break and I missed out?"

"What Olive means is, you'll spend what you think is four hours in a theatre doing rehearsals only to find out it's been five minutes," Doug explained.

"And you'll be in someone's dressing room one day and when you go to find it the next, it won't be where you left it," Howard chipped in.

"And all the hiding places you think are secret are never quite secret enough!" said Sammy from the doorway with her great big rucksack perched on her back and her dance clothes on underneath her coat.

"And finally, she arrives!" Olive cried, getting up from the floor and rushing to hug her friend. "How'd it go?"

"How it always goes." Sammy rolled her eyes and wiped her dark hair off her sweaty forehead.

"So you nailed it then?"

"They want to see me again, but you can just never tell, can you? They keep their cards so close to their chest."

"Well, the fact they want to see you again is amazing," said Olive, taking Sammy's bag from her and putting it in the corner with her own.

"And Oscar?" Sammy was shrugging off her bag and her coat but paused to say, "Ghosts exist. There's no debate. And if you don't believe, you'll just attract more ghosts to haunt your disbelieving arse, so I'd watch it if I were you."

"All right! Back to it!" Michael suddenly interrupted, aiming his coffee cup into the bin and missing.

"Well, that told me!" Oscar laughed.

"You're a theatre boy now, Oz! You've got to learn our ways at some point and it's probably best you know before we get into the theatre and you come face to face with a ghostie!" Olive poked him in the ribs and sauntered off to take up her position in the scene they were rehearsing.

"Oz . . ." Oscar smiled, enjoying the nickname he'd never been given and enjoying even more that it'd been given to him by her.

"I really don't want to be here," Olive shouted to the bartender over the music, knowing full well that no one would be able to hear her and those close enough to potentially lip read were too drunk to care.

"No one does," he groaned back and slid a rhubarb gin with elderflower tonic into her hand. "On the house, Olive. We never see you here any more."

"You remembered." She smiled, raising the glass to him. "No, my days of hardcore partying are over, I think. I got too old, too fast!" She laughed.

42

"Well, it's nice to have you here for a night at least." He reached over and squeezed her hand and Olive felt incredibly guilty for not remembering his name.

The entire cast seemed to have eluded her. Familiar faces swam through the crowd but were lost the moment she blinked. It was only then that she spotted the sweaty faces of Tamara and Jane up on a platform above the rest of the drunken crowd, a pole between them, their hair stuck to their faces and alcohol sloshing over the sides of their glasses. Olive couldn't believe they'd had the outfits they were now wearing with them in their bags, and idly wondered if all women carried slinky dresses and high heels just in case the occasion to wear them suddenly arose, or if Tamara and Jane were anomalies. It didn't matter to Olive either way. Even if she'd known about the night out prior to leaving her house that morning, she still would have chosen to wear the same clothes.

"I really don't want to be here either." Oscar's lips brushed close to her ear and Olive was acutely aware of his hand on her hip. She could feel its warmth through the thin fabric of her London-bus-red dress. Olive took a large swig of her drink and turned awkwardly in the crush at the bar to face him.

"Do you . . . do you want to go somewhere else?" She leant closer to him, but nowhere near as close as he had dared. Oscar blinked slowly, drained the last of his beer and let his hand find hers. He tugged on her fingers and led her as best he could through the crowd. Olive had only had a sip of her drink, but she couldn't seem to focus on anyone's faces. Maybe it was the thumping bass of the music, the roar of everyone shouting over each other or maybe it was the fact that every cell in her body was now fixated on the feel of Oscar's warm fingers wrapped around her palm. Everything else was simply secondary.

The cold air was welcome against their sweaty bodies as they emerged onto the bustling street. They walked mainly in silence past the loud bars and clubs full of people enjoying a night out. Hundreds of words spilled out of the open doors and splashed at their feet. Their own conversation would have been lost amidst the noise, so they spoke only in nervous smiles and in the briefest of brushes with their hands. That said more than enough for both of them. They turned a corner and Oscar finally took Olive's hand in his, clutching it to his warm chest. It was half past ten at night and he knew just the place to take her.

"Home!" He grandly gestured to a large square in front of them, lined with houses. In the centre was a small fenced and gated park, in which Olive could just make out brightly coloured children's climbing frames through the gaps in the hedges. "Well, it used to be for a while, anyway."

"No way! I love it around here," Olive cried as she crossed the road with Oscar, his heartbeat thudding against the back of her palm.

"See where the light is up there?" He took her by the shoulders and pointed to a window on the third floor of one of the tall and narrow houses. "That was my room."

"Your room?" Olive queried, looking up at the cream-coloured walls.

"Well, our room. It was Zadie's flat."

"She doesn't live there any more?"

"No. We were going to move into a house together before we split up. She went ahead with the move without me. Still, the bad memories haven't managed to fog up this place just yet. I miss living there, despite not really missing who I was living with."

"She can't have been that bad?" Olive laughed. *I bet she was*, she thought.

"She was," he said. *Called it*, she thought.

"I'm sorry," said Olive, and she really did mean it, despite enjoying that he didn't seem too attached to his ex even though they broke up only a few months prior. They were still facing the flat, Olive not wanting to look at Oscar. She always felt more comfortable talking when no one was looking at her and so she afforded him the same courtesy.

"No need to be. I hated the house she's in now. It was the house she wanted for her, not the house she wanted for us." She felt him shrug. "I miss that flat, though. And it means I can't get into this park any more." He turned to face the gated shrubs. "BUT, if you're willing to climb the railings . . ."

"You've been watching too many movies," she laughed, walking to the black railings and giving them a jiggle to test their strength.

"Just one," he confessed.

"*Notting Hill?*"

"Bingo." He kicked a stone with his shoe that pinged against the gate.

"Well, I'm not willing to climb these railings," Olive said, taking a step backwards.

"Not even if I hoist you over the top?" He interlinked his fingers and spread out his palms as a foothold.

"Not even then," she said, taking another step away from him, her back hitting a green electrical box.

"Really?" Oscar looked into the park he used to love so much. He'd never been in at night, but he thought it might have a bit of magic to it when it was free of screaming kids and exhausted parents.

"Only because there's no need." Her hands rummaged behind her back and after a swift bit of feeling around, Oscar heard six short beeps followed by a long one and then a thunk. Olive brought her hands in front of her and presented him with a key.

"What on Earth? How the hell have you done that?" Oscar snatched the key from her fingers, examining it closely.

"A friend of mine lives in one of these." She pointed to one of the lit windows in a house on the square. "That one, I think. After shows we used to meet up here for a drink and then crash in his flat. He keeps his keys in this little coded box here because he's sure he'll lose them otherwise. Once I learnt the code, I never forgot it!" She grinned. "I'm sure he won't mind us borrowing them."

"Well, I'll be damned!" he laughed.

"What?"

"Nothing . . . I just didn't have you pegged as a late-night-drinking, throwing-caution-to-the-wind kind of gal!"

"Oh, I'm full of surprises!" she winked, hoping her moment of coolness wasn't short-lived.

Up until now, Olive's life had seemed to consist of a series of wacky events. She'd trained at drama school and had been plunged headfirst into the industry as a leading lady with little to no time to adjust. Olive had soon discovered that when you were a name in theatre it often meant nothing in the "real world" outside of the stage door. Sometimes fifty people could be waiting for you when you finished for the night, but then you'd get the bus home with the spare change at the bottom of your pocket and eat Super Noodles for your dinner.

Outside the bubble of the theatre, she was simply Olive Green. No fame, no fortune, but that didn't matter to her because the love of it was more than enough. The love of it was the reason. The lights, the costumes, the sequins, the programme that listed the names of all the people that contributed to the magic on stage . . . Olive had wanted to be a part of it from the first performance of *Beauty and the Beast* she had seen aged six.

This was the job of a lifetime for her and although she often had less experience than most of her peers in the principal cast, Olive made up for it in her dedication to the craft and simply by being easy to work with.

Oscar wrapped an arm around her shoulders, pulled her into him and ruffled her hair. "Come on, then!" He skipped ahead of her to the gate with a boyish bounce. The key slotted into the lock and he paused before he turned it. "You better not be lying to me, Green."

"Turn the key and see," Olive laughed.

"There'll be hell to pay, Green!" he said as he turned the key and pushed the gate open. "YES!" He cheered and a light flickered on in a house above them.

"Shhhh!" she hushed, running into the park, closely followed by Oscar who shut the gate behind them and shushed Olive back until the cacophony of shushes was louder than his cheer had been in the first place.

Inside, the children's play area was small and a little lacking. A small green slide, a yellow plastic horse on a thick spring that wobbled about when you sat on it, and a platform with red handles to hold onto that spun round and round.

"I'm sure to little kids who don't really know any better, this is brilliant," Oscar laughed.

"It might look a little disappointing to your jaded adult eyes, but when you're a bit drunk, this thing is the best," Olive said, expertly hopping onto the spinning platform and making it turn in one smooth glide.

"Who'd have thought innocent Miss Green was such a rebel, eh?" Oscar said, taking the handles and slowly starting to spin her around.

"Oh, hardly. Everyone goes out in their first few years of jobbing in the West End. Yearly contracts on half-decent money seems to equal a lot of getting the first train home in the small hours of the morning." She rolled her eyes at herself.

48

"And a lot of hangovers, I presume?" Each time the handles came past him, Oscar gently pushed her around on the platform again.

Olive had been brought up to say no to drugs and to know your limits when it came to alcohol. The first she obeyed without objection, but the second she felt she could only really discover by testing those limits. As a result, Olive had often found herself waking up in several strange places after a particularly heavy night. These included a church pew, the floor of an abandoned old people's home and, most strangely, in the dressing room of Christine Daaé in Her Majesty's Theatre without any recollection as to how she got there or why. She'd quickly realised that her limits were not as high as she'd imagined.

"Absolutely. That novelty wore off quite quickly for me. A hangover renders me useless these days."

"You sound like you're eighty-five!"

"I feel like I'm eighty-five!" she laughed. "I've only drunk half a free gin and tonic and I'm already giddy!"

"Free?" Oscar stopped spinning her and just let the platform glide on its own momentum.

"The barman recognised me from when I used to go in there a lot."

"Oh. Right," Oscar replied, slowing the spinning down.

*Is he sulking?* she wondered.

"Is it awful that I couldn't even remember his name?" she confessed.

"Utterly terrible, Miss Green!" he cried, spinning her faster. "Tomorrow's headline will be 'West End Star

Thinks Herself Too Important To Remember The Names Of Those Kind Enough To Give Her Freebies'!" He spun her again faster still.

"How catchy!" she squealed as she held on for dear life.

"And now you're having a go at my journalism! How DARE you!" Oscar whipped the platform with a mighty force and Olive lost her grip. Her clammy hands slipped on the handles and she was sent flying into Oscar. They both landed next to each other with a thud onto the grass. Olive laughed until Oscar groaned.

"Are you all right?" She rolled onto her knees and he groaned again. He was clutching his arm and panic suddenly kicked in for Olive. "Oh God! Oh, no, no no! The producers will absolutely *kill* me if I've injured their big star!"

Oscar's eyes, which had just been scrunched in agony, quickly snapped open. "That's really the first thing you think of?" he laughed.

"You GIT!" She hit him. "Of course that's the first thing I think of when it's in the contracts we *both* signed that we wouldn't do extreme sports!"

Oscar sat up on his elbows and looked over at the kids' playground where the platform was still gently turning.

"I know that's not exactly an extreme sport," she said, hitting him again, "but we *have* signed our lives away and part of that is making sure we don't break any of our limbs. If you'd got hurt I could have easily been sacked!" She batted him again, but a little softer this time.

"They're not going to sack you on account of me, Olive." He sighed. "If they lose you, they lose the show! You're what holds the whole piece together!" He sat up, brushing grass off his T-shirt.

"Hardly!" she scoffed. "You could put my understudy on and it'd make very little difference."

Oscar scoffed back. "Do you really not realise just how good you are in this show? Screw that, in *any* show you've ever been in?"

Olive fiddled with some grass and shrugged. "Oh, you've not seen some of the disasters I've been part of." She winced, thinking back to when she played the role of a zombie who'd fallen in love with a ghost in a play that attempted to ride on the back of the success of *Twilight*.

"Sure, some of the shows you've been in may have died on their arse but that doesn't mean to say you weren't brilliant in them, eh?"

"Sure, sure," she laughed.

"You're not taking me seriously, are you?" He sighed.

"No, I am! I am!" she lied.

"Am I being stupid?" Oscar pouted, ducking to catch her gaze as she continued to rip out clumps of grass from the ground.

"Only a little." She smiled. "But in a sweet way."

"In a sexy way?" His pout turned sultry with the simple raise of an eyebrow.

"In a *sweet* way." She threw her handful of grass in his face, but as she did he caught her wrist in the air. A few blades of grass had caught on the stubble above his top lip and momentarily she forgot herself. Forgot the nervousness that came with being desperately attracted to someone new, or her worries of being seen as just another girl throwing herself in the path of a celebrity in order to gain a little bit of fame. And she would probably have forgotten her own name had she allowed herself to be taken in by his blue eyes any more than she already had been.

She stretched out her fingers and gently brushed the grass from his lips, lingering only a little longer than she needed. Just before she pulled away, Oscar turned his head and kissed her fingertips softly. Her first instinct was to withdraw again, to forget the giddiness she felt rising in her and the potentially all-consuming feelings this may lead to. *How exhausting this could be*, she thought.

And then Oscar moved her hand to his cheek, still kissing her fingers, her thumb, her palm over and over, his eyes closed and his face calm. He slid his warm hand up her outstretched arm to her shoulder and paused there a moment before caressing her cheek, a few blonde strands of her hair caught between his palm and her face. Gently, he pulled her in towards him. She had to lean awkwardly on her knees to reach him, but it was worth it to hear him whisper, "How exciting this could be . . ." before he hungrily planted his mouth on hers. Their lips fit together like two pieces of a puzzle, and Olive gently bit his bottom lip as his tongue found hers, and there they stayed and explored until the morning light started to seep into the sky.

# CHAPTER
# THREE

## Coffee

Olive's flat in Turnham Green wasn't large, but it was big enough for her. In those rare moments when Olive might complain about its size, her cast mates would gently remind her that she'd been able to buy her own place when she had been only twenty-two whilst the rest of them still rented. But she'd worked hard and saved and now any leftover money she had was spent on doing the place up to reflect her own personality as much as possible. The walls were painted green, her furniture was oak and signed posters of the shows she'd been a part of hung in ornate silver frames in every room. For Olive, knowing she could come home to her own space and her own bed made her not want to waste a moment getting the Tube after work. However, since meeting Oscar, spending time at work had become more and more enticing.

On this particular morning, Olive awoke with a definite "morning after the night before" feeling. She wasn't hungover and she didn't have that horrible "what have I done?" dread — after all, the only thing that had occurred was a kiss, and a good one at that. But something had changed. A connection had been established between her and Oscar that was more than just their onstage chemistry, and Olive's brain was whirring with wondering What It Meant. She poured herself a cup of tea and spoke out loud in her kitchen, mentally laying out every scenario before her.

"Was it just . . . a mistake? He was a bit drunk. But not so drunk that he didn't know what he was doing, I don't think . . ." Olive stirred her tea without looking until the teabag had made the water far darker than she usually liked. "Do I mention what happened when I see him today? And if I do mention it, will it happen again? Or does it mean that it *won't* happen again?"

Olive opened the fridge to get the milk and noticed last week's edition of *Burn* magazine sat on the kitchen counter. On the corner of the cover, a little yellow circle with a picture in the middle caught her eye and she flipped to page sixteen to read the rest of the story.

And there he was. On a beach with his top off holding hands with Zadie Lanette. Her smile was wide, as if she was mid-laugh, but Olive noticed that Oscar's didn't quite reach his eyes. And whilst Zadie clung to his bicep with what looked like unnecessary strength, Oscar's gaze was focused only on the sand at his feet. "Do I *want* it to happen again . . .? Why are you even asking that? Of course, you want it to happen again. The real question is, does he?"

Little did Olive know that wasn't a question that needed to be asked.

Over in Bow, Oscar sat up in his bed, sipping his black coffee with Google open on his laptop.

"Olive Green . . ." he said as he typed. "No, I don't want Dulux paint swatches . . . Olive Green, Actress. Ah, here we go." Oscar clicked on *Images*. "Wow." Olive was almost unrecognisable in some of the pictures but in most, Oscar could make out her distinctive green eyes. Olive had played four roles since college, with each one being bigger than the last. And if her adult career seemed impressive, it was nothing in comparison to the acting work she'd done as a child. She was certainly building up a bold body of work and judging by the rave reviews she received it would only continue to grow. Oscar shook his head as he read through a list of her special talents. Horse-riding. Juggling. Grade six piano. "Is there anything this girl can't do?"

Olive arrived at the theatre earlier than she would have liked and sat in the auditorium twiddling her thumbs. The dressing rooms were still occupied by the cast of *Gone With The Wind* and she would have to wait until their final week of rehearsals before she could bring in her pictures and keepsakes that travelled with her to every theatre she performed in. Olive couldn't wait until the theatre started to feel like home rather than visiting someone else's house. She pulled her phone out of her bag, but the signal wasn't good enough to browse social media and she was yet to ask for the wifi password. She rummaged through her bag to see if she had anything else that would help pass the time, but in her haste that morning she'd forgotten to bring her headphones and her book that she'd purposely placed on the kitchen counter.

"What is it they say about the early bird?" said Oscar, loitering in the doorway to the stage left stalls. He held a coffee in each hand.

"Something about catching the worm but really I'm just in it for the best seat in the house."

"And the free coffee?" he asked, walking along the row behind Olive's and handing her the larger of the two drinks.

"Oooh, you can stay," she said, taking the warm paper cup from him, removing the lid and peering inside.

"It's a latte," he said, flipping one of the seats down and sitting diagonally behind her. "I was a few people behind you in line at the coffee shop across the road the other day and heard you order one."

"Stalker," she said, reaching into her bag with one hand, careful not to spill her lidless latte.

"I'm sure lots of other people in the cast would happily take a free latte!"

"Yes, but this one literally has my name on it." Olive pulled out a bottle of honey and expertly squeezed a long and oozing dollop into her drink. "And my honey in it." She smiled, putting the bottle back into her bag and the lid back onto her drink.

"Honey? Really?" He raised an eyebrow.

"Yes, really. And don't call me honey!" She was trying to be cool, but inside her stomach fluttered at the idea of him actually calling her "honey" like it was the most natural thing in the world.

"Well, we've kissed now, so I feel like I know you well enough to call you honey, don't I?"

*Oh god, he's mentioned it,* Olive thought, her jumper suddenly feeling clingy and hot.

"I think that's for me to decide, isn't it?" she said from behind the lip of her coffee cup before taking a gentle sip.

"Would you decide to kiss me again if the option was there?" Oscar said, a little too fast. He swept his dark hair back off his face but looked her directly in the eyes, waiting patiently for her response.

"Depends if the option *is* there . . ." Olive said, not able to keep the smile from creeping onto her face. Oscar immediately shuffled himself onto the edge of his seat, placed his hand under her jawline and gently pulled her towards him. Without reluctance, Olive let him guide her to his lips. She could almost feel the electricity between them fizz on her tongue and the more they kissed, the more she wanted, but Oscar pulled away far too soon. He looked to the door into the auditorium.

"I guess . . ." he winced, "I guess there's no easy way to say that I don't really want everyone knowing about this . . ."

"I get it," Olive said, pulling back and fiddling with the edge of her coffee cup.

"You do?"

"Yeah, of course. It's new. Even we've not had a proper conversation about what this is . . . or what this isn't."

Oscar took her hand gently. "Let's talk properly at some point today."

"Okay," she said, not meeting his eyes.

"You know it's nothing to do with you though, right?" He squeezed her fingers and her eyes flicked up to meet his.

"I should hope not." She half smiled.

". . . and so I just slammed it down on the counter and walked away . . . oh. Hello, you two." Tamara seemed to always make an entrance, even if she was walking into an empty room.

"Looking cosy," said Jane without any degree of warmth.

"Well, it is cold in here. Got to wrap up warm!" Oscar said, pulling his scarf tight around his shoulders.

"I don't think that's what she meant," Tamara smirked, taking the row behind Oscar and sitting in the seat directly behind him so that she could massage his shoulders with the pads of her fingers.

"I know what she meant," Oscar said, his shoulders tensing, "but I've never been keen on rumours."

"Amen to that!" Olive raised her coffee cup and took a large gulp, wishing it was gin.

Time dripped by like treacle, and Olive awaited the conversation Oscar had promised, but every break seemed to bring with it a reason they couldn't speak. The first tea break Oscar had to work through a scene with the director and lunch brought with it press interviews for which he had to stay inside whilst she ate alone in the front of house café. Frustrated that they

58

hadn't had a moment in private together, Olive nabbed her chance in the final tea break.

"Can I borrow you?" she whispered, touching his arm as she followed him down the tiny wing to the auditorium.

"Sure! Coffee?"

"Yes. I'll buy." Olive raced to get her coat, as did Oscar, but just as they were slipping out the door Jane grabbed Oscar's hand.

"Oooh, coffee run? I'll come! I could murder a frappuccino!" she said, sidling up to Oscar and rubbing her cheek against his bicep like a dog nuzzling its owner.

"Actually, Jane, I was hoping to have a little conversation with Olive here."

"What can you say to her that you can't say to me?"

"It's about the show."

"Well, I am her first cover! Surely I should know these things?" Jane pulled away from Oscar sharply and was one stamped foot away from showing her age as the baby of the cast.

"Don't hold your breath to go on, though, love." Doug slung his arm around Olive's shoulder, giving her an unpleasant waft of his sweaty pit. "I've worked with this one before and I'm sure she still holds the record for least sick days taken. What was that number again, Olive?"

"Is this necessary?"

"ONE! One sick day in two years of solid work," Doug shouted.

"I had holiday, Doug, it's not like I was never off! And I have holiday in this run too," she reassured Jane with a smile.

"Exactly. See, this is all stuff I should know," Jane nodded, and Oscar looked at Olive who simply shrugged, annoyed that her chance to speak with him had been stolen again.

"All right, come on then." He huffed and followed Olive to the coffee shop sporting a new and annoying accessory on his arm: Jane.

The queue at the coffee counter was long and the crowd waiting for their hot drinks was three people deep.

"I'm going to the toilet. Can you order me a peppermint mocha frappuccino?" asked Jane.

"Aren't they iced?" asked Oscar.

"Yeah?" Jane shrugged.

"It's freezing out!" Olive laughed, blowing into her clasped hands.

"So?" And she started pushing through the throng of caffeine-deprived hipsters.

"Right, quickly, before she comes back," Olive whispered.

"What?" Oscar said, browsing the cookies through the glass.

"You said we were going to talk?" Olive said, glancing over Oscar's shoulder and watching Jane's perfect straight hair swish away from them.

"Now? Here?" Oscar already felt clammy from the overcrowded coffee shop, but now he was being put on the spot he felt a wave of heat rush through his entire body.

"It's not like we have an abundance of opportunities! The only time I've really spoken to you today is on stage via a script." Olive tried to smile and keep her tone light and breezy, but she knew they had to talk now and they had to be quick.

"True." He nodded.

"So shoot." She prodded him playfully, worrying that she really was being too pushy.

"I don't know where to begin." He tried to rub the creases out of his forehead.

"Well . . . what do you want?" she prompted.

"You're forward!" he laughed.

"And you're panicking. I just want to know where we stand and we don't have time to not be forthright," Olive said, going up on her tiptoes to try and spot Jane's imminent return.

"I want this," Oscar gestured between them.

"What is this?" *I wish he'd just say what he means,* she thought.

"Fun!" *I wish she understood what I meant,* he thought, squeezing her hand.

"Casual?" she suggested. Olive's father had always told her that when she wasn't able to make a decision she should flip a coin. Not to see how the coin would land, but because you would always know what you truly wanted once the coin was in the air. Much in the same way that it was only until she suggested being casual that she realised she was hoping he'd say no.

"I guess?" He shrugged.

"Right." She pulled her hand away.

"Doesn't have to be." He took her hand back and raised it to his lips, kissing it gently. "I just can't do serious. Or committed. Not right now."

"Okay. We want fun, not casual and not serious," she said with a small but noticeable sigh.

"Yes. That sounds right." He nodded, strands of his hair curling over his eyes.

"So . . . ..what is that?" She sighed again.

"Does it have to be anything? Can't we just be us?" Oscar felt a twinge of guilt twist in his gut when he saw her face change. It was only a small difference, but he could plainly see the idea of being casual didn't appeal to her, and probably never would.

"Doesn't that feel a little fragile?" She blinked slowly and breathed a little deeper.

"Isn't that half the fun?"

"I . . . I guess."

"Who's fragile?" Jane bustled back over to them, jostling several people's coffee cups as she went.

"He is. Our poor Oscar here has a jippy tummy. Is the loo free? I think he might need to go." Olive started pushing Oscar in the direction Jane had just come from.

"What the . . .?" Oscar wriggled against Olive's hands as her fingers tickled him.

"Go on, before we need to get someone over here with a mop!" Olive shooed him away, trying to hide her laughter from Jane. Oscar widened his eyes at her but couldn't keep the smile off his own face.

"You little . . ." He raised a fist in mock anger but then he opened out his palm, kissed it and blew it in Olive's direction.

"Did he just blow you a kiss?" Jane asked, as Oscar retreated to the bathroom.

"Hmm? What?" Olive rejoined Jane in the queue. "Oh, no! No, no. I think he had some dust on his hand." Olive opened her purse and absently flipped through her cards, but inside she was replaying how Oscar's lips had moved when he'd kissed his palm and how she couldn't wait to kiss him again when they were alone.

"Because you know Tamara would be furious with you if he did," Jane tutted.

"Furious that someone else blew me a kiss?" Olive stepped forward in the queue.

"Furious that you're spending time with Oscar. Making him blow you kisses." Jane stared up at Olive with her black kohl eyes.

"Hang on, Oscar's spending time with me too and I'm pretty sure it was his choice to blow *me* a kiss."

"Sure."

"Okay, Jane. You tell Tamara whatever you like. I'll just be here. Living my life."

"What'll it be, ladies?"

"A flat white and a latte, please."

"Er . . . and a peppermint mocha —"

"Oh, I'm getting yours too, am I? I don't think so, after the way you've just spoken to me. Just the flat white and the latte, thanks." Olive paid for her drinks and walked to the collection counter whilst a flustered

Jane had to try several attempts to get out the name of her coffee.

"Everything all right?" asked Oscar, wiping his hands on his coat.

"Yep," said Olive, not looking his way.

"You sure?" he said, placing a hand on the small of her back, but Olive stepped forward, looking over the counter to see whether their drinks were any closer to being made.

"Of course." She half smiled.

"Olive, c'mon. I know we're not best mates yet, but I can tell when something's up." Oscar watched as Jane argued with the barista when her card wouldn't work in the machine.

"No, we're not best mates. We're not anything, really," Olive shrugged.

"Don't do that."

"No, it's fine. I get it. We're just us. Unattached and having fun."

"Is that not what you want?"

"Of course it's what I want, I just don't like the uncertainty that comes with it."

"Uncertainty?"

"Yes, uncertainty — especially when you've got so many other options."

"Options? Olive . . ."

"Flat white and a latte!" called another barista who placed their drinks down so quickly they would have toppled over had Olive not been there to catch them.

Olive handed Oscar his coffee and darted back through the crowd with half a mind to head straight into the theatre without waiting for him, but her heart tugged her back. She heard the door of the coffee shop open behind her.

"Hey, now. What's all this? I thought we had things figured out?" he queried as they slowly made their way back to stage door.

"I don't want to be a placeholder for you for when something or someone better comes along. I don't want to be a crappy filler episode. I want to be a . . . a Christmas special."

"They're usually terrible."

"Thanks." She rolled her eyes. "Then a season finale."

"That sounds serious . . ."

"You know what I mean!" Olive lightly punched his arm, which made his coffee slosh out the little hole in the lid.

"I know! I get it, I get it. But what can I do? I'm not ready to delve into anything serious yet but . . . I like you. A lot. I haven't had fun with a girl in ages. It always gets angsty and expectations get thrown around and I just can't do that, right now. But I can do this. This is cool."

"But you've got —"

"Options? So do you! You're an extraordinary woman, Olive Green. That's why I choose to spend my time with you."

"But Tamara —"

"Tamara what? Fancies me? Let her! Doesn't mean I suddenly choose her. I choose you."

"You *choose* me? What am I, a Pikachu?"

"And you choose me too, right?" Oscar ignored her joke and took her hand, pressing it against his face. When she didn't answer, he pecked her palm with kisses over and over and over until —

"I choose you!" she giggled, trying to tug her hand away. "I choose you!"

"Yes!" Oscar swept her up in his free arm and nuzzled his face into her hair. Olive worried that someone might see them, but Oscar didn't seem to care, which made her smile all the more. He offered her his arm and she gladly took it.

"Er . . . HELLO?!" Jane opened the door and it crashed against the wall with a loud bang.

"Everything okay, Jane?"

"I didn't get a coffee," she said to Oscar with a nod to Olive.

"Didn't fancy one?" Oscar squeezed Olive's hand where she had it rested in the crook of his elbow. Olive squeezed his arm back.

"Well, I don't have any money with me!" she scoffed.

"That seems odd to come out to buy coffee and not bring any money with you . . . almost as if you expected someone else to pay for you. But it's all right, Jane. I know you're a nice girl who would never do such a thing, would you?"

"Well . . . no . . . but . . ."

"And you'd never expect a man to pay just because he's 'the man', right? Equality and all that! It's okay, Jane. Next time, we know coffee's on you. Come on!" Oscar gave Olive a tug and turned her sharply towards the direction of stage door.

"Don't turn around! Don't turn around! Just walk, walk, walk!" Oscar whispered as he frog-marched Olive back through stage door.

"Was that mean? That felt mean," Olive said inside the safety of the theatre as Oscar signed them in.

"Olive, she's young and never going to learn she can't always get what she wants if people don't teach her. That, out there, was Learning Not To Be A Spoilt Brat 101."

Walter lowered his paper a little to see the pair signing in and couldn't help but chuckle. Olive glanced his way and could only see his twinkling eyes over the edge of the paper but still gave him a timid smile which Walter, after folding his paper, returned. Oscar held the door open for Olive but before he followed her through he also caught eyes with the stage door man and, wondering how much he had heard, gave him a small roll of the eyes and a cheeky smile.

"You've made a smart move there, boy," Walter said to Oscar, nodding his head in the direction Olive had walked, and whilst the old man's words were complimentary, Oscar noticed the smile had gone from his face.

"I'm aware." Oscar nodded, not knowing why the man at the stage door seemed to be so serious with him. The lamp on Walter's desk flickered, followed by the light above their heads and then the light further down the corridor. Holding the door open, Oscar followed the flickering until it eventually stopped.

"Blimey. No wonder everyone thinks this place is haunted!" he laughed, nodding his goodbye to Walter and following Olive up to her dressing room.

Walter reached under his desk and turned his lamp off at the mains. Then he unscrewed the lightbulb and opening his desk drawer, brought out a torch which he taped to the top of his lamp. He turned it on, feeling pleased with himself until that began to flicker too.

"You have no idea."

# CHAPTER
# FOUR

## Life and Death

"Oscar, can we have you on stage, please?" Michael called out to him from the stage as soon as Oscar and Olive stepped through the door. He didn't wait for a response.

"Technically we still have six minutes of this break left but ... sure. Don't drink my coffee," Oscar mumbled to Olive, shrugging off his coat and handing his cup to her. She took both to the far side of the auditorium, knowing that Jane would be walking through the door at any minute. She didn't want to face her at all and definitely didn't want to without Oscar.

On stage, Oscar was immediately handed a gun.

"You're the murderer, then?" said a man who by the looks of his white and tufty hair must have been in his sixties but from the looks of his green velvet tracksuit, he thought of himself as a lot younger.

"Oscar, I'd like you to meet Toby. Our go-to stunt and weapons man. You'll be handling a gun in this production so we thought it'd be wise to get you acquainted with your weapon."

Oscar turned the gun over in his hands. The handle was wooden but the hammer and trigger were gold,

**69**

while the cylinder and barrel were silver with gorgeous swirling patterns carved into the metal.

"Is it real?"

"Looks like it, dunnit?" said Toby. "This is a Colt 45 Peacemaker revolver replica. This model dates back to eighteen-seventy-three but Michael here insisted on this one because it's 'pretty'." Toby rolled his eyes.

"I think it makes an impact, don't you, Oscar?"

"I bet it certainly would make an impact . . ." Oscar took the gun by its handle and pointed it towards the back wall of the stage.

"A real one might. But this one is what we call a 'blank firing gun'. The barrel is blocked off so nothing's gonna come out the end and even then we use blank bullets that don't have what we call a 'projectile'. There's no bullet. Just a cartridge with a bitta gunpowder. You pull the trigger, the hammer hits the primer, the primer ignites the gunpowder, the gunpowder goes bang, give the audience a flash and, hey presto, no one gets hurt and you've got yourself a show!" Toby took a bow.

"Yes . . . well, Oscar isn't actually going to be the one loading the blank into the gun every night. That will be a job for the assistant stage manager. All Oscar needs to know is where to aim and how to fire it."

"He won't be the one loading it?" Toby asked.

"No." Michael shook his head but Toby covered his mouth and chuckled.

"Well then, I feel sorry for whoever's playing the lady in this show. Whaser name?"

"Olive," said Oscar.

"Eliza," said Michael and Oscar felt himself blush.

"Why?" Oscar said, glancing over at Olive in the auditorium, flipping through her script.

"Well . . . 'cause of what happened."

"Toby, I don't think this is the best time for this . . ." Michael warned.

"Nonsense!" Toby gave him a playful yet forceful shove. "It's only a story, big boss man."

"It really did happen, though," Michael said, turning away from Oscar.

"Yeah, but it's not gonna happen again! Not if everyone's careful! And there's no harm in telling the fella! Probably best to, actually. Scaring him into doing things prop'ly. Come over 'ere." Toby led Oscar through the black curtain into upstage wing on stage left. "Now, we don't usually allow people up the ladder but on this occasion I think we can turn a blind eye. Eh, Michael?"

"Well, I just don't think it's —"

"Up you go!" Toby roughly took the gun out of Oscar's hands and handed it over to Michael who held it out at arm's length before dispensing of it on the quick change table. Oscar started to climb the ladder until he reached a metal grated walkway which he hopped off onto, closely followed by the old man.

"You believe in ghosts, mate?" Toby asked, dusting down his tracksuit. Oscar sighed.

"No, but I think I'm the only one around here who doesn't."

"Yeah, probably best not to give stock to old fairy tales but . . . even so . . . interesting, isn't it?" Toby gestured to a wooden case fixed onto the wall. Behind a glass panel was a revolver, much like the one Oscar had just been holding, except this one was black and this one was *real*.

"What's this?"

"Well, issa revolver," Toby shrugged.

"I can see that, but why's it all the way up here?"

"Last time this production was done, right here in this very same theatre, someone died, din't they?" Toby wiped his nose on the back of his hand. Oscar recalled the conversation from the rehearsal room.

"Oh, yeah. Someone mentioned something about this. Is this the gun that killed them?" Oscar got up close to the case.

"Yeah. They used a real gun in the show. Bunch of idiots, the lot of 'em. Used hollow wax bullets with a bit of gunpowder in 'em. Usually when the trigger is pulled the little bit of wax would disintegrate. Harmless, but still stupid to use a real gun."

"So what happened? What went wrong?"

"What always goes wrong when you're playing with fire. They got burned! Some idiot put something down the barrel of the gun. Playing silly buggers, I s'pose. Dunno how this poor girl ended up getting shot in the side of the 'ed. She wasn't even s'posed to be in the line of fire but . . . she was. Died on stage. Brain blown out. In front of an audience. For everyone to —"

"Yeah, okay, I get it. 'Fawn Burrows. 1931–1952'," Oscar read on the little gold plaque underneath the gun.

"So, I'd suggest you keep a close eye on this ASM loading your gun every night and I'd also suggest checking it before that final scene." Toby tapped the glass. "You don't want that revolver downstairs getting put in a case like this one."

"I doubt anyone here has any reason to shoot anyone else," Oscar scoffed.

"I bet that's what *they* all thought back then, too and yet, here lies Fawn Burrows, may she rest in peace." Toby started to climb down the ladder but caught Oscar taking one last look at the gun before he followed. "Guns always look so harmless when they're not in the hands of fools, don't they?"

# CHAPTER
# FIVE

## One Week To Go

Rehearsals seemed to be over before anyone was a hundred per cent sure of what they were doing, but the theatre was ready for them to move into in their final week of preparations. Opening night was only six working days away and tensions amongst the cast were starting to rise.

"I have never felt so fucking ridiculous in all my life," said Sammy, waddling out of her dressing room in a tight — but not ill-fitting — gold-sequined dress that stopped just above her knees. "If I'd been told I'd have to wear a dress like this for the next year of my life, I never would have walked into that audition."

"If I'd known I'd have to share a dressing room with Tilikum I never would have auditioned either," whispered Tamara, and Jane giggled so hard the beads on the hem of her dress rattled.

Samantha was tall and beautifully built with thick thighs and strong arms and the way she moved was second to none, which explained why Michael had cast her as one of the "dancing girls" in a heartbeat. However, as proud as she was of the way she looked, in the superficial world of entertainment, hearing her fellow cast members compare her appearance to a famous whale could make a girl doubt herself.

"What was that, Tam?" asked Sam, having heard full well.

"The dress looks great, Sammy! Nothing to worry about. Just ask to stand nearer the back if you're feeling self-conscious."

"D'ya know what, Tam . . ." Sam glanced around at the faces of her peers, all of whom gave her encouragement in their individual ways, "Tilikum got more fame by passing away than you'll ever get whilst you're alive. So, I think I'll be all right." Jane gasped and clutched Tamara's arm. "Also, Tilikum was held captive. You can do us all a favour and quit any time you like."

A deep shade of red filled Tamara's face and Samantha might have regretted saying anything at all had it not felt so good.

"You little b —"

"*Everyone to the stage please. That's everyone to the stage please, thank you!*" crackled the deputy stage manager's voice over the tannoy. Sam pulled on the hem of her dress and with more grace than she gave herself credit for, sauntered past her cast mates through the double doors towards the stage. Doug clapped.

"Beautiful show, Tam. Really, well done. Now if you could just turn off the outbursts of outward hostility and turn on the constant inward seething animosity that we all know and love, that'd be great."

Tamara huffed and rolled her eyes as she strutted past in her heels.

"Shut up, Doug!" Jane said as she click-clacked after Tamara.

"What have I done?!" Doug whined, reaching into his dressing room and picking up his bowler hat.

"Give it a rest now, Doug," Oscar said, walking up behind him and taking him by the shoulders. "We don't want anyone pulling out of this show a week before we open."

"It's good to ruffle a few feathers every now and again!" Doug laughed, and Olive sighed pointedly as she swept past them in her burgundy dress.

"Hmm. Let's not be causing bad feeling where there wasn't bad feeling before," Oscar said, watching the train of Olive's dress disappear as she followed the others.

"Oh it was just a bit of fun, Oscar!"

"For you, maybe!" Oscar laughed. "Just leave the girls to it. If they want to fight, let them fight without any encouragement from us."

Doug held up his hands. "Okay, mate! But, remember, those girls are going to have each other by their throats before this week is out, whether I say anything or not."

Oscar sighed and followed the rest of the cast through the doors towards the stage. Although he'd been given a tour around the theatre, he knew it would take him at least a couple of months to get his bearings. The multitudes of corridors seemed endless and had twists and turns that just led to more nooks and crannies. Even when he was certain he was going the right way, he was almost always wrong, so he'd taken to letting people go first and then following them, as he did now through both sets of double doors and into the upstage, stage left wing. It was inconceivably dark and he could only just make out the outlines of the others at the back of the set. A light popped on and the shape of a quick-change table appeared. On it were a stack of baby wipes, an industrial size pump bottle of anti-bacterial hand sanitiser and sandwich bags filled with make-up with the ensemble girls' names written on them in Sharpie. There was a mirror leaning against the wall that Oscar could just about see his silhouette in, and he leant in close to check his teeth for the remnants of the croissant he'd scoffed down earlier. He looked up at the towering wooden walls, the backs of which were clean and well sanded, but a smudge of black caught his eye. He went onto tiptoe and squinted and strained his eyes in the darkness as hard as he could, just making out the words **SET BUILT BY THE TEAM AT LIGHTFOOT LTD**. He assumed all the squiggles around it were signatures and Oscar wondered how many more signatures would be up there when the set was finally deconstructed.

The TV set Oscar was so accustomed to was always small and snug, the room often full of people, all jostling to view the monitor or pass each other polystyrene cups of lukewarm coffee. Despite the Southern Cross Theatre being one of the smallest venues in the West End, its space seemed so vast that Oscar couldn't imagine it ever feeling full. He suddenly felt a chill run through him and he stepped into the lights of the stage, hoping they'd warm his bones.

The rest of the cast had gathered on the black-painted textured floor in a vague semi-circle facing their director, Michael, who stood centre stage, his feet shuffling back and forth.

"Hello, everyone. Lovely to have you all here. How are you all feeling? Good? Good?" he nattered. There was a mumble of general approval from the cast.

"Good! That's good. Well, then. Let's begin with the more technical parts of the show, and then once they're out the way we'll do a full run-through of the show after lunch." Michael shuffled off stage, cracking his knuckles repeatedly, and reappeared in the auditorium where a little desk had been settled over the tops of three rows of chairs and a lamp was lighting his reams of notes.

Crew members carried tables and chairs onto stage, putting them on the little pieces of tape stuck to the stage that marked their place. The ensemble girls took their positions in the upstage centre, ready to act as the entertainment in a 1940s bar, and Doug and Howard took their places behind the bars either side of the stage where they pretended to clean glasses, pour drinks and ogle the girls in their short, rattly dresses.

"Is this a terrible show?" Oscar whispered to Olive as he took his starting position on a chair opposite her at the furthest table stage left.

"No. It only seems like that now because we're having a terrible time."

"I'm not having a terrible time." Oscar smiled and brushed her leg under the table. "Are you having a terrible time?"

"Not outside of work I'm not. But this cast and this production are having a terrible time because we're just not ready to open in a week. A *week*! Once we've done a full run and the show can actually take a bit of shape things will start looking up."

"Is this normal?" Oscar asked, swirling his glass like it was full of sloshing whiskey.

"Oh, Oscar, this isn't even bad."

"*Really?*" He stopped his glass mid-swirl.

"Put it this way," Olive put her elbows on the table and leant across to him, "I was once in a show when on opening night, we had to announce to the audience that the male lead, who, may I add, was a big star that shall remain nameless, was 'indisposed'," she air quoted, "and would not be performing."

"Why was he 'indisposed'?", he air quoted back.

"Drink, drugs, more drink. Who knows! But he definitely couldn't perform. His understudy had to step in and take his place but because his understudy hadn't rehearsed and his costume wasn't ready, he'd had to perform with his script in his hand and in his ensemble costume . . ."

"And who did he play in the ensemble?" Oscar covered his face with his hand and peeked through his fingers.

"The *court jester*, Oscar. He played the dashing leading man . . . dressed as a court jester."

"Wow."

"Oh, it doesn't end there. One of the ensemble girls broke her ankle mid-show during the first week causing not only the show to stop, but the performance being cancelled! Then two weeks later, the backers pulled their funding after reading the terrible reviews."

"Okay. This show is a breeze," he sighed.

"Yeah, we're fine," she laughed.

"We've still got a long way to go, though."

"Miles. But I reckon we'll just about get there before opening night. I just need to learn to walk in these heels!"

"Can we keep the noise down on stage please! Thank you!" called Michael from the auditorium, his hair sticking up at all angles.

"I need to knuckle down and make sure I know all these lines!" Oscar continued to whisper.

"You need less distractions," Olive sighed, sitting back in her chair.

"What do you mean?"

"I'll leave you alone for a while," she said, looking over at Doug who was twirling his dishcloth so that the end of it whipped about in a circle.

"What? No! Why?"

"It's probably best I don't distract you from what *really* matters . . ." She glanced at Oscar, whose eyes were wide and glistening.

"If that's what you want," he said, swirling his glass again.

"It'd be that easy to get rid of me, would it?" Olive stopped his glass with her fingers.

"What? No! Of course not! Ugh, you're such a tease, Miss Green!"

"Just keeping you on your toes!" She laughed and nudged his leg with her foot under the table.

**80**

"Okay, people! Let's pick it up from Eliza's line, 'You're always lurking in the shadows. Come and dance,'" said Michael, reaching over and dimming the lamp on his table a touch. The girls disappeared behind the little red curtain that fronted their mini stage on the real stage. Olive rose from her seat and dusted little specks of chipped black paint off her lap. She hadn't realised she'd been picking it off from the underside of the table.

Eliza
You're always lurking in the shadows. Come and dance with me, Lars.
[Eliza holds out her hand.]
Lars
I think it's best for both of us if I stay in the shadows.
[Lars takes a large swig of his whiskey.]
Eliza
No one will find us here, darling. I've got people watching at every entrance. Any sign of Melvin we'll be gone before he's even in the door.
[Eliza offers Lars her hand again, but he waves it away, downs his glass and gestures to the bartender for another.]
Lars
No, it's not that.
Eliza
Then what, Lars? Why can't you dance with me?
[Eliza holds out her hand one last time.]
Lars
I can't dance.

[The music crescendos. Dancing girls erupt onto stage with a high-pitched squeal and the bartender comes out from behind the bar, slides a fresh glass of whiskey over to Lars and takes Eliza's hand himself.
The four dancers wave their arms, kick their heels and their dresses rattle and sparkle in the lights. Other customers take to the floor but none of them dance as expertly as Eliza and the bartender. Centre stage, he twirls her effortlessly, her burgundy dress rippling across the floor, missing people's feet by a hair's breadth. Eliza's smile sparkles as brightly as the sequins and beads on the dancers' dresses but with her eyes closed, her fingers wrapped tightly around the bartender's hands and the trumpets blaring, she can't see Lars' pained expression or the sound of his cry as a strong pair of hands reaches out from the shadows and bundles him into the wings.
A scream pierces through the music. Eliza's head snaps up to see a burly man standing tall, clutching a handgun in his thick fingers. The dancers scatter and duck behind the bar. The bartender kisses Eliza on the cheek before darting behind the bar himself and shielding two of the girls from any potential harm. People race past Eliza, pushing her this way and that, stopping her from reaching the table where she had left Lars, but she can already see he is missing.]
Eliza
Lars! LARS!

[The lights black out and the stage is plunged into darkness.]

"Okay! Thanks everyone!" Michael shouted, interrupting the action on stage. "Um . . . okay . . . um . . . Let's do that again but this time let's try . . . actually I'm coming up there. Gimme two seconds."

Olive pushed a loose pin in her wig back into the hair until she could feel it poke her head. Doug jumped up and slid himself onto the bar, waving at Olive and giving her a thumbs-up.

*You too!* she mouthed, but her eyes danced into the wings. She looked around. Everyone seemed busy fiddling with their dresses or their shoes or surreptitiously flicking through script pages to brush up on lines before they got to the scenes they were unsure on. Olive took her chance to dart into the wings.

"Oscar?" she whispered but there was no reply. The wings were dark when the lights on stage were low and her eyes hadn't yet adjusted. She felt her way along the wall up to the upstage entrance, and although no one seemed to be around she was sure she sensed another presence amongst the props and rails of costumes. She paused and then realised it was more than just a feeling. She could actually hear someone breathing.

"Doug? Is that you?" She could imagine Doug's little smirk as he waited with bated breath to pounce and make her jump so hard her wig fell off. "I'll hate you for ever if you do this!"

Then someone moved out of the shadows, and Olive's heart knocked against her ribs so hard she thought it would burst clean through.

"Sorry," said a voice she didn't recognise. It sounded dry and unused but warm nevertheless. "Didn't mean to startle you there."

"No worries! We've not properly been introduced; I'm Olive. Playing Eliza. In the show." She gestured to her costume but she wasn't sure he could see in the dim light.

"Yes. I know. You're very good," the man said, straightening his cap.

"Oh, thank you. Do you know this show at all?" Olive could hear Michael's voice on stage and looked back into the wing. Suddenly, with a great click, they were swathed in a clinical white light.

Olive could now see that she was speaking to an elderly gentleman in a flat cap who she vaguely recognised.

"I know the show well." He nodded. "But I don't want to keep you."

"No, I'd best get back. You work on stage door though, don't you?" she asked. "I feel like I've not really been introduced to anyone behind the scenes. I'm doing my best to learn all the crew's names, though!"

"Yes, I work at stage door. Have done for many years. Walter," he said, but didn't make a move to shake her hand as she would have expected.

"Lovely to meet you, Walter. I'm sure I'll be seeing a lot of you." Olive gave him a small smile and hot-footed it down the wing just as she heard Michael call her name.

Walter retreated through the double doors, trying to ignore the dull yet persistent ache in his chest. He leant against the wall in the corridor before slowly making his way up the stairs. As he did so he glanced upwards and shook his head. "Why did they have to cast someone who looks so much like you?" he sighed.

"Olive?" Oscar gently tapped on her half open dressing room door.

"Hello, you." Olive was sitting in a green armchair wiping dark lipstick from her mouth. "I'm sure this stuff is staining my face." She scrubbed a little harder, desperate to be rid of it in case Oscar wanted to kiss her. He walked behind the chair and leant his arms and his head along the top of it, speaking to her via their reflections in the mirror and for a brief flicker of a moment, everything around them seemed to pause. As their eyes met through the glass, the noise of London outside the window became muted, and even the tiny specks of dust seemed to swim through the air a little slower. Then in an instant, the moment was gone.

"What are you doing tonight?" he asked softly.

"Going home?" she said, her eyes flicking up to his face in the reflection.

"Is that a question?" He smiled, a wave of warmth making his back sweat under the weight of his black rucksack.

"No," she laughed. "I'm going home but it sounded as if you were going to try and change my mind. I guess

I didn't want my riveting plans involving sitting on my sofa staring at my telly for the evening to sound too set in stone."

"So, you'd be happily persuaded into doing something else?" He raised his eyebrows. Olive's heartbeat had picked up speed from the moment he'd walked into the room, but now he seemed to be asking her out for the evening, she could feel it in her fingertips.

"Well, it depends on what that is. I won't change such irresistible plans for just anything, y'know."

"Or just anyone?" Oscar rested his chin on the back of his fingers in an attempt to look sweet and innocent.

"Or just anyone." She nodded.

"Well, I was wondering if you fancied coming back . . . with me tonight. Maybe." He ran his fingers across the velvet on the chair and fiddled with a frayed edge of the fabric that had come loose.

"Maybe?" She shrugged, hiding a smile underneath the make-up wipe.

"Definitely." Oscar stroked a stray curl on the back of her head and she shivered.

"No dinner? No movie? Just a straight invitation to go back to yours." She turned to face the real him, rather than his reflection. "Bold move!"

"We can have dinner and a movie! At my place." He grinned, showing all his teeth, like a child being asked to smile for a photo.

"Is this about sex? It sounds like it's all about sex." She turned back to the mirror and started to scrub at her eyes. *Please don't let it be just about sex*, she thought.

"It's not about sex!" He laughed and placed his hands on her shoulders, giving her a light shake.

"So, you're saying if I came back with you tonight . . . we wouldn't have sex?" She tossed her make-up wipe aside, slid her make-up bag towards her and looked only at her own reflection.

"If that's what you wanted." Oscar glanced up at himself to see if his sincerity was showing.

"Am I that easy to resist?" she asked, pulling her dressing gown tighter around her shoulders. *How much are you supposed to make a guy sweat before it starts being cruel*, she wondered when she caught his pleading eyes in the mirror.

"What? No? I want to have sex with you!" he said, a bead of sweat dripping down the small of his back.

"So, it *is* about sex?" She squirted foundation onto the back of her hand and then started smearing it onto her cheeks with her fingers.

Oscar sighed. "No! Let me be perfectly clear. I want to have sex with you, but this isn't just about sex."

"Sure," she laughed. Olive's romantic past hadn't been squeaky clean and although it hadn't put her off putting herself out there for life, she was much more cautious as to whom she was handing her heart over to. She couldn't help but think of the actors she'd had romantic encounters with over the years. Whilst many had been brief spontaneous affairs which had eventually simply fizzled out, one in particular had been rotten from the word go.

Jason Butler had been a dancer with muscles in places that Olive hadn't realised you could even have muscles, and although the conversation between them was never particularly riveting they seemed to be able to talk about nothing for hours on end and never get bored. Although Jason had had a girlfriend when rehearsals had started, they'd split up in the first week of performances and he'd made his move on Olive when they'd been out celebrating the end of a successful run of the first eight shows. From that point onwards, Olive and Jason were inseparable. They would kiss in her dressing room during every interval, and they'd elongate their days by going for drinks after the show at the pub across the road, just so they had a little more time together.

Every relationship that's formed in the West End will move at the speed of light, but when Olive and Jason had finally had sex, despite it being nearer the end of their run in *Little Shop of Horrors*, Olive felt it had happened quite quickly. She knew that was the consequence of the theatre bubble — when you spend that much time locked up with a group of very liberal, free-thinking, creative people, sooner or later, things will start to spice up.

It was only until she came into work the next day, thinking nothing had changed, to find actually everything had changed. Jason had avoided her eyes across the stage in warm-up and sought conversation elsewhere. He hadn't come to her dressing room in the interval, and when she went to find him he was missing from his own. She tried to shrug it off, hoping that if something were truly wrong, he'd talk to her about it, but with the contract nearing its end, Olive found herself wondering what would happen when they were no longer in each other's pockets. Being loved-up was easy when you were forced to be in the same place as each other, but when you lived at opposite ends of the city and weren't going to be seeing each other every day, it was harder to keep the momentum going on a relationship, especially when one of you had decided to ignore the other without rhyme or reason.

Olive had never been one to beat about the bush. She liked everyone's feelings out in the open where she could see them and keep an eye on them.

"What's going on?" She caught Jason's arm at stage door before he whizzed past her, his beanie hat pulled down around his ears and his backpack high on his back.

"I have to get my train," he said, pulling away from her, but he hesitated and Olive took her chance to touch his arm again.

"Jason . . ." she pleaded.

"Look." He pulled her to one side so that none of the fans crowded around stage were within earshot. "I'm not into . . . this any more," he said, his eyes darting from her to the fans behind them.

"What do you mean you're not into this any more? What changed from yesterday to today?" She shook her head.

"You can't be angry at me for changing my mind," he huffed.

"Oh, I'm not," Olive had answered, feeling her fingers ball into fists, her nails digging into her palms. "Change your mind all you want, Jason."

"Then why are you so pissed off at me?" he said, like she was someone he barely knew. Someone annoying that he was trying to cut loose.

"I'm angry at you for avoiding me. For making me feel like it's me who's done something wrong."

He sighed and rubbed his temples with his hands and Olive knew it wasn't because of anything other than a desire to hide his face from her. *You know you've been an arsehole*, she thought.

"You're just . . . wrong for me. Or we're not right. Together. Or something like that," he said.

"'Something like that'?"

"Yeah," he said, taking a step away from her. "I need to get my train."

"Okay, Jason," Olive said, and she let him practically run away from her.

Two weeks later, their short summer run of *Little Shop of Horrors* came to an end and it was only once the show was over that Olive discovered what had been going on. A message dropped into her Facebook inbox from Rosanna Lime, an American actress quickly on the rise in the UK. Olive recalled that she had just started a run in *Annie Get Your Gun* with none other than Jason Butler. The Facebook message began:

Olive. You don't know me and this may be completely out of line, but . . . I need to know.

90

Rehearsals for Annie Get Your Gun began six weeks ago and I started getting more than friendly with a guy called Jason Butler who is in our ensemble . . .

Once they'd gotten to the bottom of it, it turned out Jason was not only dabbling in half-arsed relationships with Olive and Rosanna at the same time, but the girlfriend he'd claimed to have split up with in the first place was also still on the scene.

"He's a star-fucker," Olive's best friend Lou had said, sipping from a large glass of white wine.

"A what?" Olive sniffed from underneath several blankets, reaching for the chocolate caramel digestives.

"A star-fucker. Someone who just keeps penetrating the next 'big thing' on the scene until he's worked his way up the ladder to stardom." Lou shrugged as if what she was saying was common knowledge.

"People do that?" Olive sniffed.

"Clearly." She gestured to poor Olive with her mascara-stained eyes, the biscuit crumbs in her scraggly hair and the several dozen scrunched-up tissues in a sea around the sofa.

Olive had never forgotten that heartbreak, and whilst she genuinely felt it would be different with Oscar — she could feel his sincerity even when he was simply putting his arm around her — she wanted to be certain.

"Do *you* want to have sex with *me*?" Interrupting her wander down memory lane, Oscar moved round to the side of her armchair, got on his knees and faced her.

". . . I'm undecided." She squinted her eyes at him, a smile playing at the corners of her plump lips.

"Well, I'm decided," he said with a single nod.

"I'm sure you are!" she laughed.

"We don't have to have sex at all. Ever. I just enjoy your company and I'd like to spend the night with you." Oscar stretched out his hand tentatively, as if she were a wild animal and he was daring to get close. She softened a little and moved her cheek to meet his fingertips. His hand brushed along her jawline and he stroked her skin with his thumb, careful not to ruin her freshly applied make-up. "This isn't about sex, Olive."

She closed her eyes, enjoying the warmth of his smooth hands. Even with her eyes closed she could picture his face exactly, every perfectly chiselled line and even the exact shade of blue that shone in his eyes. "Haven't you got hundreds of other women to choose from?" She sighed.

"No." He shook his head, trying to push from his mind the thought of all the texts on his phone from various women. "Even if I did, doesn't it count for something that I choose *you*?"

Her eyes snapped open. "Am I supposed to feel lucky?" She pulled away, but only a little so that his hand was still touching her face.

"Olive." He sighed and took her hands in his. "I have no hidden agenda here. No secrets. I'm not trying to add you to a list of women I've managed to 'conquer'. I just want to spend my time with you. I'd love to have sex with you because I like you, but that's not my aim here. My aim is simply getting to know you better. If

92

you don't want that, then just . . . tell me. But wouldn't it be amazing if you wanted to spend your time with me too?"

Oscar's bright eyes and his smooth lips had already won Olive over. She knew he was kind, she knew he was well-intentioned and she knew that he liked her. Yet she could feel the demons in her head digging away at pre-existing craters in her self-worth, created by past romantic tragedies and men she'd trusted not to hurt her, but who'd hurt her anyway. When she pushed those demons away, they'd only come back again with bigger pickaxes and greater vengeance.

"Okay," she breathed.

"Okay?" Oscar squeezed her hands. His palms had started to sweat so he deftly swept a hand through his hair.

"Okay!" she laughed. "I will come back with you tonight," she said, turning to the mirror. "But that doesn't mean I'm going to sleep with you, though. You know that, right?" Olive rearranged her dressing table into a slightly neater mess.

"Of course! Okay. Um . . . okay!" Oscar hopped up off the floor and wriggled his shoulders to reposition his rucksack.

"Everything all right?" She raised an eyebrow at him through the mirror.

"Yeah, just . . . well, I didn't really expect you to say yes and now I'm just trying to remember what state my flat's in."

When Olive had finished putting on her make-up (which she took more time on now that she had a reason to make a little more effort), she got changed and was thankful that she'd worn one of her nicer dresses to work. Oscar had waited patiently in his own dressing room across the hall, making a plan in his head for what embarrassing things in his flat he'd have to quickly hide away when they arrived. Oscar suddenly realised he hadn't thought this far ahead. This wasn't like the few one night stands he'd had in the past because he knew Olive and although he didn't know her all that well, he already cared about her far too much for it to be a one-time occurrence. *Maybe this isn't a good idea*, he thought, suddenly starting to second guess himself. *Is bringing her back to my flat serious? No. Maybe? Do I want serious? No, I don't want serious. But I do want her. Why is this so complicated?*

As they sat next to each other on the Tube later, Oscar rubbed his eyes, trying to stop over-thinking the evening in front of them.

"You seem quiet," Olive said. Her arms were folded, and she used her concealed fingers to stroke Oscar's arm, just in case any of his avid fans happened to be on the train watching them.

"I'm fine!" he said, taking her hidden hand and kissing the back of it. Then they heard giggling. Oscar's head whipped round to see two teenage girls sitting at the other end of the half empty carriage, watching very conspicuously. Oscar gently returned Olive's hand to her own lap and gave the girls a smile and a nod, which prompted even more giggling.

"Oh no," Oscar muttered through still-smiling lips.

"What?" she whispered back.

"I think they're about to come over." Oscar took out his phone and started randomly opening and closing apps in order to look busy. Olive glanced over at the girls through her hair and they seemed to be deep in frantic conversation. One of them was rooting through her handbag and decanting the contents of it onto the empty seat beside her.

"How can you tell?"

Olive was aware of the difference in fame between herself and Oscar and the types of fans they encountered. Olive could do a show, say hello to a few respectful and often shy fans at stage door and then happily and anonymously get on the Tube home without anyone noticing her again. She'd even sat opposite people reading the programme of the show she'd just performed in who still didn't know who she was. However, she had seen the piles of letters that had poured in through stage door with Oscar's name scrawled wildly on the front, often in pink or purple with the "i" in "Bright" dotted with a heart. His face had reached the TV screens of everyone in the country and even if they didn't know his real name, they were more than happy to call him by his character name. Olive wasn't adept in recognising he'd been spotted, but Oscar was a dab hand at seeing the signs.

"I just have a hunch. Stop looking. If they think we're busy it may put them off."

Olive averted her gaze to look over his shoulder at his phone. She noticed he'd opened his message inbox which he quickly closed again when she paid an interest, and her brain went into overdrive wondering if he had something to hide.

"Don't you want them to come over?" she asked, fighting the urge to sneak a glance at the young girls again.

"If they come over, they come over. It'll be fine. It's just the build-up to it that I hate — makes me anxious like you wouldn't believe." Olive had already noticed that he had shrunk in on himself and his shoulders were no longer brushing against hers because they were up near his ears.

"Anything I can do?" she asked, squeezing her hands between her knees and feeling her own pulse quicken.

"You got an invisibility cloak in that rucksack of yours?" Oscar asked, hunching himself further over his phone, frantically scrolling through his Twitter feed and replying to every other tweet with various emojis.

"Why? Did you leave yours at the theatre?" She bumped his shoulder, just as a timid voice interrupted them.

"C-c-can . . ."

Giggle.

"Can I get . . ."

Giggle.

". . . a picture?"

Giggle.

Oscar looked up from his phone to see the teenage girl in her modified school uniform. Shirt ends tied together in Britney Spears fashion at the front, her skirt rolled up at the waistband so it sat high above her knees and her black heels which surely weren't school regulation. Her face was shiny and so red Olive wondered if she might burst with one untimely jolt of the train. Olive had never seen Oscar interact with a fan before and given his reluctance at being recognised, she worried this girl was about to be sorely disappointed.

"Of course you can!" Oscar's face burst into friendliness, like someone increasing the brightness level on a phone screen.

"Ohmigod!" the girl squeaked, alerting a few other passengers to their interaction. Oscar stood and held onto the rail above his head and snaked his other arm around her shoulders, and Olive watched as the youngster melted into him like butter. The train juddered around a corner and when Oscar held onto her a little tighter to stop her from falling, her smile became a little wider. Then the girl thrust her phone at Olive.

"Oh . . . um . . . sure!" Olive took the phone that had been primed for a photo. She stood on shaky legs, her own face now hot, her hairline sweaty as she tried to take a picture but each one came out blurry as her hands shook. "Oh, I'm sorry. I'm not very good at this." Olive handed the phone back to the girl, but Oscar took it and expertly swivelled it around in his fingers, flipped the camera and snapped two selfies.

"There we go!" he said, flopping back down on his seat as he handed the phone back to the girl.

"Thank you! Oh my goodness! Thank you! My mates are gonna be well jel!" The girl wobbled up the carriage on her heels and unashamedly squealed with her friend, instantly checking the photos.

"Are they always like that?" Olive asked, delicately nodding at the young girls behind her who were still excitedly giggling.

"No. Only sometimes." Oscar's face still hadn't returned to normal. There was something mechanical about his eyes and his smile.

"How do you cope with it? I could never deal with that day in and day out." Olive brought her rucksack up from the floor, placed it on her lap and hugged it.

"You just get used to it, I suppose," he shrugged, not being able to resist running his fingers along her shoulder.

"That's kind of sad," Olive said, glancing up. He was slowly melting back into the Oscar she knew and not the switched on, Display Oscar.

"How so?"

"You're used to people treating you as though they know you better than they do. It's like they think you owe them something because, in a way . . . they've made you famous by watching you on the telly and buying tickets to the show you're in."

"I guess. I'd never really thought about it like that."

"Just as long as you realise you don't owe them anything, it's fine." She smiled at him, but he was looking at his hand, twisting a silver ring around his middle finger with his thumb.

"Don't I?"

"Why would you?" She swivelled towards him a little.

"Well, like you said, they've made me famous . . . haven't they?" He gestured to the teenage girls who now seemed to represent his entire fanbase.

"Not at all. Did a group of fans get together and decide to give you the job in *Love Lane* when you were a kid?" she laughed.

"No . . . but —"

"No — that's all there is to it!" She raised her voice and was a little shocked at the passion in it. "If not one single ticket is sold to a single performance of *When The Curtain Falls* . . . you still get paid, right?"

"Right," Oscar nodded, still not looking at her, deep lines wrinkling his forehead.

"Because your wages don't rely on how many people come to watch you. Your wages rely on you turning up and doing the job." Olive noticed more and more people on the train honing in on their conversation.

"But doesn't me getting the job rely on how many tickets I can sell based on how many fans I have?"

"That depends. Are you any good?" she asked, more quietly. Olive could feel a rage burning in the pit of her stomach as she glanced over at the girls who were tapping furiously on their phones. *That picture has probably already been seen by hundreds of people*, she thought.

"Well . . . yeah. I should hope so at least." He gave her the briefest of smiles.

"Then that's why you were hired. The fact you've also got a pre-existing audience is a bonus for the producers."

"A big bonus!" He laughed.

"But a bonus nevertheless! You're a good actor, Oscar, and so you get hired. People with far smaller audiences, if any audience at all, still get hired in lead roles. Their careers don't rely on having a fanbase. Why does yours?"

"Because I have one?" he shrugged.

"But doesn't that show you that it's all a delusion? The only thing you owe your fans is a good performance on the night they've booked a ticket." Oscar looked at her but no words came. "Without your fans, granted, it may have taken you a little longer to work your way up the ladder but you'd still be doing this, Oscar Bright. And rightly so." She put a full stop to her point with a final nod, but she hugged her bag to her chest despite feeling hot and sticky in her thick cardigan. Oscar couldn't help himself. With a gentle hand, he turned her face towards him and kissed her full on the mouth with a tenderness that made her whole body fill with heat. A million thoughts raced through her head.

*Are those girls watching? Is everyone watching? Does he care? Do I?*

She pulled away gently but kept the tip of her nose against his. She opened her eyes but his were still closed and she felt him take a slow and deep breath.

"Everything okay?" she asked.

"Of course," he nodded. "Thank you."

"For?"

"Being so nice." He took one of her hands and looked down at it as he fiddled with her fingers.

"I didn't realise I was." She smiled, but an odd feeling crept over her. "Are those girls watching us?" she whispered. Oscar glanced over her shoulder and sure enough, the girls were red-faced and staring.

100

"Yeah, and their subtlety is astounding."

"Oh, dear."

"It'll be fine. They're just kids. We're getting off at the next stop anyway."

"You sure?"

"Stop looking so worried! What are they going to do? Come on." Oscar stood and hauled her up by her elbow, but her legs still felt like jelly after such an unexpected kiss. She tried to smile reassuringly at Oscar, but she couldn't help but notice the two teenage girls furiously tapping away at their phones as they stepped off the train.

Oscar's place was only a short walk from the station and was not what Olive had expected at all. His ground floor flat was only slightly bigger than hers and certainly just as messy.

"Cleaner doesn't come until Monday," he lied, rushing ahead of her through the front door and picking up various items of clothing and empty cans of Diet Coke.

"I hope you pay her well!" Olive said, retrieving an empty can from the plant pot by the front door which Oscar took, sheepishly.

"Living room's through there. Make yourself comfy and please ... excuse all the mess. I'll be just a minute," he said. She guessed he was heading to quickly tidy his bedroom.

"Wow, you really weren't expecting company, were you?" Olive laughed as she moved a pizza box from the sofa to the coffee table which had several mugs of coffee on it, some still half full. She slipped off her bag and cardigan and sank into the grey sofa. Within moments, a wave of fatigue hit her like a ton of bricks, every blink feeling heavier than the last.

"Yeah, that sofa's a little bit special, isn't it?" She hadn't even heard Oscar come in.

"I feel like I'm being hugged by a cloud."

"Do you want a drink? Tea, coffee, a Ginny Weasley?" he asked.

"A what?" She laughed.

"A Ginny Weasley!" He smiled. "A gin and tonic."

"Love that. And no. I'm good, thank you."

He sat down next to her and repositioned himself a little closer to her.

"Food?" He leant in a little more.

"I'm okay."

"A kiss?" he whispered, their noses touching and his lips almost brushing hers.

"Hmm . . . maybe." She closed her eyes, but he didn't kiss her.

"Just maybe . . .?" he breathed against her lips.

"Definitely," she said and she kissed him, hungrily.

Kissing at the theatre had always come with a cautiousness and a worry that someone would burst into their hiding place without warning. Often anything that sounded vaguely like an opening door or a knock and even calls over the crackling tannoy would make them jump ten feet apart. But in the private comfort of Oscar's messy flat, such cautiousness was unneeded and Olive revelled in having him all to herself. He scrambled backwards, keeping a firm arm around her waist, carefully lifting her up from the sofa to a standing position. Oscar paused a moment, wondering whether she really wanted this, but Olive reached up once more to kiss him, this time her hands sliding up his chest underneath his T-shirt. Oscar couldn't believe that he actually missed kissing her in the brief moments it took to pull his T-shirt over his head and as soon as it hit the floor, he lifted her off the ground and instinctively she wrapped her legs around his waist and tangled her fingers in his hair. Oscar carried her the short distance to his bedroom and, without turning the light on, he gently lowered her on the bed. Immediately her fingers were unbuckling the belt of his jeans whilst he fumbled at the buttons on the front of her dress.

"Wait . . ."

"You've changed your mind?" he said, pulling away.

"No," she laughed, and awkwardly turned slightly onto her left side. "There's a zip."

"Well, that makes things easier." He unzipped the dress in one smooth glide and for a brief moment, Olive wondered how many women had been back to this room with him. *Shhhh*, she thought to herself. She felt her way back to his waist and unbuttoned his jeans then ran a finger along the inside of the waistband of his boxers. Oscar responded by lowering his head and kissing her neck.

"I thought you were undecided," he said in between kisses, his breath hot on her collarbone.

"I was." She smiled as she slid her other hand up his back and through his hair. "I make up my mind very quickly."

*  *  *

Oscar had fallen asleep within mere moments. Olive gently pulled the duvet up from the floor and wrapped it around her naked body, careful not to disturb Oscar's sprawled limbs. As soon as she lay down facing away from him, he reached his arm around her waist and pulled her into him. When he was settled, she carefully reached her arm over the side of the bed and retrieved her phone from her dress pocket on the floor. She noticed that the screen was already lit up with several text messages. She quickly turned the brightness down and held it close to her face, squinting her tired eyes until the writing came into focus.

Doug
     Just a heads up, lovely. Cat's out of the bag and your Twitter feed is going crazy. I'm here if you need me.

Mum
     You kept him quiet! I knew there was something going on between you. Mother's instinct. I could just feel it!!! When can I meet him?

LouLou BFF4EVA
     Erm . . . Excuse me?! Since when were you dating a celeb?! What happened to telling your best friend ALL your secrets. Now tell me . . . is he a show-er or a grower?!

Olive thought her hammering heart was sure to wake Oscar, but he continued to snore gently in his sleep. He

**104**

looked so peaceful, whilst she watched everything start crumbling down around her. Had she thought about it any longer she would have talked herself out of it, but her panic made her turn to Oscar and shake him.

"Oz," she said. She could see his own phone light up on the bedside table next to him. "Oscar!"

"Mmmm. What's up?" He rolled onto his back.

"Something's happened. Everyone knows!"

"Knows what?" He sat up quickly and flicked on the bedside lamp, rubbing his eyes.

"About this! About us!" She gathered up the duvet around her.

"How?!"

"I don't know. I haven't got that far yet. I've just got loads of text messages from people asking me about you." She scrolled through them all again, the words jumping out at her and each one making her stomach drop further and further towards the ground.

*Cat's out of the bag. Something going on. Dating a celeb.*

Oscar snatched up his phone and, ignoring the many messages and notifications, opened up the Twitter app on his home screen. Olive watched him scroll frantically and felt guilty that a small part of her triumphed in people knowing. Whilst Olive could maybe do without her private life being splashed across the world wide web, she'd never wanted to keep secrets in the first place and she knew if she was being completely honest, she might even be a little relieved that whatever they were was no longer something she had to hide.

But when she looked at Oscar she noticed his whole face had changed. Suddenly, his jaw was sharp and tense and the blue of his eyes was cold and uninviting.

"Oh no. No, no, no," he mumbled. "Shit!" He threw down his phone on the bed and knitted his fingers into his hair, thumping the back of his head against the wall behind him. Olive braced herself and looked down at his phone and there still on the screen was an impeccably clear photo of Oscar kissing Olive on the District Line train earlier that evening.

"We can fix this," she said.

"We can't." She watched him shake his head and her heart thumped in her ears.

"We can! It's slightly blurry! That could be anyone!"

"Olive . . ." he said, grabbing his phone and swinging his legs over the side of the bed, searching the floor for his boxers. He stayed there for a moment, his back to Olive, and sighed before slipping them on. She wanted so badly to reach over and run a hand across his broad, freckled back, to let him know she was there for him to lean on, but there was already a distance developing between them.

"Where are you going?" she asked.

"I've got to call my agent." He left the bedroom without looking at her. She watched him walk away and she begged him in her mind to turn around, to look back at her, to show her some sort of kindness. Instead he opened the door to his living room and went straight inside without a moment to acknowledge that only moments ago they'd been the most physically intimate two humans could be. Now she felt like she was floating in a sea of bed sheets and he was standing on a distant shore, unable and unwilling to be close to her again.

# CHAPTER
# SIX

## Final Rehearsal

The knock at her dressing room door couldn't have come soon enough, but Olive didn't dare turn around.

"Come in!" she said feebly, making herself look busy by tidying away the contents of her make-up bag that she'd left strewn across her dressing table.

"Just me," Oscar said, poking his head around the door.

"Hi," she said, glancing at him in the mirror, but even seeing his face for that brief moment made her stomach churn.

"You disappeared last night." Oscar closed the door behind him and leant against it.

Olive shrugged. "Did you really expect me to stay?" She hadn't wanted to leave Oscar's flat but when he'd left her, naked and alone, in his room, she'd never felt more vulnerable and exposed. After waiting for him to come back for twenty minutes she'd had a sudden urge to get out of there as quickly as possible, so she got the Tube back to her home on the other side of London before midnight.

"You know I had to speak to my agent. We had to figure out how bad the situation is."

"Damage control." She nodded.

"Exactly."

"I don't think I've ever been considered as 'damage' before," she said, rubbing a hand over her heart, almost as if she were trying to ease the pain he'd just absent-mindedly inflicted.

"You know that's not what I meant. This is a difficult situation that needs to be handled . . . delicately from now on."

"How bad is it?" She leant on her elbows and covered her mouth with her linked hands.

"Could be worse." He shrugged. "But it's not ideal. Zadie's furious. She retweeted the photo along with some pretty harsh comments."

"I know," Olive sighed.

"You've seen?"

"I've had to delete Twitter from my phone. Just for a little while. I'm not really accustomed to death threats from teenage strangers." Despite knowing there would be a lack of notifications, Olive still pressed the home button on her phone, just to make sure no more hateful words had wheedled their way onto the screen.

"Oh, Olive," Oscar groaned.

"Why is Zadie so angry anyway? You're not together any more. Who you kiss and who you're in photos with isn't any of her concern, is it?"

"Have you never seen pictures of an ex with someone else quite soon after a break-up and felt terrible?"

Olive thought back to when pictures of Jason and Rosanna had surfaced. They hadn't even been kissing, but even so, the pictures had made Olive's stomach tie itself in knots.

"Yes, I suppose I get that. I just don't think I'd ever . . . tweet about it."

"That's why I'm now stood in your dressing room trying to make things up with you and I'm very glad I'm no longer with her."

"How's it been for you? You've got triple the amount of followers I've got."

"Fine. No death threats. Just a lot of questions."

"Funny how you're the boy caught in the middle of two women and yet it's me who gets the backlash. Like I'm some home wrecker." Olive tried to laugh but she suddenly realised what she said hadn't been a joke. That's exactly what she'd been made to feel like.

"Zadie and I aren't even together." Oscar moved further into the room but still kept his distance from Olive.

"I know, but your fans seem pretty loyal to her."

"It's because we were an on-screen couple for years. You must understand why they feel that way?" Oscar leant against her dressing table, his back towards the mirror.

"Of course, I get it, but . . . *death threats*?" She shook her head, careful not to shake any tears loose.

"I know. That's out of line and I'm sorry. But I can't control the move of every individual who happens to be a fan of me or the TV show I was in. And at this point if I say anything publicly, I could make it worse. For both of us." Oscar wanted to run over to her, scoop her up and he wished he could fix it all with a kiss. *That's what got us into this mess*, he thought.

"I don't expect you to be sorry. You've not done anything wrong," Olive said as Oscar lightly scoffed. "I just don't think you realise how hard all of this is for me." She took a deep breath, feeling tears threatening to spill over, but kept herself still.

"This is hard for me too, y'know?" Oscar sighed.

"Yes, it must be really tough having two women vying for your attention, some more publicly than others, and a loyal fanbase who care about you deeply." Olive would have rolled her eyes if she thought it wouldn't force out the tears she was fighting hard to keep at bay.

"Olive, you know it's not like that. The reality is I've got a crazy fame-hungry ex-girlfriend who's trying to sabotage my new career and she's found an in with the only glimmer of happiness I've found in months." He sighed, covering his face with his hands.

Olive finally looked at him through the mirror, but she could barely see him, her eyes were so full. Was it her demons, her own insecurities making her wonder whether she was the only one he treated this way? Or had she picked up on something, and that's why she couldn't shake the feeling that she was being kept in the dark?

"Are you saying you don't want to do this any more?" Oscar held still, his face unchanging.

"Aren't you telling me we *can't* do this any more?" Olive shrugged. Her body felt heavy and her head

**111**

throbbed and she wondered if she cared enough to live through the stress that Oscar brought with him.

"No. No, not at all. We just need to be more . . . *careful*."

"More hiding." She closed her eyes.

"Not hiding. Just . . . less kissing on trains." He slid himself closer towards her.

"I don't want to be your sordid secret, Oscar. It's not even like this is a real relationship. We're just . . . playing."

"Shouldn't that mean there's less pressure? Less expectation?"

"Maybe." She shook her head. "But I can't cope with the constant game of guessing what's acceptable for two people who aren't together but are 'involved'."

"Stop guessing. Just do what feels right."

Olive turned to him and pulled her knees up to her chest in the armchair. "Did it feel right when you left me alone last night? After having a whole conversation to convince me this thing between us wasn't just about sex, you thought it was okay to have sex with me and then disappear?" Olive couldn't keep the tinge of anger out of her voice, but it was only the tip of the iceberg compared to what she felt inside.

"Olive, I'm so sorry. The whole incident with the picture got me spooked and I didn't know how to react, but I shouldn't have left you. I can't imagine how that must have made you feel." Her eyes were so big and Oscar couldn't bear seeing them filled with tears instead of that playful sparkle. "I don't want this to be over."

"No. Me neither." Olive wiped away her tears. Despite all her anger, she understood why Oscar had acted the way he had and wondered if she'd have done much better in his situation. "I'm just tired."

"Of me?"

"Of this." She gestured to her wet cheeks.

"This can be better."

"It's been what? Less than a month and I'm already in tears."

"But it means you care, right? Doesn't that count for something?" Oscar slid towards her again.

"Of course it does." There was a brief flicker of a smile on her lips and Oscar jumped at that glimmer of hope. He went to her, took her hands and pulled her into his arms.

"I'm sorry this has happened."

"Me too," she said, trying so hard not to give in and sob into his embrace.

"It'll all blow over eventually." He stroked her hair, but the moment had gone. Olive pulled away from him and without looking at him or his reflection she said, "I'm just getting tired of waiting for eventually."

Lars
She's not yours.
Eliza
Actually, Lars . . . I am.
[Eliza holds up her hand and reveals a large, sparkling engagement ring.]

"Okay, thank you! Olive . . ." Michael stood from his seat in the front row and leant over the edge of the orchestra pit. Although *When The Curtain Falls* was primarily a play, Michael had insisted that a live band played in the interludes between scenes and in the lively bar scenes to add atmosphere. The producers hated the added expense, but Michael was certain the audience would be enraptured. Olive lifted the hem of her dress and teetered over to the edge of the stage in her heels. "Yes, Olive — I need you to be a little more emotional here. Tears. I need tears. Can you do that, darling?"

"Er, yes, of course." Olive scratched a determined itch under the lace of her wig.

"You sound hesitant." Michael folded his arms. "Speak to me, Olive. Tell me what's on your mind." He sighed.

"It's just that . . . in the script, Eliza seems so strong at this moment. Unfaltering. She's putting on a brave face for the sake of Lars. I was playing it like . . . maybe if Lars believes she doesn't love him he'll leave and won't be in danger any longer? Is that wrong?"

"No, no. There are no wrong choices here," he said and smiled as Olive's brow dripped with sweat. "Just better ones. I really would like tears, Olive. Can you do that for me?"

"Of course!" She smiled. "No worries!"

Michael sat back in his seat. "From the top of the scene!"

Olive wobbled back to Oscar, slipping a little on a bump in the stage floor.

"You all right, there?" He took her elbow, but she gently shook him off.

"Yeah," she said with her hands on her hips, glancing back at Michael who sat back in his seat, furiously flipping through pages of the script. "Actually, no. No, I'm not. He wants me to cry? Is he *stupid*?" she hissed quietly, facing upstage.

"And this is a problem because . . . you can't cry on cue?" Oscar fumbled.

"I can! At least . . . I think I can. I've never had to before. But that's not the point! The point is it's totally out of character for Eliza!"

"Then don't do it." Oscar caught her elbow again and Olive wobbled over another bump in the floor and this time she leant into his warm hand. He smiled at her, a little too widely, and Olive's heart plunged downwards because she couldn't bring herself to smile back.

"I *have* to." She sighed and looked into Oscar's calm eyes. "He won't be here for ever," she whispered, "I'll do what he wants until he's gone and then I'll play Eliza how I want to play her."

"You sound like you've done that before."

"Well, when you think about it, whilst the director is . . . well . . . the director, it's still only an opinion on how the parts should be played. It's all art and interpretation, right?"

"Sure. But won't you get in trouble?" Oscar asked, and talking about other things with him seemed to distract Olive from the ache in her chest and the thudding of her head.

"When I was in *Oliver!*, years ago, we had two versions of the show: the director's version and our own version when we knew he wasn't watching. I think it's pretty common practice amongst us *thespians*." Olive placed her index finger under her nose and tilted her head with it to accompany the posh voice she'd adopted.

"Wow. Well. Noted!"

"Can we go from 'Actually, Lars', please?" shouted Michael.

"He expects me to cry in a matter of what? Three lines?" Olive whispered to Oscar.

"That's mad," he replied softly. "Can we go back a little further?" he said at full volume to Michael.

"We're really pushed for time here, Oscar," said Michael, dismissing him with a shake of the head and a shoo of the hand.

"I know, I know. I just think it might be easier for us all to get a good run into the most emotional part of the scene."

Michael looked Oscar up and down and Oscar suddenly wondered what would happen if his attempt at making things up to Olive backfired entirely.

"For someone who's spent the majority of their life in television, I wouldn't have thought you'd need much of a run-up," Michael said, slowly folding his arms across his chest.

"I guess I'm just out of practice!" Oscar shrugged, and the cast held a collective breath as Michael paused for what felt like an hour.

"Ok, Mr TV," he glanced down at the script in his lap, "we'll go from the top of the scene. And if we have to stay late, we will, and when everyone misses their trains home they can direct their anger at you."

"Lovely." Oscar nodded, turning his back on the auditorium. *Mr TV?* he mouthed at Olive and she mouthed *Thank you* back to him and when he winked at her, her heart lifted a few inches from where it had fallen.

Eliza
You were never supposed to find out this way.
Melvin
You didn't do well to hide it.
Lars
Leave her be, goddammit!
Eliza
Larson, please. Go back inside. Go home. Anywhere but here.
Melvin
Yes, Larson. Do as she says.
Eliza
Please, Lars. Not here.
Lars
She's not yours.
Eliza
Actually, Lars . . . I am.

Oscar watched Olive lift her hand where a large engagement ring glittered in the blue stage lights. His heart squeezed gently in his chest as the briefest of thoughts flickered into his head: *What if Olive got engaged to someone who isn't me?* His throat closed around his next line.

Lars
Eliza . . . no.
[Lars holds up the gun and points it at Melvin]
Eliza
NO!

Olive placed a hand on Oscar's chest and could feel his pulsing heartbeat beneath his crisp shirt. She hoped he couldn't feel the warmth radiating off her and hoped the blue lights were drowning out her red cheeks.

Melvin
Oh, Larson. When will you learn? It doesn't matter how well you scrub up or how many lavish parties you sneak yourself into. It doesn't matter how many of London's finest you rub shoulders with or even how many wealthy women's beds you wheedle your way into. You will never be good enough.
Eliza
Please don't listen to him, Lars. Just go back inside.
Lars
Do you love him? Do you?

Olive's breath caught as she looked into Oscar's eyes. It seemed as though Oscar had disappeared entirely and Lars' love for Eliza was seeping from his every

**118**

pore. Olive's chest tightened at the idea of Oscar ever looking at her, the real her, in that way.

Eliza
I fear you'll kill him either way.
Lars
Eliza. If you tell me yes, how could you think that
I would kill the man you love and put you
through that misery? No, Eliza. Should you say
yes, I will turn this gun on myself and the bullet
will be destined . . .

Oscar paused.

. . . for me.

He had selfishly hoped to see a flicker of *something* in Olive's face, but when her eyes filled with tears, he couldn't be sure that it was her crying and not Eliza. She was an extraordinary actress after all. *And why would it be real, you idiot? Focus*, he thought.

Melvin
Must we have all this drama? It's terribly dull. We
all know you don't have the gall to shoot a rabbit,
let alone a man. Just put the gun down, Larson.
Lars
Do . . . you . . . love him?

*If I said yes, would he care?* Olive wondered. *Or would he find another girl in the ensemble to pass the time with? Oh, I'm in way over my head, aren't I? How have I done this again?*

Eliza
I . . . I . . . do not.

Olive took her director's note and tears spilled down her face. Oscar pulled the trigger, the blank bullet flashed and smoked, and the sound of a gunshot rippled through the auditorium and the stage went black. Oscar tried to find Olive's hand in the blackout but his hand collided with nothing but darkness.

"Olive?" he whispered.

"Okay, thanks very much, everyone! Go get some rest and I'll see you on opening night!" Michael called, rubbing his hands together. Some of the cast clapped but most were already half out of their costumes on the way back to their dressing rooms.

"Olive?" Oscar called as he walked down the stage right wing. "Doug, is Olive down there?"

"I think she's gone to her dressing room," Doug called back, taking off his flat cap and ruffling his own hair back into its usual disarray. Oscar started unbuttoning his shirt himself and gently pushed aside the curtain in the wing to widen his path so he could scoot past Howard and Jane.

"Oh — Oscar! Are you coming tonight?" Tamara ran to him and stroked his bicep, Jane watching close behind. They were both out of costume and in their own dressy clothes already.

"What's tonight?" he asked, holding his shirt closed between his fingers.

"Just . . . drinks?" She shrugged.

"Again?"

"Always!" she laughed.

"Maybe. No. Probably not." Oscar backed away. "Sorry." Tamara snatched her hands away.

"Why? You gotta go snog on more Tube lines?" She tried to smile as she said it, in some attempt to make it sound like she could have been half joking — but her true feelings gave her away in the wobble of her bottom lip as she swivelled on her heels and left.

"We'll miss you!" Jane shouted after him, but Oscar was already through the double doors and heading towards Olive's dressing room.

OLIVE GREEN was displayed in a cursive font on a laminated card stuck to the door, with the show's logo in the bottom left hand corner. He knocked twice.

"Olive? You in there?" The door opened abruptly and there stood Olive in her own clothes, a make-up wipe in her hand and her lipstick smeared across her chin. She quickly finished cleaning her face before throwing the wipe in the bin.

"How are you changed already? Did I pass out for half an hour while you all got dressed?" Olive let go of the door to slip on her boots but when Oscar followed her inside she glanced up at him and he backtracked the few steps he'd taken.

"It's called 'under dressing'. Depending on the costume you have, you can probably get away with changing into some of your own clothes in the interval and putting your costume back on over the top." She sniffed.

"Olive, what's wrong?"

"Nothing." She wiped her nose on her cardigan sleeve as she pulled her purple rucksack onto her shoulder.

"Olive . . ." Oscar stepped forwards again, but she flicked her dressing room table lights off and took the weight of the door from him.

"Honestly." She gestured out into the hall.

"Really?" he asked her as she turned the key she'd left in the lock and slipped her index finger into the keyring loop. "You're sticking with 'nothing'?"

"I don't know what else to say." She shrugged.

"How about the truth? Just talk to me. Tell me what's going on."

"You already know! This!" She flapped her hands around between them. "Me and you. It's all so complicated and it's just not . . . fun, Oscar. I hate feeling like I'm a secret. I hate hiding and I hate feeling the constant threat of your ex-girlfriend and her blindly loyal fans."

"I thought we sorted all this out, and we were okay? I thought . . ."

"You thought wrong, Oscar. I don't think you quite grasp what it feels like to be kept hidden like you're something to be ashamed of. And *then*, when you see a brief glimmer of it changing, a glimmer in the form of a kiss on a train when anyone could be looking . . . that glimmer is then not only snuffed out, but you have to go so far as sorting out damage control? To attempt to cover up any trace of . . . well . . . *me*." Olive put the key back in the lock of her door and turned it.

"What are you doing?"

"I'm going in here to have a cry and you're going to go out and have a drink with Tamara. You're probably better off spending your time with her from now on. I'm sure she'll gladly be your little secret." Olive walked into her darkened dressing room, slammed the door and, without even a thought to turning on the light, she slid down the back of the door onto the floor. Tears poured out of her and she clamped a hand to her mouth, knowing Oscar would probably be able to hear her sobbing.

Oscar stood in the hallway, stunned, torn between waiting and trying to fix things or walking away, knowing there was little to be done. He could hear her faint sniffing and he knew nothing would dull the ache in his chest but he knew the best way to start was with a stiff drink or two.

# CHAPTER
# SEVEN

## Reawakening

Olive scrubbed at her eyes with a half used baby wipe, making them even more sore from crying. She couldn't believe how foolish she'd been. She had told herself not to get too invested; had warned herself that any kind of relationship with Oscar would be complicated. She had berated herself when she knew her feelings towards him were growing, and she'd held back when she wanted to tell him all the things she'd love to hear had he said them to her.

"At least you know now," she said to herself. A single bulb around her dressing room mirror flickered twice. Olive switched the lights on and off again, hoping that old trick would sort it out, except when she turned them off again the bulb that had flickered was now on . . . even though she'd switched them off at the mains.

"Weird," she whispered. She switched the lights back on and the singular bulb turned off again. "What the hell?" Olive muttered and reached up to give the bulb a twist, thinking there was some loose wiring which could be fixed with a jiggle, but before her hand could even touch the bulb, it shattered into pieces. She retracted her hand quickly with a yelp as the pieces of glass scattered over her dressing table.

"Okay, time to go," she said to the empty room, her heart beating wildly in her throat. In one swift movement, she grabbed her coat and her bag and ran out the door. She quickly turned the key in the lock and relished the feeling of being distracted from her boy troubles, even if it was due to being well and truly spooked.

"Here's my key," she said as she put it through the little hatch where Walter sat on the other side.

"You're late tonight, Miss Green," Walter said, hanging her key on its hook.

"It's Olive, please." She tried to smile but it felt stiff and odd. "And yeah. Didn't feel like going home straight after rehearsals."

"Everything all right?" Walter asked.

"Yeah, yeah. Just got some admin done. Taxes. That kind of thing," she lied.

"Well, if you need anything, just let me know."

"Actually, now that you mention it, one of my bulbs has gone on my dressing room mirror."

"It probably just needs a jiggle."

"Actually, that's the thing. I did try that but the bulb sort of . . . exploded."

"Oh," Walter said, and Olive couldn't help but notice that he looked oddly worried. "Right."

"Gave me quite a fright!" Olive tried to laugh but it sounded forced even to her own ears.

"Well, no worries. I'll get it replaced as soon as possible." Walter noted it down on the pad in front of him that already listed a couple of other odd jobs here and there around the theatre.

"Thank you, Walter."

"Careful out there," Walter called as Olive pushed open the stage door which almost got pulled out of her hand by a fierce gust of wind. "Weather's looking grim."

"Just my luck," she said, putting down her rucksack and shrugging on her hoodless coat. "See you Monday, Walter." She swung her rucksack back into place, huddled her neck in her coat's collar and stepped out into the rain, closing the door behind her.

Directly opposite stage door was a bar that always seemed to be bursting with people and buzzing with music and chatter no matter the time of day. Howard stood outside, a cigarette in one hand and his phone in the other. He looked up and saw her but didn't smile. She gave him a slight wave, adjusting her heavy bag on her back and doing up the wooden toggles on the front of her grey coat. Howard returned the wave with his phone but glanced behind him through the window of the pub. When he looked back at her, his face was drained of colour and expression.

"What's up?" she shouted as she ran across the street, her boots splashing through the big puddle that had collected outside the bar.

"You've been in the theatre for ages. We all thought you'd gone home," Howard replied, almost nervously.

"Just had some stuff to do."

"Are you staying for a drink?" Howard took a large step to his left, blocking the entrance to the pub.

"I don't think so . . . why?" she said, glancing behind his shoulder, but he took another step in front of her.

"I just . . . I don't think it's a good idea you go inside."

"What? Why?"

Just then Doug burst through the door, his beer sloshing over the side of the glass as he slammed it down on the large windowsill.

"Babe, let's go," he said, taking her hand.

"What's going on?"

"Let's just go and we'll talk in a minute."

"No, Doug, tell me what's going on." She snatched her hand out of Doug's grip and it was then that she caught a glimpse of some of the cast through the window. They all seemed to have made a little circle and were looking at a central pair who were uncomfortably entangled.

"Is that Tamara?" Olive would have recognised her perfectly sculpted talons anywhere, even when tugging at the hair of the unfortunate man she happened to have her lips locked onto, like a leech sucking out his life and soul.

"Yeah, it is," said Doug, taking her hand again.

"Who's she kissing?" Olive felt her heart fall down a deep, dark pit of despair when she looked at Doug's sad eyes. She looked back though the window and the light glanced off Oscar's face as he drunkenly tried to wrap his arms around Tamara's tall and bony frame, as though he didn't know how to hold someone who didn't fit so well in his embrace. His lips tried to find hers, but her tongue was too busy trying to reach his tonsils. It looked sloppy and awkward, but they didn't stop. *Why won't they stop?* Olive thought, but she didn't cry. She felt numb, like her whole body had gone into shock, and even the icy rain that was hitting the back of her exposed neck didn't seem to chill her.

"Olive, stop watching," Doug said, squeezing her fingers.

"I can't," Olive replied, but her voice barely came out as more than a whisper.

Finally, Tamara and Oscar broke apart and even though she could see Oscar's slow drunken blink, how he fumbled for his beer as Tamara disappeared to the toilets, she couldn't find anything to excuse his actions, as much as she wanted *something* to explain away the pain she knew she'd have to endure when the numbness had worn off. Oscar brushed back his hair, looking slightly dazed, and almost stumbled backwards into Sammy, who gave him a shove forwards. Olive watched Sammy mouth a few choice words at Oscar, and it was only when she pointed at the window directly at her that Olive realised Sammy knew she was there, watching the night's sordid events unfold. Oscar's eyes widened when they locked with Olive's and his hands went to the sides of his head, like he was trying to stop his brain from spinning.

"I need to go."

"Olive . . ." Doug let go of her hand as she pulled away and stepped backwards into the road.

She turned just as a car pulled into the street, its tyres racing through a puddle and throwing a fan of water up into the air, soaking Olive from the waist down.

"Text me when you're home safe!" Doug called after her as she crossed the road, ran down the side of the theatre and turned right to walk along front of house.

"OLIVE!" She heard Oscar's voice call out behind her and instinctively she slowed down, but she didn't turn around. "Olive, please stop!"

"We'll talk when you're sober," she called back to him over her shoulder.

"Please don't leave it like this."

"*Me?!*" She whipped around, and Oscar almost bumped into her. "I'm not leaving it like anything, Oscar. You're the one who's decided to end this."

"I thought it was already over!"

"We had an argument!"

"In which you ended it! You told me to go off with Tamara!"

"Which I see you took *extremely* literally." The bulbs around the theatre's sign glared obnoxiously brightly and Olive was so glad there were no staff left inside to watch this spat between them.

"I'm sorry. I know that doesn't seem like anything right now, but my God, I'm sorry. I'm drunk and stupid and a total loser. You don't need me in your life."

"Don't you dare self-deprecate and think that's going to get you an out of jail free card, Oscar. I don't care how insecure you are. I don't care if you think so little of yourself you need to get with every and any airhead who throws herself at you in an attempt to boost your self-worth. Nothing excuses the fact that you've spent the last month trying to hide me away and doing damage control when the world caught the slightest glimpse of me . . . and then kissed someone else in the middle of a bar where the whole of Soho could watch."

"I know —"

"I AM NOT FINISHED." Olive's anger came to the boil. "Not only have you kissed someone else so publicly, but you've kissed someone else *in the cast*! Do you realise how humiliated I am going to feel walking back into work on Monday morning, on opening night no less? And on top of all that, Oscar," *Oh no, don't cry,* she thought, "you've confirmed my worst insecurity." *Shit,* she thought as a sob rose in her throat and the tears gathered in her eyes again. She quickly covered her face with both her hands, wishing she wasn't there and that he wasn't watching her.

"What do you mean?" Oscar's T-shirt was soaked through from the rain, but the alcohol running through his body kept him from feeling the cold.

Olive took a deep, icy breath. "I always wondered why you spent time with me instead of someone as beautiful as Tamara, but I had every confidence in myself, in my own personality. I knew that even though I don't look typically like any of your ex-girlfriends, you were spending time with me because I'm fun. Because I'm clever. Because I can talk to you about more than the latest *Love Island* contestants and which celebrities have most recently broken up or got married or had a baby."

"I know, Olive. And you do make me laugh and —" Olive held up her hand.

"But none of that matters now. Because you've confirmed exactly what that voice in the back of my head has been saying that, up until now, I've been able to quieten. Now, you've proved that it doesn't matter how fun I am, how much we can talk or how much I make you laugh, because I don't look like Tamara."

"No, Olive, it's not like that, I promise you." He took a step towards her and she took a step back.

"And the very worst part isn't even that you've made me feel like this. The worst part is . . . I let you."

Oscar looked at Olive and his drunken haze seemed to clear for just a moment. He saw her shivering in the rain, her pale face without make-up and her hair wet and slicked against her cheeks and he wanted nothing more than to sweep her into his arms and keep her warm and dry. To shelter her from all the hurt she was feeling, but knowing he couldn't because all the hurt she was feeling could be directly traced back to him. And it was this thought, that he couldn't kiss her and make this better, could probably never kiss her again, that made him realise he'd fallen in love with her.

Olive looked at Oscar and started to feel the pain pour out of her heart and seep into her bones. He was so beautiful and looked so lost, but Olive knew she couldn't forgive him, which hurt her more than what he'd actually done. She wanted nothing more than to find a way around this. To find a way to be able to look at him without remembering the image of him kissing Tamara. But she knew that would take far more time than she was willing to give. It was in that moment, that she realised he could never be hers, that she knew she'd well and truly fallen in love with him.

"This, whatever this was, is over." The bulbs around the theatre's sign all flickered for a few moments, as though too much electricity was passing through the current. And then with a loud crackle, everything went dark.

Walter poured the hot water into his mug, pulled up his blanket across his knees, and settled in for the night in his small office. Although he'd much prefer a book, his eyesight was poor now and the more tired he got the more the words danced about on the page. So, on the recommendation of the actress playing Scarlett O'Hara in the last production of *Gone With The Wind*, he'd mastered the art of Netflix. Their selection of old movies was sublime, and he even tried a few movies that had been made in the last decade and, to his surprise, enjoyed them. His laptop was open on his desk, the opening bars of the overture to *Oliver!* blaring out of the speakers when suddenly everything went quiet and the film started to buffer. The little red spinning wheel taunted Walter and his tired old legs, and he said a little prayer that it would fix itself in the next few moments so that he wouldn't have to get up and restart it. Then the screen went black and the lamp on the desk started to flicker.

"Fawn?" he whispered. "What's got you upset?" The bulb shattered with a bang and Walter couldn't help but yelp.

*Walter.*

132

He was certain it wasn't just the draughty theatre creaking, making his old ears hear things that weren't there.

*Waaaalter.*

No, it was certainly his name called in a voice he knew only too well.

*But she only appears once a year,* he thought. "Fawn? What's wrong? What's going on?" Walter still hadn't moved. Working in such an old theatre, knowing full well he was constantly surrounded by ghosts, it was rare that Walter felt scared or encountered the unexpected. Yet here he was, stuck to his armchair, his palms cold yet clammy, clutching his blanket up around his shoulders. From his chair he could see that a light had started to flicker somewhere in the corridor that led backstage. Whatever force was within the building was moving from light to light down the corridor and making its way towards Walter, each light shattering before it moved on to the next.

"Fawn, please answer me?" Walter's voice was loud but audibly nervous. The light moved from the ceiling fixtures in the corridor to the small desk lamp at stage door. It started off as just the tiniest of glimmers, barely visible to Walter's eyes but definitely there, wobbling in the dark. Then the light steadily grew brighter and brighter. The bulb cracked, and the light dimmed for a moment before it began to grow again, shining through the cracks in the bulb, a thread of gold light spun like silk. It spilled onto the floor and started to ravel itself into a tight ball that grew up and up and Walter could see that it was starting to take the shape of a pair of heeled shoes. The light began to ravel itself faster and suddenly there were ankles, legs beneath a long dress, wide hips, hands, arms, a cinched waist, slender shoulders, a delicate neck and before Walter knew it, there she was. Fawn Burrows. Standing before him, golden and glowing.

"Fawn?"

"It's me," she laughed, looking at her own sparkling hands.

"But how? How are you here? You can only come back once a year. On the anniversary of your death! What —"

"Walter, I don't know the rules. Something's woken me up," she said, spinning, the hem of her dress fizzing.

He let go of the blanket, his knuckles stiff and cramped. "What's wrong?"

"I'm not supposed to be here. I've never been here on any day other than the day I died. So, whatever's brought me back . . ." the flames in her eyes crackled, "it's big."

HAMISH BOATWRIGHT PRESENTS
A BRAND NEW PRODUCTION
BY C. H. FLETCHER

# FAWN BURROWS and
# LAWRENCE BAKER in

# *When the Curtain Falls*

Directed by
## WILLIAM HURDLE

---

# THE SOUTHERN CROSS THEATRE

SHAFTESBURY AVENUE, LONDON
OPENS 1 APRIL 1952

# CHAPTER
# EIGHT

## Right Place, Right Time

Walter Brown was a city boy through and through. He knew how to weave in and out of people in crowds, which side streets were shortcuts and which coffee houses sold the best brew for the cheapest price. He'd grown up amongst the smoke and the soot and although he never could get the grime out from under his fingernails, there was no place else he'd rather be. London was, and always would be, home — but nowhere more so than Soho. The lights down Shaftesbury Avenue ignited a spark inside Walter that glimmered no matter where he went. It wasn't that he wanted to be an actor, on stage or screen, even if he did spend all the money he had on trying to look like James Cagney. No, Walter was simply enamoured by the glitz and glamour of the theatre. It was a love affair that had begun as a child, and one he knew would last a lifetime.

Before the war, Walter had lived a very simple life. Clothes were patched and mended, all the food in the cupboards had to be used up before they even began to think about heading to the shops and even when they did, cheap tins of spam and beans were always at the top of the list. When Britain had declared war against

Germany, Walter's mother had taken no chances and Walter had found himself on a ferry to the Isle of Wight, placed into the care of his kind and overly zealous Auntie Maureen and his quiet Uncle Harold on their farm. His father, a fighter pilot, and his mother, a housewife, were both cruelly claimed by the Blitz a year later and Walter could not and would never understand the destruction and the lives lost, all in the name of King and country.

Home schooled by patient and intelligent Uncle Harold, Walter had stayed with his aunt and uncle until he reached the age of eighteen. He learned invaluable skills in the country such as how to ride a horse, how to shoot a rabbit and how to milk a cow, but every other weekend when his uncle didn't need him for sheep shearing or his auntie for baking, he'd borrow his uncle's bike and ride the five miles to the nearest picture house in Newport and spend the money he'd earned helping on the farm on watching the latest movie. The rim of moving lights around the movie's title on the board outside glimmered in Walter's eyes, the images of Irene Dunne and Judy Garland dancing around in his head long after he had returned home. And despite filling his days with activities, Walter seemed to have an itch that just couldn't be scratched. Finally, after a lot of tears from his Auntie Maureen and a test on a map of London from Uncle Harold, Walter convinced them that it was time for him to spread his wings and return to his hometown. And so, on his eighteenth birthday he booked a ticket on the eight o'clock ferry to Portsmouth and a train from there to London for the following day.

As soon as his feet touched the platform at London Victoria, Walter knew he would never leave. He'd secured a job as a caretaker's assistant at a school in Greenford, and although it was a little further out of central London than he'd have liked, he needed to work, and the school were paying more than he thought was usual for a caretaker's assistant. It was only when he met the caretaker that he knew why.

"Here's ya list. Gerron with it." Mr Lancaster was tall, yet exceedingly round, and his face was a shade of red Walter thought you should only ever see on a strawberry. The list was scrawled in an illegible hand on a thick notebook and Walter could see it was a few pages long with some of the work needing to be done dating back at least a few weeks.

"I'm not due to start until tomorrow," Walter said, desperate to put down his trunk.

"You're due to start when I tell ya to."

"But — excuse me, sir, it's Sunday and I thought —" Walter said but Mr Lancaster simply shouted, "Sling yarook and gerron with it!" He slammed the door, knocking Walter's trunk into his knee. Walter found his quarters — a room with a bed and a sink — and got to work. He scrubbed floors and toilets, removed chewing gum from the undersides of desks with a butter knife, fixed windows and curtain rails and even unstuck a bird from a chimney. By the time he'd finished the first page of his list, it was almost midnight. He was tired and hungry, but the exhaustion outweighed the hunger and he was asleep before his head even hit his uncomfortable pillow.

Walter stayed at the school for six months before Mr Lancaster drove him so insane he could no longer bear it. He saved enough money for three months' rent on a small flat nearer central London and found a new job as a pot washer at The Langham hotel in Marylebone who were desperate for a new boy to start immediately and Walter fit the bill. He almost scrubbed and rinsed his fingerprints into oblivion, but The Langham paid him well and he scrubbed his way to as many months rent on his flat in Lewisham as he needed. He didn't necessarily love the work, but he loved that he was living in the heart of his favourite city, and that his work brought him only a short walk from London's West End. On his lunch breaks Walter could often be found stood by various stage doors, and whilst he didn't want to speak to any of the actors nor did he really want them to notice him, he enjoyed hearing their conversations, seeing the remnants of make-up line the edges of their faces and watching these extraordinarily talented people sit next to regular people in cafés between matinees and evening shows. Walter was fascinated by the world beyond the stage door and longed to see on the other side.

It was on one particularly sunny day when Walter was waiting by the stage door of the Southern Cross Theatre that both doors suddenly burst open and a young boy hit the floor with a grotesque crack. He was followed by a short, stocky man neatly dressed in a grey, well-pressed suit with greasy slicked hair and a thin moustache above his sweaty lip. Walter took his appearance in quickly, his attention swiftly drawn by the gun held in his hand, the barrel of which was pointing directly at the centre of the young boy's forehead.

"If you ever so much as look at this theatre again, I'm gonna know about it and, so help me God, I will squash you under my boot." The man pulled the trigger. The young boy yelped, and Walter couldn't help but scream too, flinging his arms over his head and cowering against the theatre wall. There was a bang and a fizzle and when Walter cautiously opened his eyes and peeked through his tangle of arms and hands, he saw a thin trail of smoke snaking out of the end of the gun.

"Now get out of 'ere." The man gave the boy a hard kick on one of his shins and the boy scrambled up off the cobbles and hobbled down the street, soon lost in the hordes of people.

"It's a prop," Walter laughed, breathing heavily and clutching his chest, trying to calm his heart. "It's a prop!" He laughed some more.

"Well done," said the man, rolling his eyes. "You ever worked in a theatre before?" He used the gun to gesture to the open stage door, twirling it expertly in his hand, and Walter realised this wasn't the first time he'd dealt with a firearm.

"No, but I've been a caretaker." *I did more than assist Mr Lancaster*, he thought, *I practically did his job for him!* "And a pot washer. Basically, I can fix and/or wash anything you like."

"Can you answer a phone?"

"Yes."

"Can you sign for packages?"

"Absolutely!" Walter held his hands behind his back, his feet apart and nodded.

"Do you often lose things? Like . . . your keys for instance?"

"Never."

"That's good enough for me. Get inside." The man disappeared through the door.

"You're kidding?" Walter ran after him.

"Do I look like I'm kidding?"

"Definitely not."

"Then get inside!"

Walter followed the man through another set of double doors and down a long corridor. They passed posters for various different musicals, all signed with messages of love and well wishes from cast members. Kiss marks in vibrant lipsticks had been dotted around the walls along with girls' names and the running dates of their shows underneath. Every nook and cranny was filled with a hidden history that you wouldn't know was there unless you were invited through the stage door to see it.

"Wow," Walter breathed.

"You keeping up, boy?" said the man. Walter hadn't realised he'd become so engrossed in reading all the messages, he'd stopped in the middle of the corridor.

"Yes! Sorry! I'm here!" Walter bounded to the burly man and as he turned the slight bend in the corridor, Walter saw he had been joined by someone else.

**142**

"Lenny! This is your new protégé." Lenny was almost half Walter's height and his flat cap threw a shadow over his eyes so Walter could only see his bent nose, his wrinkled cheeks and the cigarette hanging out of his lips.

"Bit young, ain't 'e?" Lenny wiped sandwich crumbs from the stubble on his chin.

"I'm twenty-two," mumbled Walter.

"All right, all right," Lenny sighed. "Anyfing's better than a thief." He grabbed Walter by the arm and pulled him through a door, under a sign that read SILENCE! YOU CAN BE HEARD ON STAGE! Walter held his breath as they entered into the upstage, stage left wing and found themselves in a small quick-change area that could only comfortably hold maybe four people. Large set pieces hung above them and swung gently from strong ropes and wires. Even though Walter knew they were probably as secure as the crown jewels in the Tower of London, he tried not to stand directly underneath anything. Just in case. From the back the sets were clearly made of wood but as he caught a glimpse onto the stage, he could see the brickwork so convincingly painted onto the other side. Lipsticks were lined up along the edge of a wooden desk fixed to the back of the set, in front of a crooked mirror hung from a rusty nail. All the lipsticks were open, ready for the evening's performance. The smell of dry ice was thick in the stuffy, almost moist air and caught in the back of Walter's throat.

"This way!" Lenny tottered down the cramped stage left wing. Walter's shoulders were gently grazing the

143

wall and the black cloth that hung to hide anyone from the audience's view. Lenny opened up a door and climbed three steps into another carpeted quick-change area, this one with a mirror with lightbulbs around the rim and a full set of make-up laid out in a neat row beside a gold box of tissues. Walter caught Lenny's eye and realised he'd been watching him take in every detail.

"That's for our new leading lady. Quiet girl but nice enough. Very young. In over her head. Don't get any funny ideas," said Lenny, pointing at him with one of his lumpy fingers that had clearly been broken at some point in his lifetime.

"Of course not," said Walter, nodding emphatically, but Lenny simply laughed.

"Out here, then!" Lenny produced a key and opened up another door leading out into a well-lit, ornate corridor and Walter figured this must be front of house. "What the audience can see is a right side nicer than what we get to slum it in. Funny that, innit? We're doing all the work and we get all the shit. Dirty stone floors. Chipped paintwork. This lot get carpets, velvet cushions *and* a show? Makes no sense if you ask me!"

Walter wondered how much work Lenny actually did at stage door, compared to the actors and the crew in the show, and whether his bitterness was valid. They walked down a set of stairs past pictures of famous actors from years gone by who had performed on the stage of the Southern Cross, and Lenny pushed through a set of polished wooden doors with a little

144

more aggression than was necessary, bringing Walter out into the auditorium.

"Excuse me?" A man was sitting in one of the stalls seats, sunk down low on its cushion with his legs outstretched and his ankles crossed on the backs of one of the seats diagonally in front of him.

"Sorry mate, just showing the new boy around."

"Mate?" The man swung his legs down, stood and straightened out his clean and well-pressed suit jacket. "Who do you think you *are?*"

"I'm Lenny. Stage door." Walter glanced sideways at Lenny and wondered how good he was at gauging situations. "You know the theatre's closed, right?" *Clearly not very good at all,* Walter thought.

"Lenny, I think he may be someone important," he whispered.

"What?" said Lenny, quite loudly.

"Yes, boy, care to share with the group?" The man walked slowly towards them down the row, making every step more decisive than the last.

"I was just saying you're clearly someone of great importance and so I'm sure you wouldn't be here without reason," Walter replied.

The man quickly looked Walter up and down and nodded. "Well done, boy. Finally, someone with a bit of sense. I think you'll find, Mr . . . *Lenny,* I am the producer of *When The Curtain Falls,* Hamish Boatwright."

"When the what?" Lenny shrugged.

"*When The Curtain Falls,*" Hamish hissed through his straight teeth. "The new production due to open in two days!"

"Right." Lenny shrugged again.

"The whole of London's talking about it," Walter said, adjusting himself behind Lenny's tensed shoulder.

"They are indeed," smiled Hamish, his moustache curling up at the ends.

"You're not the director, then?" Lenny probed and Hamish's nose twitched. The show's director, William Hurdle, wasn't a fan of Hamish wanting to produce the show and play the part of Melvin Banks. They clashed at every rehearsal and most days ended in a blazing row until, finally, Hurdle quit. However, Hamish couldn't afford to lose William Hurdle's name attached to the production. His body of work was astounding and his high profile was just what the show needed to get off the ground. Hamish knew how loud money could talk, so he paid him off. If Hurdle kept his name attached to the show and let Hamish take over direction, Hamish paid him more than directing any show in town possibly could. It didn't matter then to Hurdle if the show flopped. He'd already be in America spending his money on women and whiskey.

"No, I'm the producer," Hamish said through gritted teeth.

"I've not heard anything about it," Lenny said. Walter glanced sideways at Lenny's face and could see that he was lying; stubbornness may as well have been written across his forehead in bold lettering.

"Then maybe it's time you started listening." Hamish tugged sharply on the hem of his suit jacket, straightening out its creases, and turned on the heels of his shiny black shoes. "Fawn. We've got scenes to

**146**

rehearse." There was movement and a rustle of papers from the far side of the auditorium, and a tangle of autumnal burnt orange hair bobbed up above the sea of red velvet seats.

"Of course, Mr Boatwright." Fawn stood and brushed down her cream dress that was cinched in at her waist with a thick sky blue belt. She brushed off the fluff and quickly collected the many sheets of paper she'd scattered around her on the floor, stuffing them back into her brown leather satchel.

"Please, darling," Hamish smiled with all his teeth as he moved to her. "I've told you a thousand times. It's Hamish." Hamish Boatwright delicately snaked one arm around Fawn's shoulders, but the fingers of his other encircled the wrist that held the strap of her satchel. Walter could see by his whitening knuckles that his grip was just that little bit too tight. "And what have I told you about sitting on the floor?"

"I know, Mr Boatwri — Hamish." She half smiled. "I just find it so much easier to learn the lines when I have the entire scene laid out in front of me."

"It's not about what's easier. It's about what's ladylike. West End starlets don't sit on the floor. Don't make me repeat myself, Fawn, dear."

Walter watched Fawn flinch and stop on their journey to the door and Hamish snatched his hand away from the wrist that Fawn was now gently rubbing. Walter coughed loudly. Hamish quickly glanced behind him and locked eyes with Walter, who wondered whether the producer's next move would have been different had he not been watching.

"Lunch, my dear? My treat." Hamish offered Fawn his arm and hesitantly she slipped her own slender arm through his. They disappeared through front of house, but not before Fawn's green eyes found Walter's and silently said *thank you*.

# CHAPTER
# NINE

## Letters and Keys

Walter's job at the theatre was straightforward enough. As the stage door manager's assistant, he arrived at nine in the morning, after the cleaners had started at eight but well before Lenny had even stumbled out of bed. As merely an errand boy for Lenny, his main duties were signing for any parcels and storing them accordingly before they were collected, taking note of anything broken or faulty and making sure everyone signed in and signed out. Lenny was very precious about keys and wouldn't let Walter touch the wooden box on the wall where they all hung in neat rows on their hooks. The amount of packages and post that arrived at the theatre kept Walter the busiest and although it was a menial task, the feeling of purpose kept Walter happy. By the time Walter had sorted through everything the postman had brought with him, Lenny would have stumbled in at around half nine, still bleary-eyed and stinking of last night's ale.

"This one's for Hamish," Walter said, brandishing the biggest of the last three or four letters. It felt thick and heavier than the other letters as if it contained more than just one sheet of good quality paper. The

**149**

writing on the envelope was almost illegible, but Walter could tell from the big swirling "H" who it was meant for.

"Put it in his pigeonhole then." Lenny sat in his little cubby with his feet up on the desk, the ash from the end of his cigar peppered across every surface and trodden into the carpet. The smell made Walter want to vomit. Walter turned his back on Lenny to face the pigeonholes above the little table, and pushed Hamish's letter into the correct slot.

"Who are the others for?" Lenny asked, as Walter shuffled through the other letters and saw that the last one was for Fawn.

"Erm . . ." Walter said, turning Fawn's letter over in his hands. "Just . . . ensemble." Walter quickly put her letter in his inside pocket and put the remaining two in their corresponding holes.

"*Just* ensemble? Don't let anyone catch you saying that. They'll have your guts for garters, boy."

"What?" Walter said, the letter burning a hole through his pocket and into his chest.

"The ensemble carries a show! Those dance numbers would look pretty empty with only a few principals scattered about. Those choral numbers would sound pretty naff with only two or three voices, wouldn't they?" Lenny tapped his cigar, more ash joining the carpet.

"Of course," said Walter.

"Then show a little respect inside these walls, all right? It's the people in the background that matter the most."

**150**

"And who told you that?" The double doors swung open with gusto and Hamish burst through, his long tan coat swinging about so violently the letters bustled about in their pigeonholes.

"That's just theatre." Lenny shrugged, removing his feet from the hatch. He cautiously rolled his eyes so that only Walter could see.

"A show wouldn't be a show without its stars."

"It wouldn't be a show without the people in the background, neither," Lenny said, sucking hard on his cigar.

"If it makes you feel better. As long as you remember *your* place."

"And what exactly is *my* place?" Lenny stayed seated, but Walter could see his short nails digging into the wood of his desk, the end of his cigar burning bright.

"Perhaps young Wally here can tell you." Hamish tapped the end of Walter's boot with his black silver handled cane.

"Walter," Walter said but his voice came out as a crackly whisper.

"What?" Hamish snapped, and Walter cleared his throat.

"My name is Walter."

"You're talking back now too, are you?" Hamish raised his cane and held the end of it against Walter's chest.

"No! No, not at all!" Walter stepped back but Hamish stepped forward.

"Then tell him. Your place is . . .?"

". . . Stage door?" Walter fumbled.

"Exactly, and your job is . . .?"

Walter and Lenny exchanged a vacant look. Hamish pushed his cane harder into Walter's chest.

"Ahhh . . . letters?" Walter offered with a half shrug. "And keys?"

"And who do you hand those letters and those keys to, exactly?"

"Actors?"

"Very good, Walter. Actors. Your job is to serve the actors but above all your job is to serve me, the producer." Hamish gave Walter a gentle but firm push with his cane before placing it back on the floor with a click.

"Yes, sir," Walter said, resisting the urge to rub his chest.

"Your *place* is to man this door without complaint and do as I say. My key."

"Please," said Lenny.

"What?" Hamish spat.

"My key . . . *please*."

"Give me the damn key." Hamish opened his black gloved palm, waiting for Lenny to obey orders.

"No." Lenny folded his arms. "Not until you show me the courtesy and respect I deserve as someone who works for you, *sir*."

Hamish's head whipped around at Lenny so hard Walter almost heard the fluid in his head slosh. "I'm warning you," he snarled.

"Is it that hard to say please, Mr Producer?" Lenny answered, taking the keys to dressing room one out from the wooden box on the wall.

"It'd be far easier to have you fired." Hamish picked up his cane once more and pushed it into Lenny's chest so hard he stumbled backwards into the wall, hitting his head on the shelf behind him and dropping his cigar.

"All right, all right! No need for that! I've just been trying to teach the boy that a little bit of kindness is free, Hamish, that's all!"

With another twist of his cane, which caused the shelf behind Lenny's head to creak, Hamish pulled away.

"Key."

Still reluctant, Lenny placed the key in Hamish's upturned palm as he snatched it away. "Out of my way." Hamish swept past Walter, bursting through the second set of doors and down to his stage level dressing room.

"*Letters. Keys*," Lenny mocked. "Whose side are you on, kid?" Lenny brushed his shirt somewhat straight and picked up his cigar, the end of which was surprisingly still glowing.

"I didn't realise I had to take a side," Walter shrugged, rubbing his own chest.

"Well, you do. There's us, the little people who work our arses off for next to nothing and then there's them. The people who do very little and have everything to gain from everything that we do. We keep this theatre clean and in good working order, and it's him who benefits." Lenny plonked himself down in his rickety chair. "Make yourself useful," he said and shooed him away.

Walter had learnt that *make yourself useful* actually meant *leave me alone* so he scurried through the theatre like one of its resident mice, through the backstage corridors, down the stage left wing, through the pass door, down the stairs and into the auditorium and . . . there she was.

He hadn't realised he'd smelt the fresh scent of her jasmine perfume in the corridor, but it was definitely drifting over him now from where Fawn sat in the stalls in row G, rustling through sheets of paper and talking to herself. Walter cleared his throat and Fawn turned her head to the left, saw nothing, and returned to her script. Walter wanted to say something, but Fawn continued, engrossed in her work.

"*You're teasing me, Lars!* . . . Ugh, no . . . *You're teasing me, Lars. You must stop it immediately or I'll . . . I'll* . . . argh, why can't I remember this line?"

"Need any help?" Walter finally plucked up the courage to speak, and Fawn jumped.

"My goodness me! You can't sneak up on people like that!" she snapped, a hand delicately laid across the base of her pale throat. Walter couldn't help but laugh as he walked further towards the centre of the stalls down row J.

"I didn't mean to startle you."

"You're the boy from the other day!"

"Boy?" Walter laughed again but stood a little taller. "I'm twenty-two. I'd definitely consider myself a man."

"Of course you would." She pursed her lips but still managed to smile, her eyes sparkling. "Girls are considered to be women through a means of physical

154

changes, it seems. Not about how much they know of the world because they're not really *allowed* to know much about the world. A boy, however, becomes a man when his mind is enriched, his heart hardened through experience and he's had his way with a handful of women. Wouldn't you agree?" Fawn shuffled her pages into a neat pile as she talked.

"Well, I . . ." Walter took off his flat cap and ran his sweating palms around its rim.

"So, tell me, Walter . . . are you a man?" She placed the pile of papers on her crossed legs, leant her elbow on the back of the seat and casually placed her chin in the palm of her hand. Walter took a deep breath.

"Not by that definition, no."

"Is there another?" she asked, and Walter took another large breath, not feeling like there was enough space in his chest for both his lungs at once.

"I would say a boy becomes a man when he's seen enough of the world to know what he thinks of it, can earn an honest and decent living and knows his own mind and heart if ever someone asks one of them a question."

"What if someone asks both of them a question? Your mind *and* your heart?" She brushed her curtain of autumnal hair back from her eyes.

"It's rare that they have the same answer. You're better off asking just one of them." Walter took a seat in his row.

"How ever do you decide?"

"Depends which one's better suited for the task! If it's work or money, you gotta ask my brain. If it's matters of romance, however, you'll need to conspire with the ol' ticker."

"What if you need to decide something simple, like . . . what to have for dinner."

"Ah, see. My eyes are bigger than my belly so sadly, that's always a lost cause." It was then that Walter heard Fawn laugh for the first time and he thought it was a good job he was sitting down because his knees would have collapsed underneath him. It was melodic, almost like she was singing a song, and although Walter hadn't listened to a great deal of music in his lifetime, he already knew it was the most beautiful song he'd ever heard.

"So what exactly is your job here, Walter?" Fawn swivelled in her seat to face Walter a little more, bringing her white shoes up onto the red velvet upholstery in front of her and leaning her arms flat across the back of her chair, her cheek resting against the back of her fingers.

"You remembered my name?"

"Well, you know mine, don't you?"

"Fair enough. Well, Susan . . ." he smirked, "I'm the stage door manager's assistant."

"Are you really an assistant in the sense of the definition or are you one of those assistants that actually does everything your boss should do and receives none of the credit?"

"Bingo," he said, firing his fingers at her like hand guns. "Well, no, to be fair Lenny does a hell of a job at guarding that key box. I'm not allowed within ten feet of that thing."

"Oh, and I was so hoping to have at least a moment with you each day." The tone of her voice suggested she may have been joking but Walter caught a fondness in her eyes that gave him a glimmer of hope.

"And you still can, as long as your fans keep writing you letters." Walter opened his jacket pocket and produced the letter he'd hidden from Lenny earlier, suddenly pleased with himself for having that spontaneous moment of weakness.

"Oooh, how exciting! Pass it here." Walter stood and leant as far as he could over the seats but still couldn't quite reach Fawn's outstretched hand. He pinched the very edge of the letter between his index and middle finger and tried again but this time it slipped out from his grasp and fluttered to the floor in row H.

"Argh, damn," Walter said, as they both lost sight of the letter. He looked up to see Fawn had already sauntered a few seats along to the end of the row, but stopped moving as soon as she noticed he was watching. Walter moved along a few seats too with a nonchalant whistle, but he found it hard to make any noise at all when all his lips wanted to do was stretch into a smile. Fawn hopped one seat along with a leap. Walter did the same. She raised an eyebrow at him and before he knew it she was scrambling along to the end of the row and darting into row H. Walter seized his chance and heaved himself over the rows of chairs between them like he was a hurdles champion, but Fawn got there a split-second sooner. She peeled the letter off the floor and whipped it into the air, catching Walter fully in the nose as her arm came upwards.

"Oh my!" she wailed as Walter yelped and stumbled backwards a couple of steps, catching his foot on the leg of a seat and landing with a thump on his rear. Holding his nose with both hands, he let himself fall onto his back. Without hesitation, Fawn hoisted up her skirt and went over to him, getting to her knees until she was straddling one of his legs, her hands either side of his chest. Walter's palms covered his throbbing nose as his fingers tried to staunch the flow of tears streaming from his eyes.

"I'm sorry! I'm sorry! I'm sorry! Are you all right?" she whispered.

"Fine!" he lied, but Walter hadn't realised just how close Fawn had dared to get and as he brought his arms away from his face, he used the momentum to catapult his body into a sitting position . . . and head-butted Fawn.

"OUCH!" Fawn sat back on her knees and clutched her head.

"OH, NO!" Walter instantaneously forgot about his own pain and swivelled his legs underneath him so he could get a closer look at her.

"I'm all right!" she said, blinking back tears but laughing all the same.

"You're not, I can already see a lump!" Walter said, taking her wrists and pulling her hands away from her head.

"Please tell me that's a joke. Make-up can hide bruises but I don't think it'll disguise a golf ball sticking out between my eyes!"

"Don't worry, I think everyone will be too preoccupied with your smile to notice," Walter said and the silence that followed made him wish he could suck the words back into his mouth, chew them up and swallow them before she heard. Fawn looked at him with curiosity.

"Well, that was sweet." She smiled, gently shaking her wrists out of Walter's grasp. He noticed a group of three or four dark circular marks on the inside of her left wrist.

"Where did these come from?" he asked, carefully taking hold of her wrist and trying to examine the bruises.

Fawn gently pulled her hand away from his inspection. "I may look elegant on stage but I'm not the most graceful of creatures," she laughed. "Always walking into things."

"They look like fingermarks, Fawn."

"Can't think why." She pulled herself to her feet using the theatre chairs to help her stand, but slipped a little when the seat she'd held onto started to flip forwards. "Whoops! See. I'm never on my feet for too long before I've slipped over again."

"It's Hamish, isn't it?"

"Walter . . ."

"You can tell me, Fawn."

"I don't even *know* you." She backed away from him and skittered back into her original row, gathering up her belongings.

"I know, but —"

"And it's Miss Burrows," she said. Her face had hardened; the bright smile and sparkling eyes had dulled, and Walter could tell, despite not even really knowing her, that she was scared.

"Miss Burrows," he took a moment to compose himself, "I mean you no harm. I am an employee of this theatre and therefore a friend to you. If ever you need someone to deliver your mail, someone to pop out and get you food between performances . . . or someone you need to confide in, I'm your man."

"No," she sighed, her eyes searching his for something more than she found, "you're a boy."

And she left.

# CHAPTER
# TEN

## Fawn

Fawn Burrows was a *woman*. Undoubtedly so in her eyes, because everything she was convinced made one a woman she had made sure she had accomplished. However, she had very little chance to prove it as the majority of people around her thought all women were needed for was to care for their man, have his children and learn how to make the perfect Victoria sponge. There was no question that Fawn would potentially disappoint her family in her life choices. After all, when you plan to study your way into a job so you don't need to rely on a man, you tread a fine line between "strong woman" and "disowned little girl". Fawn persisted regardless and had her sights set on RADA to follow in the footsteps of her favourite actress, Vivien Leigh (despite the fact that Leigh had dropped out) and thankfully, Fawn's mother and father supported her dreams of being in the spotlight.

Warren Burrows was a quiet man who spoke only the language of money. And boy, was he fluent. If his little girl wanted to be an actress, she would be an actress. But before Fawn was able to study and train like everyone else and work her way to the top, her father had found a producer named Hamish Boatwright. He had offered to help Hamish fund his new show on the condition that his little girl become a big West End star. Hamish, a man of forty-two with a deceased wife and ambition beyond compare, took one look at Fawn and said yes with a capital "Y".

"You don't even know whether I can act," Fawn said upon meeting Hamish and pulling her hand away from his slippery kiss.

"I don't need to, and with a face like yours neither does the audience." Fawn could see Hamish was trying to compliment her so she smiled and made a mental note of it in her head: *He's ignorant and potentially misogynistic.*

"You'll have a few lines here and there. You'll be able to manage that, won't you, sweetie?" *And he's condescending.*

"And when we're at parties you won't need to say anything. Let me do the talking, handle all the business, and you stand there and look fabulous." *Definitely misogynistic.*

Had Fawn been alive when they were at their height of activity, she knew she would have been a largely involved member of the Suffragettes. It always angered her, that despite women being given the vote and the huge toll it had taken for them to be thought of as equal, there were still men like Hamish Boatwright who thought they could tell her that her only job was to be quiet, look pretty and to let men handle her business. Even though Fawn wanted to shout and scream and

162

outwardly fight, her mother had taught her another way.

"Softly, softly, catchee monkey," Hyacinth would say. "A man's ego is one of the most fragile things in human nature. One slight knock and it's broken for good and then who knows what'll happen. Whilst the Suffragettes did a great deal of good, the time for raising our voices seems to be over for now. People like you and I need to be careful. We need to be patient. Carefully tip the scales in our favour without anyone noticing. And we do that by hiding our old clothes in the bottom of handbags to take to the charity shop and secretly leaving money in the hands of the vicar at the church to distribute to the poor and needy as he wishes."

"Mother, you didn't?! Won't Father know?"

"Darling, your father gives me an allowance and what I choose to spend it on is up to me. As long as he sees me in a new dress once in a while, he thinks nothing of it. If I want to help those less fortunate it's a shame I have to do it without your father's approval but I'm never going to get that, am I? No matter, though. There's nothing like a bit of secrecy to make life a little exciting." Although her mother smiled as she said it, the smile wasn't quite convincing enough to reach her eyes.

And so, Fawn didn't snap or leer at him with disdain when Hamish said the obnoxious things that insulted her existence as a female. Instead, she bit her tongue and smiled through the pain of it and said, "Of course, Mr Boatwright," whilst counting down the hours until she could find a way to make sure he had his comeuppance.

"Oh please, call me Hamish," he said, his greasy moustache curling into a smile whilst Fawn made another mental note to only ever call him Mr Boatwright in the hope that it would annoy him as much as he annoyed her.

If only annoyance were the pinnacle of her worries. The bruises on her arm she was now having to lie to Walter about were cause for far more concern than Fawn had ever really had to muster. As a rich girl living in the heart of London, Fawn had never had much to worry about. Poverty, hunger, disease and loss had never troubled her life. Now, however, here was a man who made her skin crawl with his touch, when he wasn't turning it purple with brute force. Until now, Fawn had lived her whole life in luxury, drinking martinis at far too young an age, wearing dresses that cost more than most people earned in a year and holidaying to France whilst people got sick from illnesses that she could cure a hundred times over with just the money in her pocket.

Despite the ache encircling her wrist, she couldn't bring herself to speak up. Instead she just kept telling herself, *this is bad but it could be worse, it could be worse* . . . So she ran from Walter. She ran from the boy who made her laugh, back into the hands of a man who reminded her far too much of Foulfellow from Disney's *Pinocchio*.

Walter wasn't entirely sure what to do as he hauled himself up from the patterned carpet of the auditorium and into one of the red velvet seats. He weighed up his

**164**

options. He most certainly couldn't do nothing now that she had confirmed with her pained expression that Hamish Boatwright was not to be trusted and yet . . . he couldn't go running after the woman who had only moments ago retracted her first name from his personal use. Although, the playfulness that had just transpired between them had been more than mutual, he was sure, Walter just couldn't risk making things worse for Fawn. The overwhelming urge to protect her and keep her safe was palpable and he hoped it didn't cling to the air around him and be misconstrued as desperation. He wasn't in love with her. *She's just in trouble and I'm doing the decent thing by trying to help*, he told himself. He wasn't in love with her. *I'm not in love with her*. He wasn't in love with her . . .

# CHAPTER
# ELEVEN

## Opening Night

"Stand by, everyone!" called Eddie, the young but experienced stage manager. His voice could carry for miles in the theatre if necessary and there was a certain tone to it that made you wary of ever crossing him. However, he always had kind words to say, a gentle way about him and the safety of the company always came first. It therefore made him exactly the type of man Hamish Boatwright hated: incorruptible. When Hamish had heard that Edward Maynard was the best, he had hired him without a moment's thought. It was only when Hamish began to suggest outlandish ideas for the production, such as some members of the cast should be rigged to fly, or that someone should swing from the dress circle to the stage in the bar brawl scene, that Hamish realised that Eddie wasn't going to let him have the show he wanted. The only stunt Eddie did allow Hamish to have was a gunshot and that was only because Eddie knew a good props man who would provide that special effect for every show on the cheap.

Fawn stood in her opening position at a silver microphone on a raised platform centre stage. Bar stools and tables were dotted around her where some of the cast were seated, sipping drinks, whilst others were on their feet ready to dance as the curtain rose. Although this was only the dress rehearsal, Fawn could feel the sweat trickling down the small of her back and was hoping it hadn't created a darker patch on the back of her opening dress. Once the opening of the show was out of the way, Fawn knew she would be able to relax and then start flexing her dramatic muscles and hopefully impress the audience into reviewing her kindly. Fawn longed for a day when she was given a role, not because of her daddy and his money and status, but because she was actually, undeniably *good*. She also longed to be cut from Hamish's invisible puppet strings that he continuously tugged.

"Fawn!" She heard her name called in a loud whisper and her already humming heart chirruped in her chest.

"Stage left!" Fawn scanned the cast and could just make out a waving hand in the dark in the downstage left wing. Walter. "Break a leg!" he said and although he was mostly hidden by the black cloths draped over the wing, she could hear the sheepishness in his voice. She wondered how many times her stomach was able to tie itself in knots before she was no longer able to function. She smiled, but knew it wasn't quite enough to convey her apologies and quickly blew him a kiss before a hush fell over the cast. The curtain rose, the actor-muso behind her tinkled the ivories and Fawn took a breath . . . and sang.

The time for bowing finally arrived although the only people there to applaud were the lighting men in the gods who had already seen every scene a thousand times over. Fawn felt a huge sense of accomplishment wash over her and biting back tears proved much harder than she had expected. She caught eyes with Lawrence, the actor who played Lars, her romantic lead, and although usually quite stoic and someone who kept himself to himself, he laughed and squeezed her hand in the line-up for the bows a little harder than she was used to. Aside from a minor hiccup in the second act where Hamish had slipped on the train of Fawn's dress and fallen over, which was the cast's first challenge in corpsing, the run had gone better than they could have hoped. Even the single stunt that closed the show, in which Lars pulls the trigger of a gun and fires a hollow wax bullet and the lights black out, went without a hitch. Smiles were exchanged with the cast as they bowed together in unison and a shared sense of readiness for the night ahead filled the stage in a muggy fog that radiated from their sweaty skin. As soon as the curtain hit the floor, they whooped and cheered until . . .

"That was a DISASTER. Why are you cheering? Have you no pride? No dignity? No integrity?"

"Hamish . . ." Lawrence put a hand on Hamish's shoulder but despite being almost twice his height and half his age, Lawrence let Hamish shrug him off in a fit of rage.

"What *was* that, Fawn? Your father's money wasn't worth the damp rag you're impersonating."

"I . . . I'm —"

Hamish gripped her shoulders and shook her violently and this time it didn't seem to matter who was watching.

"You're what? You're sorry, maybe? Apologies just won't cut it! You're going to make me a laughing stock!"

"HAMISH!" Lawrence shouted, stepping in once more and grabbing Hamish by the shoulders — but he wasn't quite quick enough. Hamish raised his hand and brought the back of it down hard on Fawn's cheek, sending her to the floor with an agonising thud. Some of the girls gasped and took shelter in the wings but Fawn was quick to be back on her feet, even if she did have to hold her cheek to try and stop the sting.

"It's a shame you didn't like my performance, Mr Boatwright," Fawn said, looking him right in the eye. Then she took her hand away from her face, recomposed herself before leaning close to Hamish's ear so that her words were heard only by him, "but at least I managed to stay on my feet." Then, with a swish of the train of her dress, Fawn vanished into the wings before letting the pain in her cheek bring forth a flurry of tears that rolled down her face and neck. She walked with a steady click-clack up the steps back to her dressing room. The desire to be alone became steadily more urgent as the golden number four on her door came into sight. Once inside, she fumbled behind her back for the lock on the door and twirled it with shaking fingers until she heard it "thunk" and she knew she would be left entirely alone. Then she covered her mouth with her hand and brought forth a sob, so full of hopelessness and despair that it almost darkened the room. The pain in her cheek was intense and the marks on her wrist still purple and tender, another part of her body aching and marked by the hands of the same man. She took several deep breaths to steady her nerves and her anger and through her cascading tears she spotted something out of the ordinary on her dressing table.

Fawn walked to her desk upon which sat a champagne bucket from front of house, with a clean cloth parcel inside. When she lifted it, she could hear the satisfying jostle of ice cubes. Gratefully, she pressed the cloth parcel to the space between her right eye and cheek and revelled in the cooling numbness it brought her. Tucked underneath the ice bucket was a little folded piece of paper which she wiggled free and opened with her unoccupied hand.

*Please meet me tonight?*
   *Take the ladder on stage left to the fly floor.*
   *When the curtain falls.*
   *W.*

Although Hamish had caused such an uproar, no extra rehearsals had been called before they opened that evening. Fawn wondered whether guilt had made Hamish rethink his words and his actions but most likely she figured there was some law somewhere that stated actors are entitled to a dinner break.

The ladder was shaky at the best of times when she'd seen other people climb its steel frame, but underneath her silver heels it felt like it would shudder and collapse at any moment. Nevertheless, Fawn climbed one rung at a time, one cautious, quiet step after another. She'd hidden in the downstage quick-change until everyone had filtered off stage and through the double doors in a cacophony of congratulations. The show had gone without a hitch, and once silence had fallen over the stage and the props had been put back in their places, the set made ready for the following day, Fawn, with only excitement in her bones, climbed to the fly floor above the stage.

Walter had watched the curtain call from the rafters, eager to see Fawn, to apologise for pressuring her when he should have been more understanding. Every minute that passed was another moment of doubt. *Maybe she's not coming*, he thought and sighed, leaning over one of the cold metal railings, the stage now so dark that it looked like there was nothing below him except a dark, black endless hole.

"Don't lean over too far," Fawn said and Walter's head whipped up to look at her, still in costume and as elegant as always. "No one wants another theatre ghost." She gave him a little smile, but it was brief and looked like it caused her pain.

"I didn't hear you climb up," said Walter.

"I'm not surprised. You were so lost in thought." She stepped closer but one of her heels wobbled in the grated metal walkway, so Walter walked slowly over to her, one step at a time. "What's on your mind?"

"You," he said without a moment's hesitation. Embarrassment didn't flood him, and regret didn't immediately set in. In fact, the relief of being unashamedly honest squeezed his heart and as it did so, more words oozed through his veins, up his throat and out of his mouth. "Fawn, I'm so sorry. I never should have pushed you into answering my questions. I should have left you to tell me what you wanted to tell me in your own time. If you want to tell me anything at all." The fly floor was high up in the theatre and Walter steadied himself on the metal railing which was cool against his sweaty palms.

"I do."

"You do?" He took another step towards her.

"I do want to tell you something." Fawn leant forwards, silently wishing for Walter to be closer, even just a little.

"You can tell me anything, Fawn. Anything at all," he said. "And I swear it'll never ever go any further than right here." He patted his chest where his heart was thumping. She looked at him, her eyes full and her cheeks red from the climb up the ladder. His flat cap was pulled down too far so that she couldn't quite see his eyes, but his mousey blonde hair poked out from underneath it and she desperately wanted to feel it between her fingers. Just the thought of Walter wrapping his arms around her made her chest hurt.

"I just want to tell you that I want you around. Always," she said, quietly. Walter took another step closer, his skin tingling.

"That you're the only man to have ever treated me with the respect I know I deserve. That I've not stopped thinking about you."

172

Walter took one last step until he'd completely closed the distance between them, but he didn't dare touch her. He kept his clammy hands by his sides but all the hairs on his body were standing on end.

"I don't want to ruin the moment," he said to his own feet, the brim of his hat almost touching the end of her nose, "but . . . I barely know you." He laughed.

"You work in a theatre," Fawn said, reaching up and carefully removing his hat from his head. He quickly ran his wet hands through his hair, sweeping it all back and hoping it wasn't unruly and defying the laws of gravity. "Surely you must have seen enough backstage romances to know that people fall in love at the drop of a hat," she added, helping to sort out the front of his hair. As her skin brushed his cheek she felt a warmth in the pit of her stomach and she couldn't help but smile.

"To be honest, Miss Burrows, I've only been working here about . . . a week," he said, not looking at her.

"Oh." She laughed. "Well, how about the movies, then. Have you seen any of those?" She teased, poking his chest but then leaving her hand on his shirt. His eyes flicked up to hers and he pleaded with her in his mind to give him any sign that she wanted to kiss him.

"I love the movies," he smiled, realising he'd left it a little too long before answering her.

"Then you'll know how quickly people can fall. Love at first sight." She breathed and the mint from her mouth and the jasmine in her perfume tangled in the air and sent his senses reeling. Images of Hollywood starlets and leading men flickered in his mind. William Holden and Nancy Olson, Humphrey Bogart and

**173**

Ingrid Bergman, Ginger Rogers and Joseph Cotten, even Cinderella and Prince Charming . . . he had seen love at first sight a thousand times. Who was to say it didn't exist? Who was to say it couldn't happen? Couldn't happen to him?

"It's all fiction though, isn't it?" he shrugged. *What are the chances this radiant star of the West End stage would be interested in the "boy" that works on stage door?* he thought.

"Fiction has to come from somewhere, doesn't it?" she said, and he noticed her tone had changed. Her smile had gone, and she was fiddling with the button on his flannel shirt pocket with a seriousness he couldn't explain.

"Are you saying . . . you're in love with me?" he asked, breathing deeply, feeling her hand rise.

"No . . ." She smiled and although she'd said no, she let her answer hang in the air for a little while.

"You're not in love with me," he said, wondering why he felt a pang of disappointment in his gut.

"No," she said again, looking down at the fingers of her other hand which she moved to gently brush with his.

"How 'not in love with me' are you?" Walter stretched out his own fingers and slowly intertwined them with Fawn's and a fire raced up from his hands, through his arms and around his neck. His cheeks burned. Fawn tried to lean in but one of her heels had become wedged in the grated floor again, although she tried to keep her cool and not let her inelegance show. She looked up at Walter, who shuffled a little closer so

174

that their faces were so close that even a whisper was too loud. He placed his other hand over hers on his chest and pressed it closer so that maybe she could feel how she was making him feel.

"Only a little not in love," she whispered.

"Well," he said, his lips already touching hers, "that's enough for me."

Fawn returned to her dressing room that night where her dresser berated her for her lateness and unbuttoned her dress with such a force that Fawn wobbled in her heels and had to steady herself on her dressing table.

"Where have you been, sweetie?" Hamish poked his head inside her dressing room with his attempt at a sickly-sweet smile. He came into her room without knocking or permission and motioned for her dresser to leave, before closing the door behind him. Fawn wrapped her dressing gown around her as tight as she could, wishing she had got changed a little quicker or that her dresser had stayed a little longer.

"Nowhere of any importance." She shrugged, fixing her make-up in the mirror.

"Well, wherever it was it is keeping you from somewhere important. You're the star of the show, after all. People will want to meet you tonight at the party."

"I'm actually a little tired. I thought I would go home and —"

"Go home? And leave me without a date?" Hamish tried to laugh but it sounded forced and panicked. Fawn's insides squirmed at the idea of going anywhere with Hamish in a romantic setting.

"It's been a long day," she said, trying to remain calm and kind. "Not to mention the matinee we have tomorrow."

"I'm trying to give you a career, Fawn. You need to mingle, socialise. The producer of your next show might be at this party."

"I just think the show would benefit from me having a good night's —"

"You are *coming* to the party!" Hamish snapped and instinctively Fawn flinched and covered her already bruised cheek with her hand. "Oh, Fawn, hush now," he said, racing to her side and caressing her face as much as she let him. "No need to be like that. No need to be frightened. What happened earlier was merely a hiccup. A little blemish on an otherwise perfect day," he said, ignoring the tears in her eyes. "No need to let it ruin the evening," he said, stroking her hair.

Fawn started to pull away but his grip tightened at her slight show of disobedience and so she stayed very still. "What's going to happen now, is you're going to get into a nice dress. You've got one of those with you, haven't you?" He patted her hand and she nodded whilst biting her tongue. "Good. You're going to get into a nice dress, put on your heels and come to the party. I will meet you there and introduce you to anybody who's anybody and you're going to smile, be polite and be *grateful*." He gave her cheek a stroke and as he stood he leant in just that little bit too close to her face and her breath caught in her throat.

Hamish walked to the door with a swish of his long tan coat. "After all," he said, opening the door an inch, "there are hundreds of actresses out there who could do this job better than you. You're just awfully lucky you've got a father whose wallet is larger than his brain." Hamish left and closed the door with unnecessary force, leaving Fawn alone once more with tears in her eyes. But this time they didn't fall, and instead of dwelling on that awful moment, she got dressed, re-did her make-up, then ripped a clean sheet of paper out of the notebook on her dressing table and scribbled on it as fast as she could. She folded it twice and wrote an address on the blank side then folded it once more, concealing the name.

Despite her heels, Fawn took the stairs down to stage door two at a time. She reached the bottom and pulled her thin shawl around her cold shoulders and clutched it tightly in her hand, the piece of paper clenched in the other. As she reached the first set of double doors, she could see Hamish was already waiting for her on the pavement outside, a cigar between his thin lips. A young girl outside was first to see her through the small window and she raised a pen and an autograph book and called her name before Fawn had even opened the door.

"Looks like you've got some admirers," smiled Lenny from his seat through the hatch. "Well done tonight, Miss. You did good."

"Thank you. I don't suppose I could ask a favour, could I?"

"Anything," Walter said, moving to lean against the table where the sign-in sheet sat. Fawn smiled at his eagerness but not too widely as she could feel Hamish's looming presence.

"I have a letter of great importance that needs to be read rather urgently. I just know that *you* are the one to get it where it needs to go." Fawn gently winked with her right eye so that Hamish wouldn't be able to see were he looking, which he most likely was. Walter took the letter, careful not to touch her hand although desperate to.

"Absolutely." He nodded. Fawn stepped to the left and Walter followed. She stepped to the right and Walter stepped the same way.

"Sorry I just need to . . ." she mimed writing.

"Oh! The sign-in sheet. Yes, of course." He stepped out of the way. Fawn looked at the clock above the desk and wrote the time in the "out" column next to her name.

"Coming, sweetie?" Hamish put his head through the door and breathed out a plume of stinking smoke that practically filled the small space between both sets of double doors.

"Yes," Fawn replied without a trace of feeling. Hamish held out his arm and Fawn took it with cold fingers and a grip lighter than a breeze. Fawn stepped out onto the pavement and the air filled with voices calling her name, camera flashes filling the street.

"Seems like she won a few hearts tonight," Lenny said, closing the double doors to drown out the rabble outside. Fawn turned and caught Walter's eye the split second before the door clicked shut, but it was just enough time for her to flash him a smile that made his stomach flip and his cheeks burn.

"More than a few, I'd say."

TOASTIE PRODUCTIONS PRESENTS A
PRODUCTION BY C. H. FLETCHER

## OLIVE GREEN and OSCAR BRIGHT in

# WHEN the CURTAIN FALLS

## LIMITED TICKETS REMAINING!

# THE SOUTHERN CROSS THEATRE

SHAFTESBURY AVENUE, LONDON

OPENS 1 APRIL 2018

# CHAPTER
# TWELVE

## For What It's Worth

Olive collected her coffee from the barista with a nod and an attempt at a smile, but the weight of her heart was dragging down the corners of her lips. She wrapped her cardigan more tightly around her as she stepped out into the crisp morning air, enjoying the peace and quiet of the usually bustling streets of London's Soho. Today is going to be a good day. *It'll all be fine*, she repeated in her head, not only to convince herself it was true, but also to push away any other unwanted thoughts that had a habit of clouding her mind. *It's a new day and an important one so you gotta be on top form.* Olive stepped off the curb and as the stage door of the Southern Cross theatre came into sight she noticed Oscar walking up from front of house and Tamara walking up to stage door from the adjacent side. Olive's steps slowed, and she prayed Oscar wouldn't see her. Her plan had been to put her stage make-up on inside the theatre, ready for the dress rehearsal, and she knew her face would currently look blotchy and swollen from crying the night before.

But Oscar glanced up and caught her eye and it took all the strength Olive could muster not to smile at him.

Not even a little. Oscar stopped on the pavement, tried giving her a little wave and stepped towards the kerb, about to cross the road towards her, but Olive quickly took her phone out of her pocket and held it to her ear, averting her gaze. No one was on the other end of the telephone, and she made little effort to make it look like she was talking to someone, but she just needed something, anything to avoid a conversation with him. A conversation she knew would eventually have to be had but just not now. Just. Not. Now.

Oscar remained on the kerb and with a pain in his chest, turned back towards the stage door where Tamara was waiting for him dressed in a pink hairy coat and sunglasses (even though it was overcast and was probably going to rain at any moment), holding back her neatly straightened hair with one hand to scroll through her phone with the other.

"Oh hi, Oscar!" Tamara said as she threw her arms around him before he'd even registered who it was underneath such a flamboyant coat. The smell of her perfume, the one he'd not been able to get out of his clothes since their night in the pub, made his stomach turn and served as a sharp reminder that the arms encasing him belonged to Tamara Drake . . . the woman he had kissed instead of Olive.

"Tamara," he said, firmly removing himself from her embrace. Tamara moved in to kiss him square on the mouth and from across the road Olive's heart lurched; she had to stop herself running over to try and intervene. "Tamara!" Oscar raised his voice but quickly composed himself. "I think we need to talk."

184

"What's there to talk about?" She flipped her hair back into place and tried to smile but Oscar could tell it was forced, as though she was fighting off the embarrassment of his rejection.

"Look, I'm sorry. I seem to only ever be apologising to everyone these days, and I know it's because I just keep making stupid mistakes but . . . I'm sorry," Oscar said, struggling to get his words out.

"For what?" Tamara replied snippily.

"For . . . leading you on? If you felt led on? I don't know. But that kiss on Saturday night should never have happened. I've got a thing going on with someone else and although that's still kind of casual, and not official . . . we're still . . . a 'thing'."

"A . . . 'thing'?"

"Yes, and I don't want to hurt her. I really like her."

"You like *me*," Tamara said, trying to interlink her fingers with Oscar's, but he shook his hand from her grasp and stepped away from her.

"Of course, I do, but I *like* like her." He shrugged.

"*Like* like. Are you twelve?" Tamara snapped, her words now even more clipped.

"You know what I mean, Tamara. I fancy her. I want to spend my time with her. I want to kiss her."

"You can kiss her *and* me," she laughed, but it sounded too high-pitched and sent a shiver down Oscar's spine.

"No, I can't." Oscar tried to step around her and into the safety of the theatre as he noticed a couple of people on the street turn their attention towards them, the faint hint of recognition in their eyes.

"Why not? Because *she* says so?" Tamara hissed.

"Yes!" he laughed. "Well, actually, no. Because I say so. We say so. If kissing you or anyone else hurts her, then I don't want to do that. How she feels matters more to me."

"Oh, right, so if you saw her kissing someone else you'd be furious, would you?" Tamara scoffed. The thought hadn't yet occurred to Oscar what his reaction would have been had the roles from the other night been reversed.

Oscar thought about how the excuse of being intoxicated would have meant nothing to him either, had Olive been the one to have drunk far too much and locked lips with another cast member. He knew the image of her kissing someone else would haunt him for longer than he cared to guess and how difficult he would find it looking at her the same way again. Finally, Oscar felt the sting of humiliation at the idea of coming back into work, and facing an entire cast of people who would all know exactly what had happened, and wondering whether they were all discussing what it was about him that had made Olive find comfort in another man's arms. "Actually, yes I would," he said, feeling his eyes inexplicably start to brim. "I think it'd break my heart."

Tamara pulled down her sunglasses to check if she was seeing things or whether Oscar Bright really was getting emotional.

"Ugh, whatever." Tamara pushed her sunglasses back up her nose and turned into stage door with a toss of her hair. Oscar took a deep breath to recover his

**186**

emotions and took out his phone to check the time. He had a couple of minutes before he needed to be inside, so he could afford to give Tamara a little bit of distance before he followed her. Oscar turned back towards the way he'd come, thinking maybe he could quickly grab a coffee, when he realised someone was now standing close behind him.

"Olive. Hi."

"It'd break your heart, would it?" she said, trying to laugh but even feigning amusement at the man she was so furious with felt near impossible. "You're a better actor than people give you credit for, Oscar." Olive walked past him and turned the big silver handle on stage door.

"Olive, please just . . . give me a chance to explain." Oscar reached out to touch her and when she didn't flinch or pull away he squeezed her arm.

"Okay," she said without looking at him.

"Okay?"

"Doesn't mean it changes anything between us, but I'd be very interested to hear how you explain this." Olive went inside and only ticked the sign-in sheet next to her name, leaving Oscar to sign himself in. It was a small gesture of defiance and detachment, but it made her feel a little bit triumphant at least and that's what she felt she needed today. Oscar followed solemnly behind her, the silence feeling heavier with each step.

"Did you have a good day off?" Just the sound of his voice felt like a ball and chain around her heart. The fact he was asking questions she deemed utterly ridiculous made her grip and pull on the straps of her rucksack so tightly that her shoulders started to ache.

"Small talk, Oscar? Really?" she snapped.

"Just . . . making conversation," he said to the back of her head, where her hair was still slightly damp from the shower. She stopped on the landing before the last flight of stairs to her corridor and turned to face him.

"No, I didn't have a very good day off, Oscar. Did you?" Now that he got a proper look at her face he noticed her cheeks were pale and her eyes puffy from crying. He shook his head as he realised he'd been the one responsible for causing her pain.

"I guess not."

Once inside Olive's dressing room, Oscar closed and locked the door behind them and Olive sat at her dressing table, taking her laptop and her make-up bag out of her rucksack and setting them up ready for the day. She caught his reflection in the mirror, still at the door with his bag and coat on.

"Well?"

"Right . . ." Now that he actually had to explain, Oscar found himself at a bit of a loss. "I have no idea what to say," he confessed.

"That's a great start," she said, squirting a little blob of foundation onto the back of her hand.

"I have a lot to say, I just don't know where to start," he said, sliding his bag off his back and walking to the radiator on the wall behind her, the heat warming his legs through his cold jeans as he leaned against it.

"How about with you kissing Tamara?" She shrugged.

188

"I know, I know. I never should have done that. I'm sorry," he said, looking at her reflection.

"Then why did you?" She tried to hide her anxiety as her heart raced in her chest.

"I don't know." Oscar shook his head, replaying the events for the thousandth time. All he could remember was seeing glimpses of everyone's warmly lit faces, the stickiness of his skin in the hot pub and then Tamara's lips, thick with lip gloss, lapping against his mouth.

"Again, great answer." She rolled her eyes.

"I *really* don't know! There was no logical reason. No thought process that I can even remember, let alone follow. You and I had had an argument, I was drunk, and she was ... there," he said, rubbing his now sweating palm on his thighs.

"Of *course* she was there."

"What's that supposed to mean?" Oscar asked, confusion showing on his face.

"That must be a joke?" Olive stopped rubbing foundation onto her cheek and turned to face him.

"No ... what are you talking about?" Oscar's head had started to thump. He'd continued to drink through his day off, alone in his flat, and had slept badly since Olive had screamed at him on Shaftesbury Avenue. Thinking straight wasn't coming to him naturally.

"Oscar, Tamara's been trying to get her claws into you from the day we started rehearsals. I've lost count of how many times she's touched your biceps and how many snide remarks she's slid my way as a result of the attention you've been paying me and not her. Of course she was there. Tamara isn't stupid. She waited until she saw her opportune moment and then swooped." Olive felt a little smug at how coherent she was being compared to the bumbling mess of Oscar who stood watching her through the mirror.

"I think you're overthinking things a little bit there."

"No. I'm not, Oscar," she laughed. "Sadly, I'm not."

"Who *does* that?" Oscar said but then immediately thought of his ex-girlfriend, Zadie, and the lengths she had already gone to in order to get her own back. The stories to the tabloids, the tweets, the occasional text message containing a barrage of hate. Oscar knew people like that existed in the world, so was it really beyond the realms of reality that he had found himself working with someone like that, yet again?

"Tamara. *Tamara* does that. Stories about her have floated around for a long time and now that I've worked with her myself, it's horrible to know that they're probably all true."

"What stories?" Oscar asked, feeling the pressure on his chest lessen a little now that he wasn't the focus of her hard stare.

"She picks up the latest guy who's on the rise, uses them to get a little bit further ahead in her career, and then dumps them. She's what we call a 'star-fucker'." Olive said, turning back to the mirror before she got so angry at Oscar that she threw him out of her dressing room without the conversation coming to a proper conclusion. *Keep calm and get closure*, she thought to herself.

"She has always been quite full on . . ." he admitted, thinking back to only a few minutes earlier when

Tamara had tried to plant one on him in broad daylight, as if their drunken kiss now tied them together and his relationship with Olive was merely a thing of the past.

"She has. And you never did anything to ward her off because she's a pretty girl and you liked the attention." Olive dusted powder over her face and enjoyed the excuse of being able to close her eyes briefly and not look at his puppy dog eyes pleading at her in the mirror.

"Is that so awful?" he said, fiddling with the frayed fabric on the rips in his jeans.

"Not when you're unattached, no. Not at all." Olive blew powder off her brush and for a moment was lost in the way the particles billowed into the air, catching the light of the bulbs around her mirror.

"Exactly," he said, more quietly than if he'd been feeling confident about the situation he was currently in.

"And you'd describe yourself as unattached?" Olive asked.

"Well . . . I'm single. *We're* single. We said this was casual. I technically didn't do anything wrong here!" Oscar replied, knowing any answer he gave might upset Olive so opting for honesty being the best policy.

Olive stood up, her emotions now far too large to be contained by such a small chair.

"Oh, Oscar. If that's where your head is at then we can't have this conversation."

"I don't understand —"

Olive took a step towards him, cutting him off, her blood hot, the colour flooding her cheeks and the tips of her ears.

"Do you really think you can get *that* close to someone, sleep with them, share yourself with them as much as you've shared with me and vice versa, do you think you can tell someone you '*choose* them' and spend every waking moment with them and . . . then think it's okay to kiss someone else based on the technicality that we said it would be casual?"

"But we said —"

"Yes, we *said* casual, but we didn't *act* casual. You didn't act casual. We have never been casual. And you know that, Oscar." Olive felt the familiar tingle behind her eyes and her throat started to close around those last few words. Her arms were limp by her sides and she felt exhausted before the day had even begun. *Why don't you get it? Please just . . . understand*, she pleaded with him in her mind.

"I don't know what to say." He shrugged, and she threaded her fingers through her hair, almost ready to tear it out.

"Oscar, I don't know if this is some kind of macho, laddish front you're trying to put on but I'm not an idiot. You're making me feel like some kind of psycho for knowing with a hundred per cent certainty that you have feelings for me. But you can't behave how you've behaved around me and then tell me I'm just some casual work fling that was bound to end when the next pretty face came along. Am I wrong?"

192

"No, you're not wrong. Of course, you're right. You know that." Oscar sighed.

"I only know that because I've had to piece it all together. You've never actually told me how you really feel about me. If this is all some kind of game to you . . . like . . . you playing hard to get then . . ." Olive trailed off, not knowing what she would do if that were the case. To purposely kiss someone else in an attempt to get her to like him even more would be completely unforgivable.

"Olive, of course I have feelings for you. You aren't just some casual fling. I understand that we've not exactly been casual, right from the off, but I was telling the truth when I told you I can't handle anything more than what we are right now."

"I'm not asking you for anything more. I understand not being able to handle a relationship. I get that, honestly. What I don't understand is essentially starting one anyway but getting rid of the label, just so you could get out on a technicality when you got bored and started kissing other people."

"Please don't think of me like that. You know me better than that. It was *one* person. *One* mistake." Oscar's voice had also started to wobble.

"If these are the kinds of mistakes you make then I don't know if I can handle any more of them." Olive sat back down heavily, two nights of missed sleep suddenly catching up with her.

"There won't be any more. We said we'd be casual, but . . . that doesn't work for us. We're closer than that and it hurts more than it should when we're with other people. So . . . let's not do that," he said, the bags under his eyes creasing as he gently smiled. *I can do that*, he thought. *I can just be hers. I want to just be hers.*

"But you don't want to be with me," she heard herself say, and it sounded so pathetic and childish and so unlike herself that she welled up.

"I *do* want to spend my time with you. Just you. I like what we have and I really . . . *really* don't want this to be the end, Olive." Oscar stood up straight, the back of his legs now burning from the radiator, and walked towards her.

"You need to give me some time, Oscar. To think about all of this," she said, holding her palm out towards him.

"Please let me hold you?" he said, his own eyes starting to prickle.

"I'm — I'm sorry," she said, trying to keep strong and not give in to the irresistible idea of his arms around her. "I just need a little bit of time."

"Okay." He nodded, picking up his bag and turning to the door before she noticed a tear had escaped and made its way down to his chin.

"But for what it's worth," she said before he left, "I don't want this to be over either."

# CHAPTER
# THIRTEEN

## Two Dozen Roses

The theatre should have been ablaze with nervous energy. Jitters should have been rife, and butterflies should have been fluttering in many a stomach, but a spanner had certainly been put in the works.

"Do you want me to hurt him? Because I will happily hurt him," Doug whispered to Olive, leaning across the back of her seat in the stalls.

"And do you want me to have a quiet and calm word with him after I've stopped Doug from hurting him?" asked Howard, flipping down one of the seats and sitting next to Doug in the row behind.

"Now, now boys. No need for any of that. We just . . . plough on. It's opening night, after all! Lots to be excited about!" Olive said, turning her head over her shoulder only slightly just in case her face was still a little red from yet another bout of tears after Oscar had left her dressing room.

"You're a saint, Green. A bloody saint," Howard said, giving the back of her neck a squeeze, careful not to disturb her already prepped pin curls.

"But if you ever feel like . . . y'know . . . not being a saint, dressing room fourteen is a safe place for slagging off anyone and everyone. We won't breathe a word!"

"I'll bear that in mind!" She laughed, genuinely, and reached her hand over her shoulder. Doug interlinked his own fingers with hers and gave them a squeeze.

"By the way, don't look now but Little Miss I-Wear-Sunglasses-Inside has just walked in," Doug whispered as he kissed the back of her hand and slid along one seat, as did everyone else to make room for Tamara and Jane who were the last to join the cast for notes from their director. Olive groaned but found it very easy not to look. She knew seeing Tamara's undoubtedly smug face would make her insides squirm more than they already were and Olive couldn't risk actually vomiting before the dress run.

"Here we are, gang! Let's not mince words, tonight is the big night!" Michael seemed already dressed for the opening show that evening. The shoulders of his black jacket were speckled in diamonds, making it look like he'd been caught in the rain and had not yet brushed off the droplets. "You've all done marvellously up until now so I say we just get up there and give it everything we've got, eh?" He seemed oddly cheery for a man whose show wasn't as tight as it should be for an opening night, but Olive was thankful. The pressure of an angry director may have been enough to make her crack and that was the last thing she needed. "Just a couple of things before we get on our feet . . ." Michael pulled his notebook out of his satchel and flipped to a page somewhere in the middle.

196

"Where are we? Ah, yes! Here we are! Oscar, where are you?" Michael looked around the stalls and his eyes settled somewhere a few rows behind the main group. "There you are! I just thought that maybe, in the scene with Howard that you could . . ." Michael's voice muffled in Olive's ears as she heard her inner voice say *Don't turn around. Don't turn around. Don't* . . . but it was too late. Olive swivelled in her chair to see where Oscar was sitting. She saw him sitting a couple of rows behind, coat still on, baseball cap pulled down over his eyes, his feet on the back of the chair in front of him so that he was mostly hidden behind his knees, his coffee cup close to his face.

"No worries, Michael," Oscar replied.

"Wow. He looks miserable," Howard whispered to Doug.

"Yeah. Looks like you broke him, Olive," Doug laughed, nudging Olive's shoulder.

"He broke himself," she whispered back, wiping her cheek.

"He said *what*?!" gasped Sammy. She was sitting up on Olive's dressing table, cross-legged, after having moved all of Olive's stuff out the way with a careful swipe of her arm.

"He said we were casual and he was single and so *technically* he hadn't done anything wrong." Olive rolled her eyes as she took off her stage make-up with a baby wipe, still in her burgundy dress and wig.

"What a dick! Urgh!" Sammy dipped her hand into the jar of hard-boiled sweets on Olive's desk and picked

**197**

out an orange one. "Does he actually think he can get out of this on a technicality? Please tell me he's not that stupid?" she said around the sweet in her mouth.

"No, I think he's just desperate for this mistake not to tarnish his reputation with the rest of the cast. And I get that." Olive nodded a little too hard.

"A mistake? You're seriously going to believe that?"

"It's Tamara," Olive said to herself in the mirror. "Any time someone knowingly kisses that nut job has got to be a mistake."

"WOAH!" Sammy slammed her hand down on the counter and made everything on its surface wobble — even Olive jumped. "Stop. The. Presses. Did you actually just say something *mean*?"

"Oh, God that really was bitchy, wasn't it? Ahh, sorry, this whole thing has just got me all . . . blah."

"Babe, are you kidding? I *live* for that shit. Is it awful that I wanna see you this pissed off more often?" Sammy laughed.

"Yes! It is!" Olive whipped her with the baby wipe and gave her a cold wet splat on the knee.

"SAMMY! WE'RE GOING!" Doug shouted as he passed Olive's dressing room door, banging on it loudly with his balled-up fist.

"Shit, I'm not even out of costume." Sammy scrambled off the desk and almost slipped over on the way to the door.

"Oh wait, Sammy! What are you doing tonight?" asked Olive.

"The drinks thing, you mean?"

"Yeah."

198

"Please don't tell me you're not coming?"

"No, I'm coming, it's just . . . my friend Lou is watching the show and as we're not allowed to bring guests to the official drinks thing, I'll probably just come for one and then go for a drink with her. Just wondered if you fancied coming?"

"Is that the *only* reason you're leaving early?"

"Yes, of course! Well, that and . . . I don't really like the idea of spending an evening with Oscar and Tamara in the same room. If they do want to make out again I'd rather not see it this time."

"Olive, I know he's been a massive, *massive* idiot but . . . everyone can see how much he likes you."

"Then why did he kiss someone else?" Olive said without a smile.

"Because he's a massive, *massive* idiot. Look I'm not making excuses for the guy but — you'd had a fight, he was drunk and from what it looks like, he suffers from serious low self-esteem."

"He seems confident enough to me . . ." Olive folded her arms across her chest.

"Oh, that's all just a front! Let's look at the facts, shall we? One. Michael calling him 'TV' all the time has probably made him feel insecure and a little unwelcome here. I know it would if it were me. Two, did you see all that stuff in the papers about him and Zadie?"

"How could I miss it?" Olive sighed.

"Oh yeah, and all the drama she caused about that picture of the two of you. He's not exactly had the best of luck with women, has he? It's all drama, drama, drama! It's hard enough having a relationship in the public eye, let alone it going so pear-shaped with everyone watching and wading in with their own opinions. He might play the confident lad but I reckon he's actually a little bit . . . I dunno . . . broken by it all? Getting with someone like Tamara, a girl who looks like she stepped off the Victoria's Secret catwalk, probably made him feel good about himself — even if it was short-lived!"

"A second ago you were ready to castrate him!"

"And I still would! For you!" Sammy grinned through a heart she made with her fingers. "I could be wrong but I'm just saying, he may have *acted* like a massive arsehole but I just don't think he *is* an arsehole."

"Hmm." Olive turned back to the mirror and started to take the pins out of her wig.

"Oh, please don't be like that!" Sammy skittered over to Olive, and wrapped her arms around her shoulders, swaying them both back and forth as she spoke to Olive in the mirror. "I'm being serious. I'm a very cynical, cut-throat person. Ruthless, I tell you! Ruthless! And if I thought saying goodbye to Oscar was the way forward, I would tell you so. But you both make each other smile and we've all loved watching you flirt back and forth since the beginning of rehearsals. We've all been dying to see where this thing between you might go." Sammy squeezed Olive's shoulders and then started helping remove pins from her wig.

"You've known about us since rehearsals?" Olive asked, and Sammy stopped and looked at Olive in the mirror, raising her eyebrows at her with a smile.

"Oh, honeeeey . . ."

"Yeah, all right. We weren't subtle, were we?" Olive sighed, looking down into her lap.

"No, babe. You weren't. Look, he's a good guy. He's just at a point in his life where he's a bit lost and he made a wrong turn. A big Tamara-shaped wrong turn."

Olive couldn't help it, she laughed.

"THERE SHE IS! Now get dressed, quickly. We're going for burgers before the big show." Sammy slapped Olive's thigh and ran back to the door.

"Who?" Olive said, her stomach rumbling at just the mention of food.

"Not Tamara. Or Jane. So you're coming."

"Only if you come for drinks with me and Lou tonight?"

"Of course I'll be there!" Sammy scarpered, skidding down the hallway to the stairwell in just her tights, calling back, "GET DRESSED, OLIVE!" and so Olive got dressed.

Olive was grateful to be preoccupied by the company of Sammy, Doug and Howard but time managed to escape them all and before any of them had finished their burgers, they realised they only had ten minutes to finish up and pay before "the half" was called. Back inside the theatre, actors were running back and forth between their dressing rooms and wardrobe, making sure they had all the right items of clothing they needed. Dressers were carrying baskets of costumes to quick-change areas and setting them out in a way that made it easier for the actors to get in and out of their clothes between scenes, and in amongst it all was Walter, worrying about how much the lights had been flickering since they'd been turned on that morning.

"Fawn, I don't know what you're up to but I'm not entirely sure I like it," he muttered.

"Hi, Walter!" Olive bustled through the door with the others not far behind who all mumbled their hellos. "This is Sammy, Doug and Howard. Guys, this is Walter," smiled Olive.

"Yes, I recognise them from the programme. Hello," Walter answered. "You've got some mail, Olive. Some in the pigeonhole and that package by your feet is yours too, I believe."

"Oh, wow. That's exciting. Thanks." Olive grabbed her letters and Howard picked up the tall black parcel from the floor. It had a picture of gold flowers printed on the side.

"Looks like someone's been rather extravagant! Says here it's got two dozen roses inside!" Howard said, reading off the receipt stuck to the side of the parcel.

"Howard!" Sammy turned and thumped Howard's arm. "Why can't you let the girl open the parcel and find out for herself?"

"It's got a picture of a bunch of flowers on the side of the box! It's hardly a surprise that it's a bouquet of flowers, is it?" said Howard, peering around the side of the box.

"Relax, Sammy! My agent texted me and said they'd be sending me something so I knew it was coming. Roses, though. That's nice."

"Two dozen. Even nicer!" said Doug, signing them all in.

"Pass them here," Olive said as she kicked the second lot of double doors open, her arms outstretched for the box.

"It's all right, I'll bring them up. You're on my floor anyway," Howard answered, carrying the large box with ease.

"Aww, thanks. See you in a bit, Walter!" Olive called back as they disappeared into the theatre together.

"How did you get so chummy with the door man?" asked Sammy as they all climbed the stairs.

"Dunno. We just got chatting. He seems sweet enough." Olive shrugged as she started opening one of the three letters she'd found in her pigeonhole.

"He's *old*. How long has he been working here?" said Doug.

"No idea, but it's nice that the theatre has kept him here despite his age. If someone wants to keep working doing what they love, and they can manage it, then why not!" said Howard.

"Well, tell him the lightbulb in our room is still broken," said Sammy, peeling off to the door on the first floor with Doug.

"That's weird, one of mine broke the other day too," said Olive, giving Sammy a hug before she went to her dressing room.

"These theatres are so old, the electrics are bound to be a bit dodgy. See you guys in a bit!" said Howard and when the door closed he whispered to Olive, "Is something going on between the two of them?"

"What? Doug and Sammy? No! I mean . . . I don't think so. Sammy would have said something," Olive said as she overtook Howard on the stairs.

"Urgh, I'm so bad at this. I just can't figure out who fancies who!"

"Stop trying!" Olive laughed.

"No, I know it shouldn't matter. It's just fun, isn't it? You spend so long with people you're bound to start fancying at least *someone* in the cast. Problem is the person I fancy only has eyes for you, it seems." Howard nudged Olive's elbow with his own, almost dropping the box of flowers in the process.

"Oscar?" Olive scoffed, keeping her eyes on the open letter in her hands but unable to focus on any of the words. "He's got eyes for more people than I thought."

"Olive, my love. Can I be honest with you?" Howard said, as she held her dressing room door open for him.

"Go on . . ." she groaned. He put the box down on her desk and slid it towards her as she sat in her chair.

"Make him sweat. He deserves that. But don't ruin your own happiness. I've seen how he looks at you when you're not looking. And if he's looking at you like that when you're not looking, it's proof that he's not just putting on a show. He likes you. Whether you believe it or not. He's just being very immature about it all."

"I know," she sighed, putting the box between her legs and gently removing the bouquet of twenty-four deep red roses that spilled out into formation as they came free from the box.

204

"He's a lost little boy who up until now hasn't needed to think about what he wants because everything has always been given to him on a silver platter. Now that he's found you, something he very clearly wants, he's just a little bit frightened."

"I know."

"I know you know. But it's easy to let the voices in your head win and convince you otherwise so I just thought I'd stick my nose in and give the good voices a bit of back up."

*Ladies and gentlemen, this is your half hour call, this is your half hour call. Thank you.*

"Right! Break a leg! God bless! Don't be shit!" And just like that, Howard was gone. Olive moved a few roses out of the way, hunting for a card and finding one at the very centre of the bunch of gorgeous blooms.

*Can we start again?*
   *Meet me tonight at stage door?*
   *When the curtain falls.*
   *Oz*
   *x*

When Olive had first seen the box of flowers in reception, she'd wondered if they'd been sent by Oscar — her agent usually just sent a bottle of champagne. All the way up the stairs she'd been debating with herself whether she wanted the flowers to be from him or not. If he had sent them, then he'd won a few brownie points, but Olive wasn't sure she wanted to give him any, even if the flowers really were quite extravagant, not to mention how beautiful they smelled. And if Oscar hadn't sent them, then why not? Not that Olive thought she deserved flowers, but he had screwed up and if he really did want to sort things out between them, then a bunch of flowers would be a lovely start.

Now that she knew he had definitely sent the flowers, she couldn't help but smile at the gesture, which made her feel so conflicted about her own feelings that she then felt annoyed with herself. In the end, Olive started crying for what felt like the hundredth time that day.

"Why couldn't you have just . . . *not* kissed her?"

She folded the card in half and as she ripped it along the crease, one by one, all of the bulbs along her mirror shattered.

"OH MY GOD!" She jumped up from her seat, thankful she still had her shoes on as there was glass everywhere. She ran to the door and fumbled in the dark to flip the switch to turn on the main overhead lights. "HOWARD!" she yelled down the hallway.

"What on earth is going on out there?!" Oscar appeared in his doorway, his costume shirt on but still undone.

"Nothing! Nothing! I just need Howard."

"Have you been crying again?" Oscar started to walk up the corridor towards her, but Olive quickly retreated.

"No, of course not!" She turned back into her room and quickly wiped her face.

"Did you . . . oh my . . . what the hell happened in here?" Oscar said as he walked into her dressing room to find glass scattered on the floor and the card from his roses ripped neatly in two lying amongst the shards.

"I don't know, all the bulbs just started . . . exploding. Howard said this building had dodgy electrics, but this was something else." She started to collect the shards of glass carefully into her hands.

"Something else? What do you mean something else? Here, let me help."

"Well . . . I don't know! Ouch." Oscar picked up the small plastic bin so she could decant the glass from her hands into it, but a small fleck of blood was already forming on her palm.

"Please don't tell me you think this was a ghost, Olive." He put the bin back down and took her hand, inspecting her palm. He wiped it clean with his fingers when he was sure no glass was still stuck in her skin and in the split second he was deciding whether or not to kiss her palm, she pulled her hand away.

"I don't care what it was, Oscar. I just want things back to normal."

"The bulbs or . . ."

"Yes, Oscar. The bulbs. I think everything else is a little harder to fix." Olive took the bin and continued to pick the glass up off the floor, their conversation clearly over, and Oscar left to go and find Walter at stage door. He was so certain the roses would have helped, even if only a little, and so to see her crying again made his heart descend in his chest.

# CHAPTER
# FOURTEEN

## Oscar Believes

Olive entered into the stage right wing, where the majority of the ensemble were huddled together and buzzing, as were the crowd.

"Awww man, I hate that sound," said Doug, running up the wing to try and get a peek of the audience in the gap between the gauze and the edge of the proscenium arch. People were jostling past one another in rows to get to their seats, sweet packets were being rustled and there was a steady murmur of people discussing what the evening might hold. But what made Olive's stomach churn the most was how dressed up everyone seemed to be. No one dressed up to come to the theatre these days unless it was a really big event. Olive liked to pretend that opening night was just a dress run or even just another performance of a show she'd been in for years. However, seeing all those suits and dresses and sparkling jewellery gave her skin a sweaty sheen.

"You and me both," Olive said, following him and peering over his shoulder. "Is there anything going on between you and Sammy?"

Doug laughed. "That was subtly asked!"

"Sorry! I know you well enough not to beat around the bush, don't I? So . . . are you beating around hers?" Olive gave his ribs a jab with her finger and enjoyed the laughter that bubbled in her throat when he flinched and grabbed her wrists to stop her from doing it again.

"Eww, don't do that," he laughed.

"What?" She wobbled in her heels, trying to release her wrists.

"You're too sweet to say things like that!" he said, holding both her hands in one of his.

"But it's fine when you say them?" she said, giving him a slight tap on the shin with her foot.

"Well, yes! I'm disgusting! I'm saving you from being like me. And oww!" he said, letting go of her hands with a push.

"You've still not answered my question!" she said, her index fingers outstretched as a warning.

"No! Of course nothing's going on! Have you asked her this yet?" said Doug, straightening out his waistcoat.

"I saw you first." Olive checked herself over for any ungainly creases in her dress.

"Stand by, everyone! We have front of house clearance! Stand by!"

"You might wanna fix that," Doug said, pointing at her chest, and when she looked down he swiped his finger up, catching her nose.

"Very funny, loser! How old are you?" she said with a smile and with a deep breath, she thought about how pleased she was to be starting the show on a good note with someone at least.

"Pssst. Olive!" She didn't know where it was coming from, but she knew immediately *who* it was coming from. She squinted from her little pedestal on centre stage into the stage left wing and there was Oscar, waving his arms about. "Break a leg!" he whispered, giving her a double thumbs-up. He'd caught her in a good mood and she couldn't help but smile back, returning the thumbs-up gesture, and even laughing at how lame it was.

*You okay?* she mouthed. Oscar held his hands out in front of him so they hit the lights and even from the middle of the stage she could see they were trembling. "You'll be fine! Just imagine everyone naked!" She winked.

"He probably doesn't have to imagine too hard for you." Sammy snorted through the curtain behind Olive's pedestal, at which Olive tutted loudly. Oscar tried to pretend he hadn't heard but Olive caught him smiling as he gave her one final thumbs-up and disappeared into the darkness of the wing. Olive took another deep breath to compose herself, and as the audience fell silent, the music began and the curtain rose.

"Not bad, TV!" said Doug, ruffling Oscar's hair as the cast filtered out of the wings and into the corridor behind the stage. Oscar was far sweatier and more exhausted than he ever thought imaginable.

"We have to do this eight times a week? I don't even think I'm gonna wake up tomorrow!" Oscar said, unbuttoning his shirt with one hand whilst needing the other to hold himself steady against the water cooler.

"You'll get the hang of it, gorgeous." Sammy winked as she ran ahead of him up the stairs.

"You coming for a drink tonight, Oscar?"

Tamara was already out of her costume, in her underwear and holding her dressing gown loosely to her front. Olive and Doug came through the double doors, Doug expertly averting his gaze and Olive . . . not so much.

"Erm . . . no thanks, Tamara. I'll be giving it a miss."

"But it's the press night drinks!" she whined.

"At least show your face, mate!" said Doug. Oscar looked at Olive and she gave him a vague sense of a smile, and something in between a shrug and a nod.

"I'll go for one, but only if Olive has that drink with me."

"For God's sake." Tamara pushed past Oscar, catching him on the shoulder as she scarpered up the stairs to her dressing room.

"Erm . . . ouch," he said, rubbing his shoulder.

"You did kiss her and then decide you didn't want her any more," Olive said with a sigh as she followed Tamara up to her own room.

"Once! I kissed her once and I was —"

"Drunk! Everyone knows!" Doug gave him a slap on the cheek.

"Ouch. Why is everyone hurting me today?"

"Because everyone's a little bit angry with you today! Look, just give Olive time. She's mad at you, but she's also mad about you." Doug started unbuttoning his own shirt, his hat and waistcoat in the crook of his arm.

"And I'm mad about her! I just want this to be fixed. I want simple and happy and so far all this job has been is complicated and miserable."

"Does she know that?"

"What?"

"That you're mad about her?"

". . . I think so." Oscar shrugged.

"Have you said those words to her? Those exact words?"

"Well . . . no, I don't think so. Not exactly."

"So . . . all she knows is you like her enough to spend time with her, but don't want to be with her."

"How do you know all of this?"

"She tells me everything."

"Great."

"And I mean everything . . ." Doug briefly glanced downwards and Oscar could feel his cheeks flush.

"Which begs the question, Oscar, why are you stood here telling me that you're crazy for her? Tell *her* that! She'd love to know! In fact, if you'd been telling her that from the start she would have had far less to be insecure about."

"Don't say that." Oscar rubbed his eyes.

"Truth hurts, mate."

"I'm not a soppy person! I don't like PDAs, I'm not good with telling people how I feel —"

"You've just told me how you feel! You never have to say anything you don't mean, you don't even have to be gushy or soppy. But if you can tell me you're mad

212

about her then you can tell her that too. Simple as that." Doug gave Oscar a slap on the back and disappeared down the small spiral staircase to his own dressing room, leaving Oscar on his own.

He reached his corridor and paused briefly at Olive's door. His hand was poised to knock but, despite Doug's words of encouragement, Olive had said she needed time and Oscar was worried that things between them would never heal if he didn't do as she asked. So he kept on walking, lost in his thoughts, until suddenly Olive's door burst open.

"Has anyone seen my clothes?" she called down the corridor, Oscar the only one around to answer her.

"Your clothes?" he laughed.

"Well, I'm not going to the after party in this." She gestured at the big purple towel wrapped around her like a dress.

"I mean, it's definitely a look!" Oscar said, trying to look anywhere but at her body.

"Have you taken them?"

"Eh?" he said, finishing unbuttoning his shirt.

"Is this some kind of weird ploy to get me to come into your dressing room? Because if it is . . ."

"I don't have your clothes, you crazy naked lady!" Oscar said, as he opened the door to his dressing room and took a step inside.

"Oh but . . ." she started. *Being angry at him is really . . . really, hard,* she thought. ". . . the least you can do is help me look for them. Someone's obviously being a dick and I don't really want to wander from room to room in a towel looking for them on my own."

"You don't have a dressing gown?"

"Wait there." Olive's door closed, and she re-emerged twenty seconds later in a long dressing gown. "There we go. At least if we don't have any luck I can pass this off as some kind of weird, trendy dress that's all the rage in Paris."

"All right, weirdo, if you say so." They walked down the corridor together and Oscar went to drape his arm around her shoulders, but then let it fall by his side before she noticed.

"We're starting with Doug. He loves a prank and knows I hate them. My money's on him." In her bare feet, Olive's pace was quick.

"And if it's not him?" Oscar asked, pulling his shirt around him as they stepped out into the stone stairwell.

"Well, my dress for tonight hasn't just vanished!" Olive pitter-pattered down the stairs, sometimes taking more than two at a time and disappearing around corners before Oscar had only just turned the last.

"You could always wear what you wore here today?" he called after her, struggling to keep up.

"No, it's all gone. I left them all in a pile on the radiator and the whole lot is missing. Not on the radiator. Not in my room. Gone." They got to stage level and Oscar suddenly realised he had never actually seen the male ensemble dressing room.

"This way!" Olive opened a door and a new metal spiral staircase was revealed which she nimbly descended. It was so narrow, Oscar began to feel a little claustrophobic, but it was only around ten steps before they were met with another dressing room door.

214

"Where on earth is this place?"

"Narnia."

"Ha ha." He rolled his eyes, but her expression didn't change.

"No, I mean . . . we call it Narnia. It's so out of the way from all the other rooms. And that over there," Olive pointed to the dark space behind them, "is costume storage."

"So they're in the dressing room behind all the old coats . . ."

"Narnia!" She smiled.

"Oh . . . okay. Well, check with Doug and —"

"DOUG!" BANG BANG BANG. Olive's subtlety seemed to have disappeared along with her clothes.

"Jesus H Christ, Green." The door opened to reveal the three ensemble boys in varying states of undress. Doug hopped over a pair of shoes lying in the middle of the floor and came to the door. "Nice gown."

"Well, it's all I've got, thanks to you!" Olive hopped from foot to foot on the cold stone floor.

"What are you on about?" Doug was topless and only now did Oscar realise just how much the other man clearly worked out. Suddenly Oscar was holding his previously opened shirt closed.

"My clothes?"

"Your clothes?" Doug said in a high-pitched voice with his face all screwed up.

"Doug!" She slipped her arm through the gap in the door and poked him in the ribs. "As much as I love my birthday suit, I paid a lot of money for that dress and I'd quite like to wear it tonight!"

"Babe . . ." he said and Oscar felt a strange twinge in his chest upon hearing the affection in Doug's voice, "I don't have your clothes. They aren't in D14. But Jane said something about her pearl necklace going missing too."

"D14?" Oscar asked and they both pointed at the gold numbers on Doug's dressing room door. "Ah. Gotcha."

"Keep up, TV!" said Doug as he closed the door. "SEE YOU AT THE PARTY!" he yelled.

"Urgh. That boy. I love him, but he drives me *up the wall*."

"You love him?" Oscar mumbled, and Olive turned sharply on the stairs.

"You kissed Tamara?"

"Ouch. Touché."

"Thank you." Olive turned to grab the handrail but as she touched it expecting to feel cold metal, her hand was cushioned by a sock. One of *her* socks.

"Erm . . . what the hell?" She held it up for Oscar to see.

"Are you sure it wasn't there before?"

"A hundred per cent." Olive ran up the stairs as quickly as she could, and found her knickers lying by the double doors that led to the stage. She quickly picked them up and stuffed them in her dressing gown pocket before Oscar joined her. She peered through the little window in the door and, although it was dark, she could just make out her leggings in a bundle in the wing.

216

"What on earth is going on?" she held the door open for Oscar and started to follow the trail of clothes. Her casual dress was draped over a rung in the ladder that led to the fly floor and as she looked up, she saw another one of her socks, her coat and just out of sight on the walkway, she could see the diamante from her dress glittering in what little light was left in the wing.

"Is that your dress?" Oscar asked, following her gaze.

"Yup," she sighed. "That is my dress."

"Someone's obviously just trying to be clever."

"Well, if it's not Doug then it's probably your new girlfriend," Olive said. She felt bad every time she snapped at him, but it was almost involuntary now. In the time it took her brain to decide if the thought was worth vocalising, her mouth was already spewing it out. She felt he deserved to hear how she was feeling but she worried that she was only pushing him further away, and seeing as she hadn't yet decided how close she wanted to keep him, this wasn't ideal.

"Out the way," he said, gently pulling her back by the shoulders.

"What?"

"Out the way!" Oscar started to climb the ladder, up, into the darkness of the fly floor.

"Oscar!" she whispered. "You're not supposed to go up there!"

"And neither was the person who put your dress up here! Just keep an eye out!" Olive's skin prickled, and her body fizzed with a mixture of nervousness and a strange excitement that she'd not felt since she was playing pranks on her teachers back at school with Lou.

"You're gonna get in trouble!" she hissed, now only able to properly see his feet, the rest of him merely a silhouette.

"And what are they gonna do? Fire me right after opening night? I'll be like, five seconds!" Oscar carefully climbed the peeling ladder, black paint chips coming off on his hands. He looked down to wipe his cold palms on his trousers and when he looked back up towards the dress, he could have sworn it was a little further along than it had previously just been. He scrambled up a little faster and hopped down from the ladder onto the metal grid.

"Hello?" Oscar called out.

"What's going on?" he heard Olive whisper.

"Anyone there?" The dress was in a silver sparkling crumpled heap on the floor. Oscar took a step towards it and this time he noticed it definitely moved an inch further away.

"Jesus Christ!" He jumped back.

"Oscar! This isn't funny! Hurry up!" Olive said, her voice a little louder now.

"Just a minute!" he whispered back to Olive as he took another step towards the dress, only to see it move a little further away from him again. He took two steps forwards and the dress moved again. Oscar straightened himself up.

"It's probably just a mouse under there. Nothing spooky. No . . . ghosts. There's no such thing as ghosts, they don't exist." He took a deep breath. "Just a mouse," and he walked towards the dress without stopping. Just as he knelt to pick it up, the fabric swirled up in front of him, the bust filled out, the waist cinched in and the silk around the hips billowed and floated as though the dress was suspended underwater.

"What in the —"

*Ossssssccccaaaaarrrr*

A tingle rippled over Oscar's skin. He looked up, hoping to see the faces of his cast mates, jeering at him. He wanted to find wires or some sort of trickery. Otherwise, he was sure his own sanity was at stake.

"Olive? Is this you? Is this some kind of joke?" He tried to scoff.

"Oscar? What's going on? Please don't make me climb that death trap of a ladder!" Olive's voice was still far away, yet solid and warm. The voice he'd heard call out his name seemed hollow and whispered and yet close enough to make every hair follicle on his body prickle.

"Who's there? This isn't funny any more." Oscar said in a hushed tone. There was a crackling noise, like the sound of a distant firework, and little warm, yellow flames burst into the air before him, enveloping the dress. They fizzled and came together and slowly, the outline of a woman formed within the dress. She appeared to be made up of fire, hissing and burning, causing smoke to rise from her shoulders and the loose ends of her pinned-up hair. Oscar could see clean through her, but her face looked soft and felt so familiar that Oscar's feeling of fear crackled itself. He went to ask her who she was, or rather, what she was, but the woman raised a finger to her flaming lips and as she shushed him, black smoke billowed out of her mouth. In quick and fluid motions, the woman whipped her finger through the air and behind it she left a trail of warm sparkling light that lingered for a moment before it disappeared. She wrote one word quickly before it fizzled out: DANGER.

"Danger?" Oscar whispered, trying to be soothing through his terror. "What danger? Who?" Again, the woman's hands moved quickly but this time as she wrote Oscar's heart thumped a little bit harder as he read each of the letters. OLIVE.

"Olive? Why? Why is she in danger? What kind of trick is this?"

GET HELP

"From who? What are you talking about?"

WALTER

"Walter? Who the hell is Walter?" The woman's eyes flared, and Oscar's dissipating fear quickly returned, burning hotter than the woman's skin. "The stage door guy?"

She nodded vigorously, her skin crackling louder.

HE'S COMING FOR HER

The woman rose a flaming hand and her fingers fizzled in the direction of the wooden plaque on the wall. Oscar backtracked a couple of steps so he could get a better look and there in the glass was nothing but his own reflection. The revolver was gone.

"Oscar!" Olive called from below, and before he could ask the woman anything else, she went up in smoke and the dress fell to the floor, back into a crumpled heap. Oscar picked it up, dusted it off and checked it over. No wires, no strings, nothing out of the ordinary. It was just a dress that now smelled faintly of smoke.

"What took you a million years?" Olive asked when he finally returned back to the wing, her arms hugged tightly around her.

"Nothing. Here's your dress." He handed it to her by the straps, hoping it didn't look too creased but instantly she sniffed the fabric.

"Were you smoking up there? Is that what took you so long?"

"What? No of course not! What makes you say that?" he asked, opening the door into the corridor, wanting to get away from the stage as quickly as possible.

"This stinks of smoke," she said, still clutching it to her nose.

"Then I'll go to wardrobe and grab some Febreze or something."

"Oscar," she caught him by the arm before he could bolt up the stairs, "is everything okay? You went up that ladder as Oscar and now you've come down as . . . I don't know, some sort of zombie version of him."

"No, I'm fine, honestly. It was just a bit . . . spooky up there, that's all." He shrugged and carried on walking, but Olive skittered up beside him.

"Ohhh, coming from the man that was so offended at the idea of anyone believing in ghosts!"

"I wasn't offended! And whether they exist or not, theatres are creepy!" A shiver ran through him at the thought of the woman calling his name.

"Oscar believes in ghosts! Oscar believes in ghosts!" Olive chanted, but as they walked back to their dressing rooms together a new sense of dread loomed over Oscar like the smoke that had billowed from the woman's mouth.

# CHAPTER
# FIFTEEN

## Something Wicked This Way Comes

"Olive, my love! You did splendidly!" Michael squeezed Olive's shoulders so hard her back cracked in at least three places. The after-show party was being held in the front of house bar which, when overcrowded, was . . .

"Hotter than satan's arsehole in here!" said Howard, joining them. "Where's the bar?"

"Over there, Howard." Michael pointed the way whilst watching the beads of sweat drip down Howard's cheek.

"Is it free?" Howard whispered to Olive out the side of his mouth.

"As a bird!" she laughed.

"See ya!"

"Honestly, Olive. You really shone!" Michael said, taking her hands.

"Wow." Olive felt like her smile might burst through her cheeks. "Thank you, Michael. Can't wait to do it all again tomorrow!"

"And another six times after that!" Oscar said, as he appeared behind her, placing his palm on the small of her back instinctively. When she didn't pull away and instead looked up at him with a smile, he didn't move it, and even went as far as rubbing his thumb in circles on the skin of her bare back.

"That dress looks amazing on you," he whispered.

"Tamara not with you?" Olive asked, taking a glass of champagne from a full tray as it passed her.

"Please don't do that," Oscar replied, taking a glass for himself.

"I need to. Just for a little while," Olive took a large sip of her drink which half emptied the glass.

"Need to what? Make me feel bad?"

"Be angry. I need to be angry for a little while longer before I can . . . be anything else."

"I'm just —"

"I know, I know you're sorry." She rolled her eyes.

"No, it's not that." She raised her eyebrow at him as she waited for him to continue. "I mean I *am* sorry, it's just . . . I'm mainly tired of us being against each other." Oscar looked away from her and took a large gulp of his own drink. "I don't know how much more I can take of feeling like you hate me. Well . . . like everyone hates me." Olive tried hard to squash down the urge to wrap her arms around him.

"No one hates you, Oscar. In fact, the few people I've spoken to about this whole mess seem to understand you better than I do."

"What does that mean?" he said, guiding her gently away from the doorway as more people arrived. Everyone was suddenly too close for comfort as the conversation erupted and people roared their congratulations. Olive pointed to a little space in the corner by

224

the bar and when her hand found his, Oscar let out a shaky breath and Olive couldn't help but squeeze his fingers.

"Everyone's rooting for us," Olive said as she put her empty glass on the bar. "Ever since that fan tweeted that picture of us online, everyone's been rooting for us. Look at us right now! Huddled in a corner, holding hands and if you get any closer to me our faces will be touching," she said, brushing the tip of her nose against his and revelling in the fact he didn't pull away.

"Yeah, I guess, even before the picture, we weren't as subtle as we thought." He smiled, stroking her cheek with the back of his fingers.

"Of course we haven't. And even if nothing was going on between us, people like to talk anyway." They both took a moment to glance about the room at their fellow cast mates and although no one was directly watching them, they both got the sense that everyone had noticed them, but had purposely decided to leave them alone. "They all want us to figure things out. They think we're good together."

"We're not together, though . . ." Oscar said and finally he pulled away like Olive had been anticipating.

"Oh, Jesus Christ, will you take a day off?" she snapped. "I know we're not together, and I'm okay with that, but do you have to keep reminding me?" She reached for another glass of champagne from the cluster of filled glasses behind her on the bar. "I meant 'together' in as much as we're together now. In the same vicinity. Spending time with each other. We make a good team, is all that I meant." She looked away from him, her cheeks burning with the rush of annoyance and alcohol mixing in her blood.

"For someone who says they're okay with it, you don't seem too okay with it," Oscar said, brushing her arm with his thumb, trying not to lose contact with her.

"It's just . . . difficult. Being with someone but not actually 'being with them' takes its toll on your mind. Especially when it's their choice and you'd love it to be different."

"Oh," Oscar said, rubbing his temples. "But you know I can't —"

"Oscar, if I hear you say that you can't be in a relationship one more time I'm going to carve the word 'relationship' into a wooden plank and beat you over the head with it." Olive took another long sip of her drink.

"Wow. You're *really* not okay with it." Oscar didn't know whether to laugh or apologise.

"Who would be?" She gestured to the people in the room, "You show me a girl who would be okay with a guy who treats her exactly like she's his girlfriend but won't actually call her his girlfriend? It's madness. It makes no sense."

"I know. I know it doesn't and I'm sorry. I didn't count on liking you so much but that doesn't change the fact that I just can't commit to anything right now and —"

"AGH, AGH, AGH! Shush! I get it! I understand! But just because I understand, it doesn't mean I'm okay with it and just because I'm not okay with it doesn't mean I'm going to bail on it. This is too good for that."

"*We're* too good for that," he said.

"And he finally gets the hang of it!"

"I'm guessing kissing you right now would be out of the question?" Oscar asked, fiddling with her fingers, and Olive's heart almost leapt out of her mouth and into his.

"Says the man who abandoned me when even the slightest hint of what was happening between us escaped onto the internet. There's press at this party. It might happen again."

"Well, maybe I've learnt my lesson."

"And what lesson is that?"

"That it doesn't matter what other people think. If other people want to speculate, let them. That shouldn't interfere with how we feel and how we act around each other and if I want to kiss you, then, damnit, I'm going to . . . as long as it's okay with you?"

"And what if it's not?"

"It'd suck. But I'd just have to deal with it and —" Without warning Olive took his chin between her thumb and her curled fingers, turned his head to face her, and pressed her lips against his. The shock of it wore off quickly and Oscar wrapped his arms around her and noticed just how easily she fit there. Olive could feel him smiling against her lips and she enjoyed the taste of champagne on his tongue, but that was only a small part of the reason she kept leaning back in for more kisses.

"I've missed you," he whispered.

"I know," she laughed.

"Haven't you missed me?" He squeezed her tight.

"Oh, you're so needy!" She rolled her eyes but couldn't keep the smile from her lips nor the sparkle from her eyes. "Please don't screw me over, Oscar?"

"I'm not a loser," he said, but she narrowed her eyes at him and he could see the cogs in her head turning. "I acted like a loser. But I'm not one. I've learned my lesson and I won't be making the same mistakes twice. I promise." Olive nodded. "*I choose you*," he whispered, brushing his nose against hers, but a large crash from somewhere inside the building made them reluctantly turn their attention away from each other.

"What the hell was that?" Michael ran up the few steps and flung open the double doors that led to the back of the auditorium. "Oh my God . . ." Michael shouted as he ran down the central aisle to the stage, followed by Howard and a couple of the show's producers.

"What's going on?" Olive took Oscar's hand and led him over to the doors.

"Stay there, let me take a look first," Oscar said, putting his hands on her shoulders, but Olive caught a glimpse of something and her stomach turned.

"Who is that on the stage?" she asked.

"Probably someone in the crew. I'll go and have a check. You stay here."

"*Someone call an ambulance!*" Howard's voice sounded panicked and Olive could see Jane scrambling to call the number on her phone while Tamara turned away from the group with her hands over her eyes.

228

"Oz, where's Doug?" Olive scanned the bar for Doug's face, but he was the only person she couldn't see. "WHERE'S DOUG?!" Olive shouted as she pushed her way out of Oscar's hands and ran as best she could in her heels towards the stage. A small crowd had formed; glass and twisted bits of metal scattered at their feet and something inside Olive already knew what she was about to find.

"Hello? Yes, I need an ambulance. It's my friend . . . something's happened." Jane fought through her tears to explain. The sound of Olive's heartbeat filled her ears, drowning out Jane's voice, as she stopped at the orchestra pit and gripped the velvet-covered rail in her cold yet sweaty hands.

As she looked towards the stage, Olive could see Doug's body lying at Howard's feet. His face was twisted towards her, but she could barely make out his features under the veil of blood coating his face. Next to his head was a large light from the rigging above their heads, crushing his shoulder and his arm and pinning him to the stage. Oscar caught Olive as her knees gave way underneath her.

"He's unconscious, Olive," Howard said, as he walked towards her. "He's alive but his arm is trapped. We can't move it because we don't know how . . . how bad it is."

"Howard, what can I do?" Oscar asked.

"Help's on its way." Jane sniffed.

"I need to leave. I can't stay here." Tamara teetered from the stage and disappeared into the darkness of the wing, but Jane stayed even though she was as helpless as everyone else.

"None of us can really do anything until the paramedics get here," Oscar said, as he felt a coldness running through his bones. He thought it was just the shock setting in but when he looked up to the fly floor and to the rigging where there was now a missing light, he was sure he saw two fizzling blue eyes staring back at him. Oscar thought it must just be a trick of the light, or something to do with him being scared and in shock at Doug's accident. But as he squinted into the darkness, he saw the eyes blink twice before they vanished as the face they belonged to turned away.

"Olive, wait here, I'll be right back."

"Oscar," she whimpered. The tears had started to come thick and fast now, and her hands were only just holding her up against the barrier of the orchestra pit.

"I'll be back in a second. I'm going to let Stage Door know to let the paramedics in." Olive nodded, and Oscar kissed her quickly. "Howard, keep an eye on her. Keep her safe." Howard nodded and sat himself down on the edge of the stage, his legs dangling over the pit, not quite able to look back at Doug.

Oscar's feet moved quickly through the pass door, through the wings and up the ladder that would take him to the fly floor. He jumped onto the metal grated floor, expecting to come face to face with the man those cold eyes belonged to. They had looked like the eyes of the woman he'd met only an hour or so earlier, but he knew it wasn't her. Her eyes had been warm and yellow but the eyes he'd seen only moments ago were blue and cold and he was certain they had been looking directly at him.

"Who's there? Show yourself!" Oscar hissed, as he looked at the scene below him on the stage. Poor Doug's body was limp and Oscar couldn't imagine the horror the paramedics would uncover underneath the light. How bad was the damage? Would he regain the use of his arm? Would they have to amputate? Oscar could hear sirens approaching through the vents and he willed them to hurry. "I don't know who you are or what game you're playing but if this is your doing, whoever you are, know that you've made a lot of enemies here tonight and we *will* find you." Oscar waited, but was met with nothing but silence. He went to put his feet back on the rungs of the ladder, when a noise made his ears prick. It was the sound of crackling, like that of a log fire. He looked up and there it was: a singular little ball of flame, yellow and bright and so close to his face it looked like a sparkler, dancing in the air. It whizzed around his head and down the ladder, and Oscar quickly tried to follow it, clambering down, losing his footing half way as he half fell, half slid to the ground. He thought he'd lost track of it until its bright light shone from the corridor through the window in the door. He threw himself through the doors and chased the crackling sound up the flight of stairs and through the first set of double doors at stage door. It darted through the little hatch where Walter usually sat, bursting clean through the door behind Walter's chair, leaving a little hole no bigger than a peephole. Just then stage door burst open and two paramedics rushed in, carrying a stretcher and boxes of medical supplies.

"We were called?"

"Yes, there's been an accident on the stage. It's right through these doors, down one flight of stairs to the stage. Please hurry. It's our friend Doug. He's been hit by a light that came loose and fell onto the stage." Oscar noticed Walter's office door had opened.

"Thank you," they said and charged past Oscar as he held the other set of doors open for them as best he could.

"Oscar, what's going on? Is Doug okay?" asked Walter but suddenly the little ball of sparks appeared beside his head and whizzed around and around so fast, Walter had to shut his eyes. The image of the flaming woman writing Walter's name in the air burned in Oscar's mind and he berated himself for not coming to ask Walter for help sooner.

"Walter, I have some questions and . . . I think you have the answers." The fireball stopped whizzing and flew straight at Oscar's chest, bursting on impact, making his black suit jacket sparkle.

"Well, in that case," Walter said, "I think you'd better come in."

HAMISH BOATWRIGHT PRESENTS
A BRAND NEW PRODUCTION
BY C. H. FLETCHER

# FAWN BURROWS and
# LAWRENCE BAKER in

# *When the Curtain Falls*

**RUN CANCELLED DUE TO UNFORSEEN CIRCUMSTANCES**

# THE SOUTHERN CROSS THEATRE

SHAFTESBURY AVENUE, LONDON
OPENS 1 APRIL 1952

# CHAPTER
# SIXTEEN

## Dying Embers

"What's the time, Lenny?" Walter couldn't stop his foot from tapping and he cracked his knuckles over and over.

"Time you stopped annoying me. That noise makes my skin crawl," Lenny complained.

"Is it before the half?"

Lenny checked his watch. "It's quarter to seven. You got ten minutes."

"I'm going to take the post round. There's a few letters for . . . for Fawn and . . . and a couple of others." Walter snatched the letters out of their pigeon holes and shuffled them into a quick pile.

"All right," Lenny smirked. "But make sure you're out of those rooms before six fifty-five. If I 'ear you were in dressing room four when Danny does his rounds to give the call, I will box your ears!"

"Keep. Your. Voice. Down," Walter warned before darting into the corridor and up the stairs. He straightened his shirt beneath his knitted vest and rapped his knuckles underneath the shining golden number four on the dressing room door.

"Just one second! . . . Who is it?" Fawn's voice rang out. Walter twisted the handle and stuck his head around the door. "Come in! Come in!" she whispered, running to him, shutting the door behind him and turning the lock until it clicked. She pulled on the door knob, giving it a rattle to make sure it was firmly bolted. "Had I known it was you I wouldn't have made myself decent in such a hurry." She threw herself into Walter's arms and kissed him. "You know you never have to knock."

"I do if we don't want people knowing about us. Me bursting in here unannounced makes it pretty obvious that we're more than just acquaintances!"

"Oh, if only they could see what happens behind closed doors." Fawn kissed him again, her dressing gown falling open. She took his hands and slid them inside her gown, against the bare skin of her waist, and all Walter could think was that he'd never felt anything softer.

"Fawn . . ." he warned.

"What . . .?" She laughed against his mouth, kissing along his jawline and down into the crook of his neck.

"I need to be out of this room in a couple of minutes. Lenny said —"

"Lenny wouldn't be able to say anything if I said I wanted you in here."

"I'm sure Hamish would love that."

"I don't belong to Hamish." Fawn pulled away abruptly, almost knocking Walter off balance. She sat in her green armchair and turned to the mirror, twirling her hair around her finger and then pinning the neatly curled clump onto her head.

"You don't belong to anyone. You're a woman, not a dog. But we're hiding for a reason, Fawn. Once this show is over —"

"Nothing changes. Hamish already has another production lined up and he's already made negotiations with my father for me to play the lead."

"Oh."

"I just . . . can't see a way out." Fawn's hand fumbled in the pin box for another pin, but she accidentally tipped the box onto its side, the contents spilling out onto the dressing table and floor. "Argh!" She threw the single pin in her hand against the mirror and, sobbing, let her head sink into her hands.

"Fawn, I . . ." Walter had no idea what he could say that would make her feel any better or make their situation suddenly brighter. There was nothing. And just as his helplessness nearly overwhelmed him, there was a knock on Fawn's door and the handle shook. Fawn clamped a hand over Walter's mouth.

"Who is it?" Fawn asked. Walter quickly whipped out his handkerchief and threw it at her as he ran to her costume rack and hid behind her burgundy dress and her other clothes as best he could. Fawn wiped her eyes and did up her dressing gown with her fumbling hands.

"It's Danny. That's the half, Miss Burrows."

"Okay, thank you, Danny!" she shouted through the door. "Call Boys will shatter my nerves by the end of this job." She turned to see Walter coming out from his very obvious hiding place. She couldn't help but smile at him, but then the tears came once more. Walter ran to her and swept her up in his arms and tried to hush her as she wept.

"What if this is it?" she whispered. "What if this is all the time we get?" Walter was quiet and rocked her from side to side, but he could feel the unsettling feeling in her creep out from her bones and wheedle its way under his own skin.

"I won't let that happen." Walter could already feel his brain whirring. A million thoughts filled his head but they all seemed to lead towards a dead end: Hamish. Just then Fawn's door rattled again as the man in question made himself known.

"Fawn?" Hamish immediately tried the handle. "Why is your door locked?" Walter felt Fawn's heart leap into the rafters of the theatre.

"Just a moment! I'm getting dressed!" Fawn ushered Walter back to the costume rack but he ran to her window, unlatched it and flung it open. It was a long way down to the pavement but there was a ledge jutting out from underneath the window, big enough for him to stand on with his back against the bricks of the theatre.

"Oh, I don't mind, sweetie." Hamish continued to rattle the door handle, trying to jimmy the lock.

"You can't," Fawn gasped, holding onto his shirt sleeve.

"I have to," Walter sat on the sill and swung his legs outside. He slowly stood up on the narrow ledge, his shaking legs making it hard to find his balance, but finally he found his footing. "Shut the window, Fawn."

"Walter . . ."

"Fawn, I will get Lenny to open this door if I have to," Hamish called impatiently.

"Come back later! Visitors in the half make me nervous."

"I'm not just a *visitor*, Fawn, I am your producer."

"Fawn, just shut the window and let him in," Walter whispered as she cautiously let go of his shirt sleeve.

"I'll get rid of him as quickly as possible. Be as quiet as you can. He hears everything and *please*, dear God, don't fall and don't give yourself away . . . no matter what you hear." Fawn closed the windows and Walter breathed as deeply and as evenly as he could, his whole body sweating.

Fawn ran to the door and before she was able to fully unlock it, Hamish twisted the handle and pushed it open, knocking Fawn to the ground.

"What on earth have you been doing?" Hamish strutted past her into the room, looking around. He beat her costume with his cane, pulling it from its hanger, and then pulled her own clothes off their hangers with his gloved hand.

"Hamish . . ." Fawn stood, but backed away from him and clamped her hands against the edge of her dressing table for support. Hamish's body seemed bigger than usual, his cloak wafting out around him as he stalked about the room. Fawn realised it was his arrogance and his possessiveness that spilled out of him and spread to every corner and crack in the paintwork of the walls.

"Hmm? Answers, girl. I need *answers*." Hamish snatched up his cane so that he had a better grip on it and pointed the silver handle at her.

"I . . . I told you. I don't like visitors before the half and so I lock my door."

"And I told you, I am not just a visitor. If I want to come into your room, then this door should never be locked to me."

"Hamish, I need some privacy —"

"AND I NEED SOME OBEDIENCE." Hamish grabbed her wrist and pulled her into him, but she struggled, twisting her body away from him. He brought the cane up underneath her chin and gripped it either side of her head, holding her there, pressed up against him by her throat. Hamish turned her head so that his lips were pressed up against her ear and whispered, "You're playing games with me, Fawn. I don't like games, especially ones I don't win. I know you weren't in here alone. Someone was seen coming in here and I will find out who and I will find out why."

"Hamish, I —"

"Shh." Fawn squirmed against his hold, but he gripped his cane tighter and she could feel the heat of his body, and suddenly she was having difficulty breathing. Hamish pressed his nose into her hair and inhaled the scent of her jasmine perfume. "You are *mine* and only *mine*. And it won't be long before we make that official." Hamish kissed her cheek and down her neck, tasting the salt of her hot tears. "I've been speaking with your father and if you want to remain a star of the stage, you'll have to marry me and if you do

240

not, I will make sure your little feet never set foot in a theatre again." Fawn struggled against him again and this time Hamish let her go.

"I will *never* marry you." Fawn backed up against the latched windows. She wiped her tears away with the handkerchief Walter had given her, but she quickly balled it up in her fist when she caught the initials "WB" embroidered in its corner.

"Well, then. Your debut was also your finale," Hamish said as he straightened his jacket and pulled his cloak around himself.

"That's a very small price to pay," she said, pulling her own dressing gown tighter and folding her arms across her chest.

"What?" Hamish spat.

"I will gladly sacrifice my career if my happiness is in far greater peril. I'll find other jobs, other careers that make me happy, but I will *never* find happiness being *Mrs Boatwright*. I'd rather die." Hamish ran towards her, but she didn't flinch. He put his hand around her throat, the crown of her head pushing against the cool glass of the window pane, but she looked him dead in the eye and he faltered for a moment.

*"Don't think that can't be arranged,"* Hamish spat as he ran his splayed fingers down her throat and down between her breasts. She grabbed his wrist and he let her push his hand away, laughing under his breath. Hamish swished his cloak out behind him but before he walked out into the corridor, he turned and said, "You *will* be my wife, or you'll have a very different curtain call."

As soon as he was gone she ran to the door, locking it once more, before running back to the window.

Walter had heard every word through the glass and had even watched Fawn's red hair, ablaze against the glass as Hamish had pushed her against it and it had taken everything in him not to kick through the windows and stop him.

"Don't look down. Don't look down. Don't look down," he'd whispered to himself, trying to ignore the sweat dripping down the bridge of his nose, but Walter couldn't help it. It was getting dark but the light from the windows at the back of the theatre illuminated the street below and there, under the awning of the pub opposite stage door, stood Randall Heaves, Hamish's right-hand man. He was taking a large drag on the last of his cigar and looking Walter dead in the eye. Finally, the window opened and Fawn reached out and tugged at Walter's trouser leg.

Walter carefully ducked in through the open window and jumped to the floor, but Fawn didn't throw herself into his arms the way she had earlier. One arm was wrapped around her waist, his handkerchief still in her fist, and she was rubbing her throat with the other.

"Fawn, it's too late," Walter said, wiping the sweat from his face.

"What do you mean?" she sniffed. Walter pulled her away from the window and just the touch of her made the blood boil in his veins. She was so soft to look at, so delicate to touch and yet her mind was so sharp and eyes were so bright. To Walter, she was pure gold and the thought of Hamish handling her like she were anything less made an anger rise up in him like he'd never felt before.

"I have to go." Walter opened up the door just enough so that he could see out into the hallway.

"Meet me?" Fawn slid her hand down his arm and interlinked their fingers, squeezing his hand with all the worry she had.

"When the curtain falls." He kissed her quickly but still managed to linger ever so slightly. Almost like each time they were apart, he forgot what kissing her was really like and when the time came to kiss her again, he fell in love with her lips once more.

"The usual place?" she whispered, caressing his cheek.

"Of course."

"Walter, what's happened?"

"Get ready for the show. We'll talk tonight." He kissed her once more and slid out into the corridor, praying that no one else saw.

Randall watched Walter and Fawn move away from the window from his roadside position. He threw the stub of his burned-out cigar onto the floor and stamped out the dying embers with the heel of his boot.

# CHAPTER
# SEVENTEEN

## An Idea

Fawn never missed a line nor a beat, even when her mind was elsewhere. But even though her body moved to her marks, her hands picked up the right props and her mouth said the lines, Fawn's brain kept replaying the way Hamish's lips had pressed against her ear, the way his cane had been cold against her throat and the way his body had pressed up against her. She felt numb and knew no amount of water would scrub away the kind of dirty she felt. When the curtain hit the floor, Fawn seized her moment. She slipped off her heels and climbed the ladder to the fly floor. Walter was already waiting for her and gingerly, she ran to him, the grated floor harsh on her bare feet. He pulled her in close and held her, gently swaying back and forth whilst she let the tears she'd been holding in come pouring out in great sobs.

"Please don't cry," Walter said softly as he stroked the back of her neck.

"I don't know what else to do. Everywhere I turn there seems to be a dead end." Fawn wiped her cheeks, her make-up coming off onto the backs of her hands. "If we run away, he'll chase us. If we hide, he'll find us.

I absolutely cannot marry him and if I just quit . . . well, I don't know what he'd do," she said, knowing exactly what Hamish would do.

"He'd kill you." Walter raised his voice.

"*Shush!* And there was me trying not to say it," Fawn laughed, despite the tears still creating troughs in her make-up.

"Surely, he wouldn't actually kill you?"

"You've seen how he treats me. How he treats everyone. He's a violent man with violent people in his employ and he's only ever been accustomed to getting his own way." She suddenly felt out of breath.

"Then we go to the police! We tell them that he's hurt you. That he's going to keep hurting you." Walter took a step away from her as if he were already on his way to the nearest police station, but Fawn remained unmoved, tired of trying to find her way through a labyrinth with no exit.

"You don't think someone like Hamish has connections? I won't have been the first woman he's treated like this and where was the law then? If they're paid off well enough, they'll turn a blind eye to anything, Walter. Having money has taught me that it really *can* buy you anything. Loyalty, protection . . ."

"Love?" he asked.

"What?"

"Love." Walter held her close and stroked her cheek. "Could Hamish buy your love if he wanted to?"

"Of course he couldn't."

"Then at least he's left me something." Walter went to kiss her, but she pulled back.

"Hamish didn't *leave* you anything. I've chosen to give you my heart based on nothing but my own wish to. It's nothing to do with him, so don't you dare go giving Hamish the credit for that now."

"I know, I know, I'm sorry." Walter pulled her into him once more and she rested her head on his shoulder.

"I wish I'd never met Hamish. I wish my father had never bought my way into his hands."

"Shhh."

"I wish men like Hamish didn't *exist*." Walter was quiet for a moment, the cogs in his head starting to whirr and clunk, churning out an idea. "I wish they didn't either," he said, stroking her hair. Fawn felt fragile in his arms, sad and shivering and the mere thought that anyone would lay a hand on her made his cheeks grow hotter and hotter with anger. Fawn had a strong will and a strong mind but Hamish had strong hands. *Men like that don't deserve women like Fawn,* he thought. *Men like that should be locked away. Men like that should . . .*

"What if he didn't?"

"What do you mean?" she said, halting their gentle swaying.

"What if he didn't . . . exist."

"I still don't know what that means, Walter."

"We can't run, hide, go to the police, you can't marry him and you don't want to marry him but if you don't he'll kill you so why don't we . . . beat him to the punch?"

"Are you suggesting I kill myself?" she scoffed.

246

"What? No, Fawn . . ." He leaned away from her, so she would look at his face. *Don't make me say it*, he thought but then he watched as the idea dawned in her eyes too.

"Walter, are you mad?"

"Why not?"

"What do you mean, *why not*? That's not who we are. That's not who I am or who you are! Walter!" She clapped a hand over her mouth.

"Fawn, what other option do we have?! He may kill you!" he hissed.

"He may not," she said without conviction.

"Only if you do what he says, Fawn."

"I know . . . oh God, I know." Fawn pulled away and started to pace despite the pain in her feet.

"Then we have no other choice." They looked at each other then, a silence and a coldness washing over them.

"I can't. I just can't." Fawn covered her eyes, wishing it would all go away.

"You won't have to. We could stage it."

"What do you mean?" She looked at Walter through her fingers.

"We work in a show that stages a murder. Lars, in the show, murders —"

"Hamish . . ."

"Well, his character at least. All it would take is something to fall into the barrel of that gun for things to go . . . slightly wrong."

"Slightly? Walter, we're talking about . . ." she lowered her voice, "about murdering someone here."

"It would look like an accident, Fawn. Stage tricks go wrong all the time. This would just be another one added to the list and no one would be to blame. It would just be an unfortunate accident." The idea settled in the air between them for a moment. Walter's eyes were wide and wild and Fawn took another step backwards.

"Walter this is madness. We can't . . . kill . . . Hamish."

"There's no other way, Fawn." Walter stepped towards her, but she kept retreating.

"Walter, you're scaring me."

"I'm sorry. I'm sorry." He rushed to her. "I just . . . don't want to lose you. Not at all but most of all, not to him."

"Fawn?" A distant voice called out.

*Who is it?* Walter mouthed. The doors to the wing opened and the voice called out again, "Fawn, sweetie?"

"It's *him*. I have to go."

"No, please don't . . ."

"Walter, I *have* to. I'm supposed to be going to a party with him this evening." Fawn looked over the railing and saw Hamish walk onto the stage behind the fire curtain. He checked his pocket watch. "Just stay here."

Fawn descended the ladder as quickly as she could and picked up her shoes from behind the wicker basket where she'd hidden them, and holding them in her hand, walked onto stage to meet Hamish. Walter could only watch from his perch above them.

"Mr Boatwright . . ." Fawn stopped at what she thought was an acceptable distance from him.

"There you are!" Hamish smiled broadly, as if their earlier altercation had never happened. "You're still in costume." His smile shrank.

"Yes, I wasn't feeling too well so I've just . . . been in the lavatory. Collecting myself." She took a deep breath, but she knew she already looked shaken up enough from her conversation with Walter for her lie to be plausible.

"Not . . . too unwell for tonight, I hope." A muscle in his top lip twitched.

"I was hoping to get a proper night's sleep tonight. There have been quite a few parties over the last week or so and —"

"They're all to further your career, darling. The people you're meeting are vital to your future success." He laughed, but it was short and shrill.

"I didn't think I had a future career in this industry." Fawn couldn't keep the bite out of her voice and took another deep breath to steady herself.

"Of course you do!" He moved towards her and put his arms around her shoulders, ducking his head so close to her face that she could smell the tobacco on his breath. Their closeness made Walter's stomach lurch and he wondered if he should be watching them at all, but a part of him felt as though he could protect her somehow if he kept her in his sights.

"When you're my wife there is nothing we won't be able to accomplish together," Hamish said as he stepped closer still to Fawn.

"I've told you, Mr Boatwright, I will never be *Mrs* Boatwright."

"AND I HAVE TOLD YOU I WILL HAVE OBEDIENCE." Hamish grabbed Fawn's pearl necklace and wrapped what he could around his fist and roughly yanked her towards him so that she had to stand on tiptoe. She dropped her shoes and clawed at his wrists to release her, but his fists were like wrought iron, unflinching and unaffected by her efforts and his face was red with unadulterated rage. The pearls dug into her neck and it felt as though his knuckles were piercing her windpipe. Walter wanted to yell, to run down the ladder and give Hamish the beating of a lifetime but he knew if he did he would be risking both their lives. And so Walter clutched his flat cap to his head, bit his tongue until he tasted blood, and watched with bated breath.

"You *will* do as I say or there is no use for you," Hamish growled through gritted teeth.

"Hamish . . ." Fawn choked and Hamish smiled, his eyes glinting.

"So this is what it takes for you to say my name. *Finally*. A little obedience." He stroked her cheek with the cold, silver end of his cane. Fawn felt a volcano erupt in her belly and without a second's thought she conjured up the little saliva that was left in her drying mouth and spat it in one huge wad onto his cheek. Hamish's fist clenched, and the necklace snapped. Pearls slipped off their chain and scattered to the floor like hailstones in a storm and lying amongst them was

250

Fawn, gasping for breath and clutching her throat once again.

"You bitch!" Hamish raised his cane in both hands, ready to bring it down onto her head, clean and sharp.

"STOP!" Hamish's head snapped up and Fawn prayed it wasn't Walter coming to her rescue. But as she looked up through her watering eyes, she saw Lenny rushing from the wings. "Don't you *dare* touch that girl," Lenny said, as he ran between them and flung his arms out wide to protect her.

"*Who do you think you are?*"

"I am the stage door man of the Suvern Cross Theatah and a friend to every cast member going. This girl ain't done a single thing except be exceptional in this show and she does just about everyfing you've asked of 'er but this is asking too much. Now, 'oo do you fink *you* are, eh?" Lenny's face was puce and the veins in his neck sprouted out so far, Walter could see them from his balcony position. Hamish simply polished the end of his cane with his black cloak.

"Leonard. Do you have trouble with your ears?"

"You wha'?"

"Because not once have you ever seemed to be able to *listen.*"

"I only listen to people I like."

"Oh, dear. I fear that way of thinking is going to get you into a spot of bother, one day. Perhaps . . . one day soon."

"Empty threats, Hamish. You throw 'em about left, right and centre, daily, and not once 'ave you ever actually walked the walk. But if I ever see you lay a hand on this girl or anyone else for that matter, so 'elp me God, I will give you what for." Lenny held out his hand which Fawn took, the pieces of her broken necklace clutched in the other hand. Slowly, she heaved herself onto her unsteady legs, as Lenny supported her as best he could and escorted her from the stage. "Come on, girl. I've gotcha. Let's get you into warmer clothes and sit you down with a nice cup of tea, how does that sound?"

When he was sure the coast was clear, Walter clambered down the ladder and ran ahead through the doors and up into dressing room four and when they came through the door, it was Walter who fell into Fawn's arms.

"I felt so helpless," he sobbed. "There was nothing I could do, I just had to sit and watch him do that to you."

"I know, I know. Oh, Walter." She stroked his hair. "Hush now." Walter caught Lenny looking at the two of them, clearly closer than theatre staff and actors usually were, but he didn't raise an eyebrow or give them a look of concern. He merely tipped his flat cap and said, "I'll leave you both to it. I'll book you a cab, Miss."

"I won't need a cab, but Lenny," she reached out her hand and even though her fingers were aching from trying to release herself from Hamish's grip, she squeezed his hand, hard. "Thank you."

"We have to do something," Walter sniffed when the door was closed.

"We'll figure it out."

"We've figured it out."

"Walter. No."

"We can't let that happen again . . . wait . . . why won't you need a cab?" Fawn was silent for a moment as she slipped the wig from her head, placed it on its block and started unpinning her hair. "Fawn, you're not going to that party. Please don't go, I can't bear the thought of you being alone with him." Fawn threw down the final pin and walked over to Walter.

"Walter, will you be quiet for just a moment." She kissed him then, every ache in her body softening, evaporating into the air above them. Walter's hands meandered up her back and she held onto him like a piece of driftwood in a rough and raging sea.

Fawn did order a cab after all, but not to her usual destination where her mother was waiting for her in the drawing room. Instead, Walter found himself in Shepherd's Bush, opening the door to his run-down flat with Fawn following behind him. She looked out of place in her clean, pristine dress and unscuffed shoes against his peeling wallpaper and the worn away carpet, but there wasn't a trace of disgust or disapproval on her face.

"I'm so pleased I'm here," she whispered in his ear as she pulled him into an embrace.

"Yeah?"

"Why wouldn't I be? It was my idea."

"I know, it's just . . . well, look at this place. It's not exactly the Ritz, is it?"

"I'm far happier here than I could ever be at the Ritz." She laughed at his worried eyes and his set lips.

"I'll never be able to offer you what Hamish can offer you." He ran his hands up the back of her stiff, boned dress while she smoothed out the creases on his shirt with her fingers.

"Bruises? Black eyes? Broken bones? Walter, money doesn't matter to me. I would give it all up in a heartbeat if it meant being with you. If it was about money, I'd be out at the party with Hamish now drinking as much champagne as I could lay my hands on and ordering more caviar and lobster than my stomach could hold." She laughed. "None of this has ever been about money."

He rolled his eyes, but she took his chin between her fingers and made him look at her directly in the eyes.

"Walter, *I love you.*" Those three unfaltering words hung in the air between them. "And I rarely say things I don't mean and when I do it's becau —"

"I love you," Walter said against her lips and he kissed her and their kiss didn't end until the sun came up.

# CHAPTER
# EIGHTEEN

## Listen

By the time Walter awoke, the working day for theatre folk was almost upon them. He left Fawn asleep in his bed with a cup of tea and a note on the bedside table, and as he headed towards the theatre later for work than normal, he didn't rush. Lenny knew that Fawn had gone through quite an ordeal the night before and was probably pleased that Walter was taking good care of her. However, when Walter arrived at stage door, it wasn't Lenny sat behind the desk, but Hamish's right-hand man Randall.

"Glad you finally decided to show up. There are parcels and letters that need to be delivered across the theatre and seeing as you're now in charge, you'll need the key to the key box." Randall dangled Lenny's set of brass keys in front of Walter's face. They jangled as Randall waggled his hand and the noise made Walter's insides jangle too.

"Where's Lenny?" Walter asked.

"He quit, Mr Brown."

"No, he wouldn't do that. He . . . he loves this job."

"Then I don't know what to tell you, Mr Brown."

"The *truth*, Mr Heaves," Walter said, and as Randall stood up quickly from his desk Walter realised just how tall the other man was. He moved quickly through the doorway and up close, Walter could smell the coffee and cigar smoke on Randall's breath.

"I have told you the truth you need to know. Now, you're already in a very bad position, Mr Brown. It is very rare that I notice something and do not mention it to Mr Boatwright; however, your dalliance with Miss Burrows is something I have chosen not to disclose as of yet. Not when the problem can be so easily fixed without upsetting the boss. So, do the job you are paid to do, stop asking questions, stop dallying with the actors and *know that you have been warned*." Randall pushed the cold hard metal keys into Walter's palm and left the building with a swift hard push of the door.

Walter looked at Lenny's set of keys in his hand. He'd seen them a million times before to know they were his, but he also knew that Lenny would never hand them over without a fight. Which made Walter believe there had been one and that Lenny had lost.

Fawn arrived at the theatre at six o'clock looking fresh-faced and more content than Walter thought he had ever seen her. She ticked by her name and leant over through the hatch to plant a kiss on Walter's cheek.

"Someone might see!" he whispered, pushing her gently back through to her side.

"Let's run away," she whispered back.

"Excuse me?" he laughed.

"I don't care if that man chases me to the ends of the Earth," she yelled.

"Shush!" Walter said, now concerned.

"I don't care if he hears me now. I have enough money to get us to America. There are a million people on that continent. He'll never find us. You can find a theatre to work at on Broadway and I can . . . oh, I don't know. Write. I'll write plays. Under a pseudonym." She beamed at him. "We'd be hidden and safe and happy, Walter. We could be *happy*."

"Are you crazy?" he said, his voice still hushed just in case Randall was skulking somewhere nearby. His words had set Walter on edge, but nothing could make him stay away from the person that made him happier above all else.

"Absolutely." Fawn reached through the hatch and held out her hand which he took and placed on his cheek.

"Let's talk about it after the show then, crazy." He kissed her palm.

"Tell me now, though. Do you want to come away with me? Would you do that?" Despite the way Hamish had treated her, her eyes were still so full of hope and an innocence that Walter himself hoped would never vanish.

"I'd follow you anywhere, Fawn."

"Then I feel there's little to talk about after the show, but I'll be there anyway."

"When the curtain falls," he smiled.

"When the curtain falls. I'll be there." She blew him a kiss and waltzed off into the theatre, her feet barely touching the stairs.

The show ended, and Fawn decided to get changed in her dressing room as quickly as she could before meeting Walter. That way, they could disappear into the night immediately. She was hoping for at least one more night, safely curled around him in his bed where she felt warm and happy. But when a knock came at her dressing room door she had a feeling she already knew who was waiting on the other side.

"Just a moment!" she called, but the door was unlocked and her guest was in her room before she'd been able to entirely cover herself up with her dressing gown.

"Hamish," she greeted him, coldly.

"Well done tonight, sweetie. One of your best performances yet," he said, running his thumb over the silver handle of his cane.

"Thank you," she said, removing the pins from her hair.

"You seem to be in a rush."

"Not at all," she said.

"Well, you should be if we're going to make dinner with Lord and Lady Peckworth. They want to talk about this new production I've been envisioning." He threw his chin into the air and breathed in deeply, as if a new wave of inspiration was soaking in.

"Okay." She swallowed. "I'll be down in a few minutes. Just let me get ready and —"

"Don't lie to me, *sweetie*." Hamish's knuckles were now white as he gripped his cane. "This doesn't need to be difficult."

"I'm not being difficult." She smiled and as she felt it reach her eyes she realised she was a much better actor than she had been giving herself credit for.

"Then I'll see you downstairs?" Hamish's shoulders relaxed, and the blood returned to his hands.

"Five minutes," she said as she playfully shooed him from the room. She waited until she heard his footsteps disappear down the corridor and then she locked the door, grabbed everything she needed and threw it into her satchel and quickly made her way down to the stage left wing. She ran quickly so as not to be heard but as she turned the corner where the double doors to stage left came into sight, Randall stepped out into view.

"Going somewhere?" Randall made quick work of lifting her around the waist with one arm, as he clamped his other hand down over her mouth when she tried to scream out for Walter. He carried her up and out of stage door, not caring who saw, and bundled her into the back seat of a car where Hamish was already waiting. Randall swiftly got into the driver's seat and drove them away from the fans and their flashing cameras and the fluttering pages of their autograph books. Hamish turned towards Fawn, and placed the cold silver end of his cane under her chin, lifting her face so the moonlight could illuminate her tears.

"You're not that good an actress."

# CHAPTER
# NINETEEN

## The Pearl

Randall didn't take Fawn and Hamish to see Lord and
Lady Peckworth. Instead, the car meandered through
London to Park Lane.

"Hamish . . ." she said softly.

"Don't think you can bargain with me," he snapped.

"I'm sorry I've upset you. I promise it won't happen
again," she said, crossing her fingers. The car pulled up
and stopped abruptly outside the Dorchester hotel.
Hamish stepped out of the car and held the door open
for Fawn.

"Out," he said.

Fawn sank back into the darkness of the car, hoping
she might just vanish.

"*Out.*"

"Not until you tell me why we're here."

"*Fawn* . . ." Hamish's voice held a warning, and
Fawn quickly pulled on the handle of the far side
passenger door, ready to run, but instead she fell
straight into Randall's arms who carried her struggling
body over to Hamish. Fawn was ready to start
screaming but Randall quietly whispered in her ear,
"Remember now, dearie. I know about the boy."

If that hadn't been enough to silence her then moving the left side of his jacket away to reveal the hilt of a gun that was tucked into the waistband of his suit trousers certainly was.

"Quiet now." Randall spat on the floor and Fawn could feel her hands shaking and her options running out. If she screamed, if she warned anyone, she'd put Walter's life in danger and yet if she followed Hamish into this hotel, she knew she was putting herself in peril. No matter which way she turned she felt walls building up around her and caging her in.

"Let's not cause a scene now, darling," Hamish said, taking off his jacket and placing it around her shoulders. "We wouldn't want to be making the wrong sort of headlines, would we?" Together they ascended the steps into the Dorchester and into a lift that would take her ever closer to Hamish's room.

Walter waited for forty-five minutes. After the first ten, he became worried and after the full three quarters of an hour he was close to pulling out his hair. When he finally decided she wasn't coming, he quickly scaled down the ladder, grabbed his bag from the stage door office and locked up at fast as his shaking hands would let him. As he bolted the padlock on the door, an overheard conversation pricked his ears.

"Honestly, there was more blood than I could handle." Walter turned to see two police officers walking past the theatre.

"Poor bugger. *Both* ears, you said?"

"Both ears, clean off. Found him just round the corner in an alley behind some bins. Not a thing left of them on 'is 'ead. Whoever did it was an artist with a knife."

"An artist and a devil. You caught him yet?"

"Nah. The victim's too scared to talk. Thinks 'e's gonna lose more than just 'is ears next time. Looks like whoever it was 'as threatened every body part on the poor soul."

Walter watched the police officers come and go, their conversation taking with it every last bit of hope he had in his body. He prayed to whoever was listening that they weren't talking about Lenny.

*Leonard. Do you have trouble with your ears?*

*You wha'?*

*Because not once have you ever seemed to be able to listen.*

Walter felt his stomach turn and he retched and doubled over but nothing came up. The cold of the night was setting in quicker than usual and his fingers were icy as he wiped away the saliva from his lips. Walter thought about running after the police officers, telling them everything he knew about Randall and Hamish and what sort of men they were, but Fawn's voice echoed in his head: *You don't think someone like Hamish has connections? I won't have been the first woman Hamish has treated like this and where was the law then?*

Walter went to run back into the theatre but there was nothing he could do from in there except hide and he'd had more than enough of hiding.

"Oh *God*." He crouched down in the street and held his head as the world started to spin and he let out a sob. He didn't know where to begin looking for Fawn and even if he found whatever lavish party, club or hotel Hamish had taken her to, he wasn't the sort of person they'd allow inside anyway. The door to the pub opposite stage door opened up and he was drenched in its warm light and like a moth, he followed it.

Walter's hand slid up his pint glass as Hamish's hand slid down the back of Fawn's dress. Bodies crowded at the bar and someone jostled the drink out of Walter's hand, soaking his shirt as Fawn threw a glass of champagne in Hamish's face. Anger bubbled up inside Walter, clouding his mind and he lunged for the man who had barged him, as Hamish lunged for Fawn. A glass crashed to the pub floor as Walter tangled with another man, while Fawn struggled against Hamish's arms and knocked over a lamp which shattered against the marble floor of the hotel room. Walter yelled in pain as Fawn cried out for help. Walter struggled, but he was smaller and weaker than the man he'd chosen to take on. Fawn was too. Walter felt himself being pinned to the ground, bracing himself for a punch or two but all he could think about as the blows came one after another was Fawn. And as she now lay silent and numb, looking up into the ecstatic eyes of Hamish Boatwright, her throat like broken glass from the screaming and her body aching from the struggle, she closed her eyes and tried so very hard to make her mind leave her body and travel to the safety and warmth of the night before when she'd lain in Walter's arms.

The whole world seemed to have increased in volume and even the sound of the key turning in the key box was too much for Walter's sore head. The noise of the keys jangling together as he passed each set over to the actors sent a wave of nausea through his body, but it was his black eyes that were causing him the most discomfort. Swollen and bruised, he could barely see through them and there was no way of sitting in his desk chair that didn't make him ache all over.

"Well, don't you look handsome." Hamish slotted his cane through the hatch and lifted Walter's chin to the light to inspect the damage. As he lifted his face, Walter could see Fawn standing behind Hamish, her eyes lowered, her face sallow and gaunt as she swayed slightly on the spot. Hamish laughed under his breath and held out his gloved hand. "Keys," he demanded, but Walter didn't move.

"Please." Walter could barely see Hamish through his throbbing eye sockets, but he took great pleasure in seeing his smug expression falter, even if just for a second.

"What?"

"Keys, *please*."

"Give them to me, boy." Walter was merely a nuisance to Hamish. A nobody. As insignificant as a theatre mouse and until now Walter had reinforced that status by behaving as such. But now, seeing the shell of

Fawn with the life sucked out of her, a defiance rose up in Walter that he didn't know he had within him.

"Just because you got rid of Lenny doesn't mean I'm going to take any less respect than he demanded. So, if you want to keep acting like an arse you'll have to get rid of me too. B-because I won't stand for it either." Fawn's eyes flickered to him and although she didn't smile, couldn't smile, Walter knew his words meant something to her.

"I don't know what you're insinuating, boy, but I know I don't like it." Hamish beat his fist down on the desk and then opened up his fingers. "*Now give me . . . my bloody keys.*" Walter took his set out of the key box and threw them over, looking Hamish directly in his eyes, to which Hamish scoffed and stormed through the doors into the building. Walter turned to fetch the set of keys for Fawn's dressing room, but he heard the sound of something hitting his desk with force. He turned back to see tears spilling down Fawn's cheek, her pale hand clenched tightly on the desk. After a moment of composing herself, she lifted her hand to reveal a beautiful pearl that shone in the lamp light.

"Tonight," she whispered, the word catching in her throat. Walter looked at her. Her face was no longer young and fresh but pale and pained, her eyes shining from her tears but without their usual wonder. Walter picked up the pearl and rolled it between his fingers. It was warm from Fawn's clenched fist and he found it utterly astounding that such a tiny object could hold so much weight and significance. This old pearl might just be their new beginning.

"Tonight."

# CHAPTER
# TWENTY

## The Curtain Call

The most physical harm Walter had ever inflicted on anyone had been in the pub the night before and so his history of inciting pain and trouble had only just begun — and what a beginning it would be. Even though he would have been able to jam anything down the barrel of the prop gun, it felt significant that it would be the pearl from the necklace that Hamish had broken whilst trying to strangle Fawn. It felt right that Hamish's own violent acts would ultimately bring his own life to an end.

At every moment he kept reaching into his pocket to make sure that the pearl was still there and he kept reaching into his heart to make sure he had the courage to carry out such a terrible act. It may have been Walter's idea, but having an idea and making that idea a reality are two very different things and he hadn't thought as far as how he would feel when the time came. Not only was Walter going to be the cause of someone's death but he was going to force someone into unwittingly pulling the trigger. Although the guilt weighed heavy on his heart, he knew that had he been the one holding the gun, his makeshift bullet would never leave the barrel.

Violence had never played a part in Fawn's life. Whilst her father was distant, cold and ruled his household like a kingdom in which the women were his subjects, he'd never raised a hand to his wife or daughter. So the idea of causing harm, let alone death, to anyone was unspeakable to Fawn. That was until she was exposed to men like Hamish and her mind had been quickly changed. It was funny how a single event in one's life could change you as a person; now Fawn believed that if you were spending your life causing pain, leaving a path of destruction in your wake, then maybe, just maybe, you didn't deserve to live that life at all.

Their plan was perfect. Once all the props had been moved to their rightful places in the interval, they were left unattended in the stage left wing, until Lawrence picked up the gun ready for the beginning of act two. The gun was loaded with a hollow wax bullet that disintegrated when fired. It made a bang and flash which convinced the audience that a real bullet had been fired. But it still was a real gun. If something small were to get lodged down the barrel, then when the trigger was pulled and the charge of gunpowder for the hollow wax bullet was ignited, that something small would be propelled from the gun and act exactly like a real bullet. Walter had no doubt that Hamish's death would be put down to an accident; it wasn't beyond the realms of possibility that a stray pearl could roll into the barrel without anyone noticing. Walter also had no doubt that the man's death wouldn't cause too much grief, if any at all. The show would come to an untimely end, leaving Walter and Fawn to escape to the life they'd been dreaming of.

The curtain was due to rise, and the hum of the audience was steadily dying down in anticipation. Walter ran down the stage left wing to try and catch a glimpse of Fawn's face, to give her the sense of hope that things were going to be all right, but her gaze was fixed in front of her, her expression stoic and almost mournful.

Fawn had been able to think of nothing except Hamish's face hovering above her. She'd not been able to get the sound of his moaning out of her ears nor the feeling of his fingers from around her weakened throat. Hamish had impounded her senses and she felt the little of herself she'd managed to cling on to slipping neatly through her fingers like smoke. She looked at Walter in the wings, trying to instill in her whatever hope there was for their future beyond this fateful performance, but she didn't see him. He may as well have been a ghost.

Walter spent the entirety of act one going over his every move. The trigger would be pulled, the hammer would hit the primer, the primer would ignite the gunpowder, the gunpowder would propel but melt the hollow wax bullet but this time, take the pearl along with it. A pearl propelled at seventeen hundred miles per hour would most certainly be lethal. What if the pearl slipped out of the barrel of the gun in Lawrence's pocket? he thought. Walter figured he'd wedge it down the barrel with a bit of cotton wool and reckoned that would still do the trick. What if it didn't work and he and his scheme were discovered? Walter thought it was better to try than surrender to the hell Hamish was putting Fawn through. His brain flip-flopped a thousand times like a coin being tossed in the air, but no matter how many times he flipped it, the decision had already been made. Hamish had to die.

In her dressing room, Fawn reached for her silk gown to cover her shivering shoulders. She flung open the windows and although she didn't like to, she rummaged in her bag for a packet of cigarettes her mother had given her for when she was in times of need. Her hands were shaking so vigorously, it took her several attempts to light one and she inhaled deeply. Fawn wasn't needed for the first three scenes of act two, and she was glad that she could stay in the silence of her dressing room until Danny came to collect her. Until those hopes were dashed in three simple knocks at the door.

"Come in," she called, not caring that she wasn't supposed to be smoking in her costume. She expected Danny or even Walter, but she certainly wasn't expecting Hamish's henchman, Randall. "What on earth could you possibly want from me, Randall?" she said, taking a long drag on her cigarette. "I don't think I've got anything left for you to take."

Randall closed the door behind him and made a point of turning the lock on the door slowly. Fawn turned away from him and looked out the window, trying to pretend he wasn't there. People passed by in the street below her, never looking up, never noticing her and she felt like Rapunzel trapped in her tower.

Never before had she had any reason to consider taking her own life. Not once had the thought ever flitted across her mind, even for a brief second. She had a loving mother, a warm bed to sleep in every night and more money than most people would make in several lifetimes. She had everything and yet just one night had made the pull of the cobbled pavement outside her window more enticing than all the luxury and money in the world.

"It's interesting what you see when you're stood on the fly floor, Fawn," Randall said as he leant against the door and took a cigar out of his inside pocket, snipping off the end with a cutter and letting it drop to the floor. He took a small box of matches out of his trouser pocket and lit the cigar, the smell instantly making Fawn feel queasy. "That's where you've been spending a lot of your time recently, so I thought I'd take a look for myself and boy, is it interesting what you can see from up there." Fawn felt the familiar feeling of dread placing its hands on her shoulders and squeezing until she was filled with it.

"How long have you known?" she said, without turning around to see his face which she knew would be plastered with smugness.

"Oh, since the beginning. Since you were chasing each other around the auditorium like children. Neither of you thought to look up to the dress circle." He chuckled, and Fawn sighed.

"What do you want, Randall? Like I said, I have very little left to give you and your *master*." She leant out the window and stubbed out the cigarette on the ledge.

"Well, it's just . . . that boyfriend of yours seemed to have a very keen interest in that gun in the stage left wing." Fawn not only felt the dread running through her veins now, but the fear and defeat coursed through her in waves as well.

"What do you mean?" she said over her shoulder, but she already knew her denial was pointless. Randall had seen Walter slip the pearl into the gun and he knew full well that their makeshift bullet was intended for Hamish.

"Fawn. Let's not play games. The second act has begun and so we're on the clock here." He puffed on his cigar, letting the putrid smoke fill the room. "Don't let Lawrence fire the gun. It's as simple as that."

"He's on stage. It's already in his pocket. There's no moment I can get to him." Fawn shrugged. She folded her arms over her chest and hugged herself tightly, feeling like she was holding the broken pieces of herself together for long enough to get through this encounter.

"*Find* a moment." Randall's face never changed and Fawn wondered if he felt anything at all. Any fear, compassion, humanity, or whether life was just money and business to him.

"Why can't you do it yourself? I owe Hamish nothing," she said, trying to ignore her trembling knees.

"Don't you? He's the reason you're here, isn't he?"

"My *father* is the reason I'm here." She spun around to face him.

"Hamish didn't have to take your father's money." He laughed breathily through his nose.

"Hamish has taken far more than just my father's money!" she spat. "He's taken *everything*! My dignity! My *sanity*! Nothing can take back what happened last night, Randall."

"You slept with the man who has begun the career you always wanted?" He rolled his eyes, which stung Fawn's already aching soul.

"I was *forced* to sleep with a man whom I do not love and will never love." She spoke slowly, trying to keep the wobble out of her voice.

"Your immaturity is astounding, Fawn. Sex doesn't always have to be about love," Randall laughed.

Fawn was fed up with biting her tongue and with wondering whether she should say what she was thinking just in case it would cause a tremor in the foundations of the fragile egos of men. In a brief moment of strength, Fawn's bitten tongue slipped from between her teeth.

"Your *cruelty* is astounding, Randall, because even after helping a man rape a woman you still can't see how you, nor Hamish, could possibly have been wrong."

Randall pushed himself away from the door and his repellant nature made Fawn retreat against the windowsill but her voice still held steady. "I'm forever marked by that man," she said, the tears catching in the corners of her lips. "It's *him* that owes *me*. He's taken far more than what may have been indebted to him and he just . . . keeps . . . taking." Fawn walked over to her dressing table, her breathing getting faster and shallower.

"Fawn —"

"And he's never going to stop, Randall." She could barely see for her tears now.

"Fawn, you're hysterical." Randall watched her fumble her way around the room, like a caged and injured animal trying to remain strong in the face of adversity. He moved around the other side of the room, always maintaining his position opposite her, wherever she went.

"And he'll just keep going and going because nothing's ever enough for him." She put her back against the door and gently unlocked it behind her, hoping to make some kind of escape. "He'll take everything I have until —"

"Fawn, I *will* kill the boy," Randall said softly and she stopped fiddling with the lock and the room fell silent.

"No!" she sobbed.

"If that trigger is pulled and Hamish dies as a result, I will be waiting to pull the trigger of my own gun which will be pointed right between the eyes of your little man." Randall stubbed the last of his cigar on the ledge and threw it out the window.

"You can't."

"I can, and I will."

"You're a monster —"

"Says the girl plotting the death of her own future husband. And forcing someone else to pull the trigger for you."

"Lawrence . . ." Fawn's lip trembled.

274

"Don't tell me it's only just dawning on you? Definitely not as sweet as you look. Your friend could go down for murder."

"No — no, it'd look like an accident." She tried to wipe the thoughts away along with her tears.

"Would it?" Randall raised an eyebrow and let the question hang in the air for a moment.

"You wouldn't."

"Neither of us is any better than the other." Fawn clutched a hand over her mouth to stifle her sobs. "Stop Lawrence from pulling that trigger and Walter won't be harmed."

"But Hamish will find out . . ."

"I'll make sure he doesn't. I'll make sure Walter gets out of this theatre safely and he can live his life elsewhere and you and Hamish can figure out whatever needs figuring out between you." There was a hint of kindness to Randall's voice. A glimmer of fondness in his eyes and Fawn couldn't have hated him more in that moment.

"You think you're doing me a kindness, don't you?" she sniggered. "You don't realise that by stopping this from happening tonight, by saving the man who has caused so much misery and harm, you are sealing my own fate. By saving him you're killing me."

"No one will die tonight, Fawn." He sighed, shoving his hands deep into his pockets, having had enough of such girlish drama.

"A life with Hamish is my death," she hissed. *Why can't he understand?* she thought.

There was a knock at the door. "Miss Burrows. This is your call to stage!" Danny called.

"Thank you, Danny." She couldn't quite raise her voice loud enough to call out. Her stomach was somersaulting, and she could feel the bile starting to rise in her throat. Randall strode to the door and gently pushed Fawn aside so he could take the handle. He opened the door while she desperately tried to push it closed again.

"I'll stop the show. I'll faint onstage. I'll cause a scene."

"No. The show continues as normal, Fawn. We don't want the punters upset. It's bad for business."

"Randall, that's the only way . . ."

"Stop Lawrence from pulling the trigger —"

"He's already on stage!" She tried to keep her panic subdued, but it was starting to take over.

"— or Walter dies."

"RANDALL, PLEASE DON'T DO THIS!" she screamed but Randall opened the door, her efforts to close it wasted, and he was gone.

She whipped off her dressing gown, slipped on her shoes and ran as quickly as she could down the stairs towards the stage. She had six more scenes before the finale but only one moment in which she and Lawrence would be offstage at the same time. That was her only chance to convince him not to fire the gun. To get him to pretend it had malfunctioned mid-scene and just wouldn't fire. She hoped Walter would forgive her and she hoped no one would figure out it was him who had sabotaged the gun but if Randall stuck by his word, no one would ever know.

During her next scenes, the ins and outs of the deal she had just struck with Randall were whirling round her head, but she kept having to bat them away. The only thing that mattered was saving Walter. Everything else could be dealt with after the show had ended but even so, the idea of spending any portion of her life in the same vicinity as Hamish, let alone as his significant other, made it hard to concentrate on stage. The moment was drawing closer to when Lawrence would exit the stage while she was dancing in the bar scene. He would be bundled off stage by two ensemble members and then her character would exit to chase after his. She only had seconds with him in the wing before he would need to enter upstage for the final scene in which the gun would be fired. She heard the familiar muffled yelp as he was taken off-stage and she was supposed to wait to notice him gone. She was supposed to "act" but tonight she gave a feeble attempt at "noticing" he wasn't there, and ran offstage, stage right, before the music had even finished. She ran down the wing through the double doors and round to stage left where Lawrence already had his foot poised, ready to make his entrance.

"Lawrence, don't fire the gun," she whispered, but the music was still playing.

"What?" he said, smiling at her.

"Don't fire the gun!" She pulled at his lapels, trying to get closer to his ear. He heard her this time and looked at her face, now serious, taking in what she had said, and a little flutter of hope soared through her . . . but then he rolled his eyes.

"Funny!" he laughed and walked through the curtain.

"No, Lawrence . . . LAWRENCE!" she hissed but it was too late. Lawrence was now Lars and Lars had a gun he needed to fire at Hamish who would do his best attempt at acting as the character of Melvin. Fawn heard the scene begin. She heard Lawrence speak and she was only moments away from entering the stage to watch Hamish and Walter be slaughtered seconds after one another. She ran down the wing to the downstage entrance and took a deep breath. She heard something move and turned her head to see Walter standing where she had just been. Fawn heard her cue and did her best to smile at Walter, knowing that whatever was about to happen would change their lives forever and she entered through the black curtain.

"You were never supposed to find out this way," she said, her voice sultry and low, no longer her own.

"You didn't do well to hide it." Hamish's acting was stiff and wooden; he was a better villain offstage than he was on.

"Leave her be, goddamn it." Fawn looked at Lawrence, pleading with him with her eyes but she knew that anything she did now onstage, he would take as her acting as Eliza and not as herself. There was nothing more she could do.

"Please. Go back inside. Go home. Go anywhere but here." Fawn looked behind her and her eyes settled on Walter in the wings.

278

Watching Fawn onstage, Walter found it difficult to breathe evenly. His clammy hands held onto a set piece, to try and steady his buckling knees as beads of sweat poured down his back. There was a dullness in Fawn's eyes that he couldn't explain. He'd watched her do this scene a million times before and usually she would glide effortlessly across the stage, but this time he noticed she stood awkwardly, and when she moved it was almost like she were walking ankle deep through a marsh. *She must be nervous*, he thought, as was he. He'd only ever seen death in the movies and here he was about to witness one he had orchestrated. He kept reminding himself that it was for the greater good. For Fawn's good.

"Yes, Larson. Do as she says."

"Please, Lars. Not here," she begged and never had the words been so real to her before now.

"She's not yours," Larson hissed.

"Actually, Lars . . . I am." Fawn held up her right hand to reveal the engagement ring and she worried how soon it would be before she was wearing a real one given to her by Hamish.

"Eliza . . . no. NO!" Lawrence pulled the gun from his inside jacket pocket and the audience gasped. Fawn looked at the gun in his hand. She realised that she'd never properly given it any attention before. It wasn't her prop and so she'd never had any reason to interact with it outside of this scene and yet here it was, right in front of her, about to seal her fate.

"Oh, Larson. When will you learn? It doesn't matter how well you scrub up or . . ." Hamish's voice became muffled in Fawn's ears as her heart started beating faster and faster. She thought of pushing Lawrence's arm away as he fired the shot but she knew that would give the game away, and what would Hamish do to her if he knew she'd tried to kill him? Then she thought of the life she would lead if she did stop Lawrence from pulling that trigger. A life of "yes, Hamish. Of course, Hamish". A life of sitting still and being quiet, of being seen and not heard. A life next to a man who thought of women as objects or trophies. A man who took things from people against their will. A man who forced himself on those too weak to stop him. Hamish was a monster. And life with a monster would be no life at all.

"Please don't listen to him, Lars. Just go back inside." She put her hands on Lawrence's arm.

"Do you love him?" he asked. "Do you?" he demanded again.

"I fear you'll kill him either way."

"Eliza, if you tell me yes, how could you think that I would kill the man you love and put you through that misery? No, Eliza. Should you say yes, I will turn this gun on myself and the bullet will be destined for me."

The audience was well and truly captivated by a scene that was more real than they'd ever know and would ever watch again. They sobbed and blew their noses into their handkerchiefs, unaware of the turmoil happening in Fawn's mind.

"Must we have all this drama? It's terribly dull. We all know you don't have the gall to shoot a rabbit, let alone a man. Just put the gun down, Larson."

"Do . . . you . . . love . . . him?"

280

"I . . ." She hesitated. Walter could feel the sadness pouring off her in waves that lapped at his feet. He wondered if maybe she'd forgotten her line. Was she having second thoughts about their plan? Had she suddenly decided Hamish *was* the man for her and didn't want to see him die?

"I . . ." A tear rolled down her flushed cheek.

*A life with a monster is no life at all.*

*A life with a monster is no life at all.*

*A life with a monster is no life at all.*

Fawn took a breath so deep it almost split the seams of her dress.

"I . . . do not," she said and immediately stepped forward into Lawrence's line of fire. The pearl, travelling at seventeen hundred miles per hour, along with the little ball of cotton wool that Walter had wedged down the barrel to keep the pearl from falling out in Lawrence's pocket, only had to travel a mere inch through the air before it pierced Fawn's left temple, shattered her skull and lodged itself in her brain. The lights blacked out and so the audience didn't see Fawn slump to the floor, but Lawrence felt her body fall at his feet.

"Bring up the lights! THE LIGHTS!" Lawrence yelled. Danny relayed the order in the wings, Eddie gave the signal and the lights slowly came up to reveal Fawn's body to the audience.

"NO!" Walter couldn't look away. Her eyes were open but glassy and he vomited at the sight of her.

"I demand to know what's happened!" Hamish shouted. The crowd jostled, and the sound of sobs echoed through the air. Some could see that this was not a part of the show at all, but some were still trying to figure out how the clever trick had been done. The crew and most of the cast ran on stage to see what the commotion was but as soon as they saw her, no one moved any closer. They all simply stood in a circle, looking down at the body of the girl they once knew, her blood pouring from her and trickling down the rake of the stage. They all knew there was nothing they could do. She was already gone.

"Someone needs to explain what's happened!" Hamish kept shouting.

"Hamish," Lawrence said, tears starting to spill from his eyes.

"I demand to know!"

"HAMISH!" Lawrence yelled. "This . . . this was an accident." Lawrence still had the gun in his trembling hand. He knelt down and placed it on the stage.

"Was it? We all know what sort of man you are, Hamish," spat one of the ensemble girls. "We all know what you did to her."

"You drove her to it," spat another. "We barely knew her because you kept her to yourself. Locked away."

"She only had to speak to someone other than you and she'd end up battered and bruised."

"*Keep your voices down*," Hamish hissed.

"Or what? We'll end up like her?" said Lawrence. "No. Maybe I was wrong and this wasn't an accident. This is . . . this is murder." Some of the boys came to Lawrence's side, let him lean on them as he covered his mouth, not sure of what else to say.

"Murder . . .?" Hamish looked at Fawn's limp body. "Who was it, exactly, who murdered her?"

Randall came up close behind Walter so that he could feel the gun in the small of his back. "Run."

Walter turned to face him. "No," he said, wiping his mouth on his sleeve.

"Walter. I'm warning you."

"They're looking for a *murderer*, Randall. You kill me now and you'll be the one they're looking for. And your boss? The finger is already being pointed in his direction and I don't know if this is the sort of thing Hamish will be able to bribe the police to overlook." Walter could feel another wave of nausea pass through him, but he swallowed it down. "This is the problem with making enemies, Randall. When things spiral out of your control, no one will have a problem pointing the finger at you, whether you're to blame or not." Randall lowered the gun as Walter's words sank in.

"As long as you remember one thing, Walter." Randall quickly put his gun back in his waistband. "It was you that loaded the gun that killed her." He ran back down the wing and left, Walter hoped, for good.

"Is . . . is she dead?" asked a man from the audience, but those on stage remained silent and staring. No one had the words to express what had just happened. All they knew was that Fawn was gone. The ensemble girls clutched each other's hands. The boys around Lawrence all held each other's shoulders. A lady in the front row wiped her tears with her handkerchief and wobbled to a standing position. Her husband in the seat next to her did the same. The man who had been concerned enough to raise his voice now raised himself out of his seat as did the group of men with whom he had attended. One by one, every member of the audience, not able to take their eyes off the actress centre stage, rose to their feet and bowed their heads, giving Fawn her final standing ovation.

TOASTIE PRODUCTIONS PRESENTS A
PRODUCTION BY C. H. FLETCHER

OLIVE GREEN and
OSCAR BRIGHT in

# WHEN the
# CURTAIN
# FALLS

## SOLD OUT

# THE SOUTHERN
# CROSS THEATRE

SHAFTESBURY AVENUE, LONDON

OPENS 1 APRIL 2018

# CHAPTER
# TWENTY-ONE

## Finale

Oscar shed his jacket. The little office room had a draught running through it so strong they might as well have been stood on the street outside, but Oscar was sweating from climbing up and down the ladder and chasing "ghosts" around the theatre. Walter had been a man of few words up until now. In all honesty, he'd been a man of little significance at all, unless Oscar had wanted his keys or his fan mail. Never had Oscar thought that the quiet old man at stage door would somehow hold the key to the strange goings-on within the theatre. If Walter held some part of the puzzle as to why Doug had just had his arm crushed under a falling stage light, potentially not by accident, then Oscar needed answers and he needed them immediately.

"What's going on? Why has this theatre suddenly been overrun by . . . well, I don't know what by! But something's going on and I need an explanation."

"There isn't one." Walter creaked as he fell back into his armchair.

Oscar scraped his fingers over his scalp, frustration starting to take over his nerves. "Why am I here, then?

Look, old man, I don't need screwing around. I've had enough of that this evening."

"There isn't an explanation anyone would believe," Walter shrugged.

"Try me." Walter looked at Oscar, trying hard to keep the amusement off his face in such serious circumstances, but he just couldn't help it.

"All right." Walter leant forward, leaning his elbows on his bony knees. "The girl who died here in 1952. I'm assuming you've heard that story?"

"Yeah, yeah. I've heard that one." Oscar dismissed it with a wave of his hand. "Fawn Burrows died on stage after a stunt went wrong during the performance and she was shot with a real bullet instead of a wax one the gun should have been carrying."

"I'm impressed. But did you know she wasn't shot with a bullet? What was in that gun that night . . . was a *pearl*."

"Okay, *now* you're having me on."

"See!" Walter sat back in his chair and pulled his blanket off the floor and onto his legs, settling in for the night.

"All right, all right! I'm sorry. A pearl . . . go on," Oscar encouraged.

"Someone slipped a pearl into the barrel of the gun that night. But it was never meant to kill Fawn. Someone else was supposed to take that shot but for some reason . . . Fawn got in the way." Walter was looking down at his wrinkled, wringing hands.

"How do you know? That it was a pearl, I mean?" Walter sighed and looked up at Oscar, his eyes beginning to shine in the lamp light.

"Because I put it there."

"You what? You were there? Wouldn't that make you like . . . a hundred?"

"I'm eighty-eight, thank you very much! A little way off a hundred but I'm sure I'll still be here when that century turns." Walter rolled his eyes. Oscar leant against Walter's desk and nudged it a little too hard. A picture wobbled and almost fell but Oscar reached out to steady it and something about it made him take a closer look.

"Is that . . . is that her?" The black and white photograph was of a young girl, her hair curled to perfection, a neat bow slightly to the left on the top of her head. Although she looked young and naive on the surface, there was a glimmer in her sparkling eyes and a little tweak in the corner of her smile that made Oscar feel like she was far more playful that she'd ever let on. He wondered how he knew all this, and then he realised it was because he'd seen that look before in someone else . . .

"Yes," said Walter, looking at the picture fondly and Oscar was looking at Walter as if he were a mirror, the same doe-eyed look on both their faces. "That's her."

"You were close?"

"Close? We were inseparable. We didn't think anything could keep us apart. Until . . ." Walter seemed breathless. He coughed a little then reached over to his desk for his flask of tea. "Until *Hamish*," he said, spluttering.

"Hamish? Hamish Boatwright?"

"You've heard of him, then?"

"Yeah, he was the original producer of *When The Curtain Falls*, wasn't he? His name's on everything."

"Believe it or not, back in the day, he starred in it too. Played Melvin," Walter said.

"Blimey. A producer *and* an actor. Was he —"

"Any good? No. On neither account. Just an all-round awful man."

"So what happened?" Oscar asked.

"I wasn't the only one that had my eye on the rising starlet that was Fawn Burrows and Hamish . . . well, he thought he had ownership of her because her father had paid for her to be in the show," Walter huffed.

"Was *she* any —"

"The best," Walter smiled. "She was better than the majority of actresses I've seen come and go over the years."

"That's quite a claim!" said Oscar. *I hope he's not including Olive*, he caught himself thinking and was surprised at his own sudden defensiveness. "So, why are you still here?"

"I'm getting there, boy. I'm not as young as you. Not as fast," Walter laughed.

"Sorry," said Oscar, quickly glancing at the clock on the wall.

"Hamish kept her close. Always kept her on his arm, showing her off at parties, practically forcing champagne and caviar down her throat . . ."

"Sounds . . . awful?" Oscar raised an eyebrow.

"It was when it was *him*. The man was a . . . monster. He'd . . . *hurt* people. Or he'd get his right-hand man to do it for him so he never got his own hands dirty. And the temper on him. If he didn't get his way he'd turn into a child and his answer was always violence. No exceptions."

"Didn't the police ever get involved?" Oscar asked, not knowing what he'd do if anyone ever laid a hand on Olive.

"Back then, if you had money, you had everything. If you wanted the police to turn a blind eye you could make it happen. Hamish had it all. The money, the sold-out show but . . . not the girl. Fawn despised him and did everything she could to get away from him but that just made him hold onto her even tighter and eventually he . . . he ruined her. Drove her mad." Walter looked down into his flask, the tea rippling and sloshing inside.

"Did she . . . kill herself?" Oscar asked, not knowing how to be delicate.

"To this day, I still don't know what went wrong. The only way out we could see was getting rid of Hamish. If we'd run, he would have followed us. He had eyes everywhere so we couldn't hide and if she quit he threatened to kill her."

"So . . . you planned to *kill* him?"

Walter laughed but this time, didn't smile. "It sounds rash to you, I suppose, but you just don't know what he was like. I look back and wonder if we were crazy but . . . there's no way of knowing now." He took one last swig of his tea to avoid Oscar's scrutiny and screwed the lid back onto his flask.

"So what happened?"

"During the final scene when Hamish was supposed to be shot ... Fawn stepped in front of the gun," he said, without flinching. "At the very last second. The makeshift bullet I'd made killed her instead."

"And you don't know why she did that?"

"I don't know why." Walter shook his head sadly. "Between you and me, I tried ending my life so many times after it happened. The guilt and the sadness never let up and I just couldn't figure out a way to live without her but as it turned out, I didn't have to." Walter narrowed his eyes at the young man sitting in his office. "You don't seem like the type for ghost stories ..." he said, trying to gauge how Oscar was handling the story so far, and Oscar tried to gauge how crazy he would sound if he admitted he may have seen a ghost.

"I didn't think I was until I came here," Oscar replied.

"Met her, have you?" Walter smiled.

"I think I have, yeah!" Oscar laughed, somewhat hysterically, swiping his hair back and feeling a sense of relief that perhaps he wasn't going completely mad.

"When I realised her ghost was still inside this theatre, I couldn't leave. I didn't have much of a life before I came here, so I dropped everything. Moved in. Kept her company."

"Haven't you asked why she did it?"

"I asked once. Maybe two or three years after she started appearing. I'd always get a little bit of time with her before she would be pulled back to the stage to re-enact her death in the final scene of the show but when I asked that question, she was always pulled away from me early. As if asking that question was the trigger that sent her away. Whether it's because she couldn't cope with telling me the answer or whether something else in this theatre was stopping her, I'll probably never know, but I stopped asking, just so I could have that time with her." Walter didn't look like a man desperate for answers. It seemed to Oscar that, in his old age, Walter had made peace with the things he might never understand.

"Usually she only appears on the anniversary of her death but ever since *you* turned up, she's started turning up more often, too."

"*Me?* What have I got to do with this?"

"You tell me! I've yet to figure it out, but Fawn said it was something big."

"She spoke to you? When I met her she just . . . spelt everything out in the air. If I'd known her ghost could speak it would have made things a lot easier!"

"Where's Olive?" Walter had already started trying to stand.

"What? Why? She was on stage with everyone else when I left her."

"Help me up." Walter held out his arm for Oscar to grab and used all his strength to try and push him out of his chair as best as he could. "NOW." Oscar did as he was told and heaved at Walter's hand and as soon as he was on his feet he was through the double doors and into the theatre. Oscar ran after him.

"Why do you need to know where Olive is? What's going on? What's wrong?"

"Fawn was never a quiet girl. Never shy. Always spoke her mind but there was only one person she was ever scared of hearing her because it meant he would know where she was. It meant he would find her."

*Hamish has ears like a bat. If he even so much as hears me breathe he finds me.*

"Hamish?" Oscar was surprised at how quickly Walter was darting down the stairs towards the stage, considering he'd just had to haul him out of an armchair.

"Yes, and if he's here, I don't think it's wise to leave Olive alone." As they opened the doors, Jane almost ran head first into them. Her mascara was in streams all the way down to her chin and when she saw Oscar, she burst into tears again, flinging herself into his arms.

"How's Doug? Is he going to be okay?" Oscar put his arms around her and squeezed. Jane may have been a nightmare but seeing her this genuinely upset proved she had a heart somewhere in there that was beating louder than Tamara's.

"They're bringing him out now. The light . . ." she wailed, "It's shattered his arm and his collarbone."

"My God," said Walter, as the paramedics brought Doug through on a gurney. He was conscious now, but so dosed up he was lying rigidly with his face scrunched up tightly and his eyes closed.

"They've said I can go with him," Jane sniffed.

"I think it might be better if Howard goes, Jane." Michael appeared in the doorway. "There'll be paperwork to fill out and Howard knows Doug a little better."

"But . . . but . . ." Jane burst into another bout of tears and transferred herself onto Michael who, oddly, started to soothe her.

"Have you seen Olive?" Oscar asked.

"Earlier, but then she disappeared." Walter and Oscar exchanged a glance. "Why, is something the matter?"

"No, no. Everything's fine. Just need to take her home. She's had a long day."

"Haven't we all," Michael said, gesturing to Jane who was wiping her nose on his shirt. "I'll send out an email tomorrow with an update on what happens with the show."

"Okay," Oscar said as Walter ran on ahead through the doors. "Thank you!" he added and followed.

They'd cleaned up on stage, the broken light collected into a pile on stage right.

"Olive?" Walter said, tentatively.

"Olive!" Oscar yelled but Walter was quick to shush him.

"Up here." Olive's voice came from the rafters. They both looked up to the fly floor where Olive was standing in her beautiful sparkling dress, but as they looked closer they could see that she herself was sparkling too. All around her skin were little blue flashes that buzzed in the air, little veins of electricity that crackled like lightning every few seconds, dancing off her arms and face. Her hair stood on end and as she tilted her head to look down at them, her eyes twinkled a bright blue. However, the most concerning thing for

Oscar was the revolver which was now in her hand and pointed at her own head.

"Olive, what are you *doing?*" Oscar started to rush to the wings, ready to climb up the ladder and stop whatever this foolishness was, but Walter held out a strong arm to stop him.

"Oscar . . ." Walter said, still staring up at her. "I don't think that's Olive."

"Very clever, young Wally. Well, I guess you're not exactly young any more, are you? Still though, sharp as a tack. Can't fault that!" Olive's lips were moving but the voice wasn't her own. Instead it was posh, clipped and almost whiny.

"If you want to settle this, Hamish, let it be just you and me. Olive and Oscar have nothing to do with this."

"She has *everything* to do with this," Hamish snapped through Olive's lips. "Why do you even think I'm here in the first place? I've been lurking in this theatre ever since my sorry life ended but never before have I been able to do anything. Except, of course, re-enact the death of that ungrateful little brat once a bloody year. I've been waiting for the moment I'd be able to return, and I knew all it would take was something strong enough to awaken the magic of this theatre once more."

"It *was* you," Walter said, turning to Oscar.

"I'm gonna be honest, I am so lost."

"Then all of a sudden, this one," Olive took the gun and pushed the barrel up under her chin, "and Prince Charming over there decided to fall in love at the exact same moment and HEY PRESTO! Here I am!"

296

"We're not in love —" Oscar fumbled.

"Oh, oh . . ." Hamish made Olive pout. "I can hear her crying inside." Suddenly, Olive's empty hand flung out and leant against the railing for support. She took in a deep breath and the blue in her eyes faded just for a moment. She looked down at Oscar.

"Oscar . . . he's in my head," she cried. "I can hear what he's thinking."

"Olive, stay with us!" Walter called up to her, but she was already crying out in pain as her skin started to crackle again, this time more furiously.

"MAKE IT STOP! MAKE IT STOP!" she begged but her face snapped into serenity and she stood up straight once more. "Goodness me, she puts up a fight. Now, where were we." Hamish made her place the gun back against her head. "*You* took my girl from *me*, so it only seems right that I take the one that replaced her. She's not quite as elegant as Fawn, a little clumsy, but pretty enough . . ." Hamish made Olive run a hand down the front of her body and this time Oscar really did run to the ladder.

"Oscar, don't!" Walter shouted, but it was too late. Oscar climbed up the ladder as fast as his body would allow him and he was met by the gun now pointing directly between his eyes.

"Hello, Oscar. How lovely to meet you." Olive was grinning from ear to ear but now that he was up close Oscar could see that, despite the blue, her eyes were still her own. They were wide and panicked with tears constantly spilling out of them, down her cheeks and collecting underneath her chin. "Originally, I wanted

Walter, but he's got so old now, the day he dies is probably sooner than expected and where's the fun in that? No, Wally, bless him, always seemed like a caring fellow when he wasn't plotting my murder. It'd be much more fun to watch the guilt eat him alive for the rest of his numbered days knowing one of you was killed because of his own foolish past mistakes." A laugh slipped out of Olive's mouth which made her lips contort in a way that briefly changed her whole face and Oscar worried that Hamish wasn't ever going to leave her. "It didn't matter which of you I killed. I thought I'd managed to crush you with that light earlier, but it turned out it was just another one of the theatre mice."

"You . . . thought Doug was me? That light was meant for me?" Oscar said, glancing down at the shattered light in the corner.

"Oh no, is the guilt setting in? What does that feel like, I wonder?"

"It feels like this," Olive managed to whisper, and she let all the guilt she could muster flood through her body. She thought of Doug never being able to use his arm again because of something she could have stopped had she not been so foolishly in love with Oscar. She stumbled backwards, Hamish clearly not enjoying the feeling of caring about anyone other than himself.

"Olive, if you're in there," Oscar said quietly, as if Hamish wouldn't be able to hear, "put the gun down."

"Do you really think it's that easy?" Hamish tried to make Olive put the gun back under her chin, but her arm started to shake, like there was a resistant force pushing against it. "You couldn't stop me taking back my revolver or stealing a pearl necklace. What makes you think you'll be able to stop what's coming next?"

"I think Olive's stronger than you think she is," Walter called up.

"This little thing?" Hamish said, but Olive's voice was shaking and changing in pitch. "She's no match for me."

"Oh no?" Oscar crossed his arms and watched in amusement as Olive fought against Hamish inside her. Hamish pushed to the left, but Olive pushed to the right. Hamish tried to pull back the hammer of the revolver, but Olive wouldn't let him lift her thumbs. Olive's eyes were still streaming but focused whilst Hamish clenched her teeth tightly together.

Walter watched from the stage, wishing he was able to do something, but his time of climbing up that ladder was long since over.

"Fawn, where are you?" he whispered and immediately the air fizzled with a warm yellow light that wrapped around him and a voice in his ear whispered, "Always here."

He followed the trail of crackling yellow all the way up to the fly floor where the little bursts of flame all joined together to create one single blazing ball of light. It floated slowly and quietly behind Olive where Oscar could see it and he got ready to warn Olive, but a soft voice hushed him in his ear. As he closed his mouth, a calmness washed through him, as if he knew everything was going to be all right. The ball started to get brighter and brighter and crackle louder and louder and the fight between Hamish and Olive ceased. Hamish turned around in Olive's body and before he had a chance to make Olive react, the ball of light flew forwards and into Olive's chest and simultaneously a ball of blue flew out from between her shoulder blades. The gun slipped out of Olive's hand, over the railing and plummeted towards the stage where Walter awkwardly dashed forward as best he could to catch it.

It was then he heard a loud crackling in his ear and along with it, a laugh he knew so well, because it often haunted his dreams. Walter turned to face the light that hovered, still, for a moment, its bolts of lightning reaching out like hands before it zipped towards him. And even though Walter's legs wouldn't have let him run away anyway, he stood still and welcomed the impact of the blow.

The force of Fawn expelling Hamish from Olive's body had sent Olive flying backwards into Oscar where he was ready to catch her. Olive's hair was singed and smoking, and her arms were peppered with little burns, like someone had held a cigarette to her skin over and over.

"Olive? Olive!" He shook her gently and patted her cheek but when her eyes finally opened, they glowed yellow.

"I'll only borrow her for a moment, I promise." The voice was more like Olive's own but much more refined — still not the voice of the girl he knew. Fawn quickly guided Olive to her feet and looked down onto the stage where Walter was bent double, his hands rested on his knees facing away from them.

"I'm too weak to fight him, Fawn."

Hamish turned Walter's body, which was overcome with blue electricity.

"Your mind isn't," Fawn smiled, and Olive let her.

"It never was but even when I was younger and stronger, I never fought for you like I should have."

"Had you fought the way Hamish fought, I wouldn't have been in love with you." She smiled, and even though Oscar knew it wasn't Olive speaking, he still felt that familiar twinge of jealousy at hearing her say she loved someone else.

"Well, that's some comfort, I suppose." Walter smiled as his shaking arm raised the revolver up to the fly floor at Olive. "Argh . . ." Sweat dripped down the bridge of Walter's nose.

"Is there anything I can do, Walter?" Oscar got to his feet and jumped in front of Olive.

"All I ask is that whilst I'm holding him off, you listen to me. That girl up there, and that's Olive, I mean . . . she's a good one."

"I know." Oscar nodded.

"No, you don't know. Don't just *hear* me, *listen to* me." Walter had never raised his voice in anger, but he thought if any moment called for it, it was in these last moments of his life. "Every molecule of that girl loves every molecule of you. Do you know how rare that is? Do you think you'd be able to find that again with someone else? I've watched you both walk past me a hundred times, together but also alone. When you're not around, I've watched her collect your mail with her own and deliver it to you, so she'd have another excuse to spend time with you. I've seen her struggle through doors with a cup of coffee in each hand to surprise you. God knows how many times she burnt herself. She's signed you in and out of this building because you've forgotten more times than I can count, and she always doubles back down the corridor at the end of the day to check your door for your key because you never remember to bring the bloody thing back." Walter's legs buckled underneath him, and his knees hit the stage with a gruesome crack. "And she never complains, Oscar! Because she doesn't have to. That's all just part of what loving someone is to her. And in the same way you're only hearing me and not listening to me, you're looking at her but you're not seeing her."

"He's right. I can feel it. She's choosing to potentially get hurt by you over and over again because she thinks what you could be together would be breathtaking . . . if only you were brave enough to take that shot," said Fawn, gazing up at Oscar through Olive's eyes.

Walter's arm was shaking vigorously now as Hamish was slowly but surely winning the battle inside him. Walter knew he had little time left to say all the things he needed to say before it was finally all over. "I've been watching you too, Oscar. And I see it, don't think I don't. There's only so long you can hide it before it starts manifesting itself in different ways. I see the way your face changes when you see she's already signed into the building and I see the pride in your smile when she's signing autographs by your side at stage door." Oscar smiled, recognising himself in what Walter said and acknowledging all of the feelings that were starting to poke their heads out of the cage he'd put his heart inside. "And Oscar," Walter laughed, "the fact that I'm knelt here with a gun in my hand proves that you've fallen for her as much as she has for you. Your love awoke the magic that this theatre lost the day Fawn Burrows died."

"I know." Oscar reached down and took Olive's hand and Fawn let Olive squeeze it back. "I know," he said and without meaning to and without warning, Oscar started to cry. It was only a little at first but instead of pushing back against feeling something, Oscar let himself feel it all. Love and sadness gushed through him, breaking down every wall he'd ever built.

"You need to look harder, Oscar. At yourself. Stop holding back. You haven't got anyone stopping you from doing the things you want to do . . . not like I have right now," Walter said as his thumb pulled back the hammer of the gun. "She's bravely put herself into no man's land and she's taken every shot you've fired at her because you're just too scared to join her."

"So, join her," Fawn whispered and nudged his arm.

"And if I may, my darling Fawn, I think it's time I joined you," Walter said, tears starting to spill from his own eyes.

"Walter?" Oscar wiped his tears away on the sleeve of his shirt.

"I've never had the courage to do what I thought was right and it's time that changed."

"I'll be here." Fawn smiled, knowingly.

"Then I'll see you on the other side, my love." Walter took a breath as deep as his tired lungs would let him and with all his strength, he took Hamish by surprise and quickly put the gun against his head. The gunshot rang out across the auditorium and Walter's old body fell forwards onto his face. His skin was still crackling gently but after a few moments, it fizzled out with a hiss and Hamish was gone.

"I'll be gentler this time," said Fawn, but Oscar knew she wasn't talking to him. Then she took a long breath and gently blew into the air like she was blowing out candles on a cake. Hundreds upon hundreds of tiny little lights came pouring out of Olive, and swirled in the air like stars. They spilled out and down like a waterfall, floating down onto the stage until they gracefully took the shape of Fawn Burrows herself. She wasn't sparkling or crackling and this time she wasn't just an outline. She looked as though she'd been drawn onto tracing paper and then pasted into real life. Olive wobbled for a second and then opened her eyes which were back to her usual, human green and Oscar couldn't have been more grateful. For a moment, they smiled at each other as if they'd been by each other's sides for a lifetime already.

"I'm waiting . . ." Fawn called out, rocking back and forth on her heels, her hands clasped behind her back.

"Calm down, woman. It's been a long time since I've been in a body as young as this." Walter emerged from the stage right wing in all his former glory. Olive couldn't help a little sob escaping at the sight of Walter as his younger self, in his shirt and sweater vest and his delightful little flat cap.

"Oh . . . oh that's much better. I didn't think you much suited wrinkles." Fawn pulled off his flat cap and touched his smooth cheek.

"That's rich coming from the girl who didn't even live long enough to have 'em!" Walter laughed.

"You two have been back together for all of thirty seconds and you're already bickering!" Olive shouted.

"The lady's right. I think it's high time we got out of this theatre, don't you? I'm sick of it." Walter laughed, taking Fawn's hand.

"Oh, I don't know. I rather like it here." Fawn smiled, looking around fondly, one last time.

"I know. You always did."

"But it's time." She nodded.

"It's time," Walter agreed. He looked back up to the couple on the fly floor. "Goodbye, you two."

"Olive?" Fawn stepped forward to get a better look at her. "Could you do me a favour?"

"Anything!" Olive nodded.

"I watched you. In this show. Every night. And I think you're just . . . *brilliant.*"

"Oh . . ." Olive felt all the breath in her lungs escape her at once.

"Go and have the career I never got to have. For me. And please know, I'll always be your most avid fan." Olive couldn't speak through the lump in her throat so she just nodded and sank into Oscar as he encircled her in his arms.

"You're not bad either, Oscar." Walter winked.

"Thank you, Walter," Oscar laughed.

"Thank *you*, Oscar. For reuniting us . . . and tell them I er . . ." Walter gestured to his old, dead body and Oscar looked down at him lying in a pool of his own blood, revolver in hand.

"I think . . . I think it might be quite obvious, mate," Oscar said.

"Yeah — I suppose you're right."

"Right, Walter, it's time." Fawn came and stood with Walter and just like they'd never been apart, his arms found her waist and she placed his hat back on his head. "I've waited a long time to do this again . . ." Fawn barely let him take a breath before she pushed her lips against his and pulled him in as tight as she could. When she pulled away, Walter smiled wider than he had in years. "Me too."

"Before we go, my lady, I think it's time you took the bow you never got for the performance of a lifetime."

"Really?" Fawn's eyes burned a little brighter for a moment.

"You deserve it," Oscar said.

"Well, only if you'll bow with me? I've never bowed without the rest of the cast before!" she shouted up to the couple on the fly floor. And so Olive and Oscar climbed down the ladder and walked from the wings to join the ghosts of Fawn and Walter on centre stage.

"It's been a pleasure knowing you," Olive said to Walter.

"The pleasure was all mine." He smiled back. "Now, ladies and gentlemen!" Walter addressed the empty seats. "You've all been waiting sixty-six years for the actress who —"

"She's here?" called a voice that broke the deathly silence of the auditorium.

"Fawn Burrows?" Another voice shouted from the dress circle.

"Erm . . . yes . . . that's me." Fawn said and suddenly, the auditorium was abuzz with noise and chatter. In every seat, a ghost faded into view, men in bow ties, women in their evening gowns still clutching their handkerchiefs.

"Oh . . . oh my goodness." Fawn couldn't believe it. Nearly every member of the audience the night she had died had returned to see her curtain call. The few empty seats belonged to those who were lucky enough to still be living.

"We've been waiting just as long as you have to see you take the bow you deserve," said a lady in the front row, whose hat was so large it was blocking the view of at least six people.

"No one likes unfinished business," laughed another voice from the back of the stalls.

"Well, then, in that case . . . ladies and gentlemen," said Walter, "it is my honour and my privilege to present to you the actress who loved her work so much she died for it, wrongfully robbed of a long and beautiful life . . . and the girl who stole my heart from the moment I heard her laugh. I give you: Fawn Burrows."

The audience burst into an applause so rapturous that both Oscar and Olive knew they would never hear anything like it again in their lifetimes. The crowd roared and cheered and Fawn looked out on an ocean of a thousand pairs of hands shimmering, a sight she never thought she'd get to see again. Fawn took Walter's hand and stepped forward.

"Take a bow too, Walter. You deserve it just as much as she does," Olive said and then clapped and cheered arguably louder than anyone else.

Fawn and Walter grinned at each other at the prospect of finally having the life they'd dreamed of in a world hereafter. Then as the audience rose to their feet, the ghosts of the rising starlet of 1952 and her stage door man bowed together . . . and disappeared.

# Epilogue

## Twelve Years Later

Olive Green, two-time Olivier-award-winning actress, is to star as Maggie in the Broadway revival of *Cat On A Hot Tin Roof*. However, this won't be Green's Broadway debut. She took New York by storm at the age of twenty-seven when she starred as Eliza Small in *When The Curtain Falls* which transferred from London's glittering West End back in 2020. Back then she was loved-up with her co-star, Oscar Bright, but where are the couple now over a decade later? We can't wait to find out when we catch up with Olive Green when she's back here in NYC this Autumn.

Olive put down the magazine on the dressing table of her new dressing room. Opening night still never failed to make her stomach somersault at any given moment. The clock on her phone said she had five minutes until she would be called to the stage and there was no turning back then. The show must go on. Olive felt like she needed a moment of calm amidst her new crazy life in the US. Yellow cabs honked their horns and people yelled outside her window and she was sure she could see more city lights than stars in the darkness. But as she put her hand to the window, tracing the skyline, no star or light glinted as brightly as the diamond on her wedding finger.

Olive went back to the dressing table and picked up the magazine once again. She must have looked at it a thousand times already but she couldn't help it. In the corner of the article, the journalist had used an old production photo from London's version of *When The Curtain Falls*. The young and chiselled face of Oscar Bright held a broody stare as he stood holding the revolver in his straightened arm with Olive draped across him in her burgundy dress. Olive automatically felt down the side of her body and wondered if she'd be able to get into that dress any more, but then she shook the thought from her mind. *I look better now anyway,* she thought, and smiled. Her phone buzzed and LOULOUBFF4EVA flashed on the screen and Olive scrambled to pick it up, the phone almost slipping out of her grasp.

"LOU!" she yelled.

"OLIVE, you big star, you! Tell me *everything.*" Lou's voice instantly filled Olive with the urge to jump on a plane and fly back home. It was her accent more than anything that made her miss London. Olive loved the sound of American voices but nothing made her feel more out of place than their unfamiliarity. People would say words to her that she thought she understood but it often turned out that she didn't and what it meant to them meant something very different to her. Olive's eyes stung but she tried to keep the sadness out of her voice.

"I need to be on stage in like . . . three minutes!" She laughed.

"Well, then you have three minutes to tell me everything! GO!" Lou started to make tick-tock noises with her tongue.

"Arghh, the pressure. Erm, the apartment they've put me in is lush, the theatre is pretty nice and tickets are selling well so that's . . . that's good."

"How are *you*? You sound stressy. No one likes you when you're stressy."

"Thanks!" Olive laughed, wiping the single tear that had escaped. "I dunno. Theatres here aren't quite the same as at home. There's no . . ." Olive twisted a bulb wondering if she could *make* it flicker, "atmosphere. And I'm missing Mr Green, of course."

"Mr Green," Lou giggled. "I still think he should have taken your name. Sounds so much better!"

"I know, but 'Olive Green' is and always will be my stage name. A perk of being an actor!"

"Is he going out there at any point?"

"We don't know yet. Just gotta wait and see how things pan out."

"Bloody actors," Lou muttered with sincerity which made Olive cackle until her eye caught the picture in the article again.

"They've used this picture from *When The Curtain Falls* in this magazine and I just can't stop looking at it, Lou. It's the one from the London version and it's just . . . weird. So much has changed since then."

"Blimey, that is a blast from the past. Almost a decade ago now, isn't it?"

"*Over* a decade! We look so young." Olive touched Oscar's face in the photo.

"You were so young! You've had a lot of ups and downs since that photo was taken but look! You're in NYC, playing another corking role to add to your never-ending list, and you and your fella will be back together again in no time."

*Ladies and gentlemen, this is your act one beginners call. This is your act one beginners call. Thank you.*

"Listen, Lou, I gotta go — but I'll call you when I'm back at the flat after the show because I need to know all about you and home! God, I miss home," Olive said, another tear or two escaping.

"Oh shush, home is boring. You're in the US of A! Blink and you'll miss it! Stop thinking about him. I know you've never really been separated for this long but he'll be fine. I'll make sure of it! SO MUCH LOVE!" Lou yelled down the phone.

"Love, love, love!" Olive said back but Lou had hung up before she pulled the phone away from her ear.

Olive ripped the article out of the magazine and pinned it to the corkboard at the side of her mirror. She slipped off her wedding ring, kissed it and put it alongside her necklace into a little pink ceramic jewellery dish she'd been given as an opening night present. With one more quick look in the mirror at her clean white dress, she turned her mirror lights off and then slid on her costume shoes ready for the opening scene. Olive took a slow and steady breath before opening her dressing room door and heading down to the stage for yet another opening night. As soon as the door closed, the light Olive had previously twisted turned itself back on.

"Could I get an extra Playbill, please?"

"Oooh, is that a British accent I hear?" said the usher, handing over the Playbill. Oscar Bright laughed.

"It is, yes." Oscar politely nodded his head but pulled his flat cap a little further over his eyes and quickly ducked away into the crowd that was filing into the auditorium, their chatter loud and their drinks sloshing to and fro. The nerves were starting to get to him. Ever since experiencing an opening night from the other side of the curtain, regardless of which side he sat now, everything inside him seemed to bubble. Although, ever since his West End debut, Oscar had stayed firmly off the stage and in front of the camera instead. A world in which he could redo takes until they captured the perfect one was much more suited to Oscar. These days, however, his role on British soap opera *Love Lane* was far less talked about than his work on set playing the sidekick in *Indiana Jane*, the new sequel to Indiana Jones, in which Indiana's daughter, Jane, takes over her father's daring archaeological adventures. Oscar played a sweet librarian who was not only extraordinarily helpful when it came to his extensive knowledge of history but also had a thirst for adventure himself, even if Jane was constantly digging him out of trouble. The first movie had been released earlier in the year and

Oscar found himself on a small break before shooting for the second would begin.

He checked his ticket three times. "M fourteen. M fourteen. Ah, here we are," he muttered to himself. "Sorry, could I . . .?" Oscar did his best to awkwardly slide past everyone already seated who did very little to help him until he plonked himself down in seat fourteen next to a smartly dressed elderly gentleman who, Oscar noticed, seemed to be alone.

"Do you come to the theatre much?" asked the man, taking off his glasses and giving them a clean with a cloth he produced from his top pocket.

"Quite a bit, yes." Oscar smiled, removed his hat and ran his fingers through his hair. "You?"

"As much as I can. Nothing quite like it, is there?"

"Absolutely not!" Oscar smiled, but it was then he heard a small gasp and his heart jumped. Instantly, his eyes scanned the audience around him until he locked eyes with two girls of, he guessed, around eighteen, sat four rows in front of him but firmly wedged in the centre of the stalls. He politely smiled; immediately the girls started scrambling through their bags and suddenly the occupants of the stalls had a mission put to them. Two tickets and a pen were passed from person to person, from row to row until the man in front of him, puzzled, looked up at the girls who were now standing and frantically waving, impossible to miss. They enthusiastically gave the man the thumbs-up so he handed the tickets and the pen to Oscar whose cheeks were now glowing so red he was sure the cast would still be able to see him from the stage when the lights went down. Oscar returned the thumbs-up to the girls and proceeded to sign the tickets.

"Are they friends of yours?" asked the elderly gentleman, chuckling at the swooning pair, one of whom had started to cry.

"Something like that." Oscar smiled, not wanting to be rude but also not too keen on explaining. Oscar passed the tickets back to the man in front who had been waiting but much to the girls' dismay, instead of passing on the freshly autographed tickets he said, "You don't know who this is, do you?" to the elderly man who was placing his glasses back on his nose.

The elderly man took a good look at Oscar but there was no recognition there at all. Just an apologetic smile. "I'm sorry — I . . . I don't!"

"No, please don't be sorry! I'm no one worth mentioning." Oscar smiled, fiddling with his flat cap in his lap, hoping the lights would go down soon.

"Don't be modest! This is the guy who's making a laughing stock out of the Indiana Jones franchise," the man in front scoffed and quickly turned back to the stage, passing the tickets and the pen along to the person in front of him. Oscar waved at the flustered girls when they received them and finally, they sat down. The elderly gentleman could sense Oscar's embarrassment and gave him a smile and a roll of his eyes at the man in front whom Oscar thought was no doubt feeling very smug. Just as the lights were going down, Oscar couldn't help himself. He leant forward and whispered in the man's ear, "Harrison Ford didn't seem to mind the new movie too much when I had dinner with him last week but hey, what does he know, eh, buddy?" Oscar patted his shoulder and sat back in his chair.

"Beautifully done," said the old man.

The show was an undeniable success. Well directed, with a tight and well rehearsed cast and impeccable acting but from no one more so than Olive Green. When she appeared to take the final bow, the members of the audience who weren't already on their feet jumped up like they were spring-loaded. Oscar put his fingers between his lips and whistled as loud as he could and there was a twinkle in Olive's eyes as she glanced towards M fourteen.

"Why are you even here?" snapped the man in front, flinching from Oscar's whistle. "Isn't theatre a little too intellectual for someone like you?"

"Oh, absolutely," Oscar said over the roar. "But you see that woman there? The one who this entire theatre is applauding?" Oscar made sure to lean over the man's shoulder and point Olive out, even though she was standing centre stage, taking the hands of her cast mates and bowing again.

"Oh, I see her," said the man, still applauding. "I plan on taking her home this evening."

"Oh, do you!" Oscar laughed.

"She and I have yet to be introduced but y'see, I'm the *producer's son.*" The man turned his head and flashed his teeth and Oscar felt a wonderful rush of triumph flood through his chest.

"Ah, well you see . . ." Oscar grinned from ear to ear and leant forward so the man had no chance of mishearing him, "I'm her husband." Even in the dim light, Oscar could see the man's face fall and he instantly stopped clapping. He collected his coat and quickly moved past the people in the row just as the cast disappeared and the lights went up so no one could see his drained face.

"I'm sorry, I couldn't help but overhear." The old man took hold of Oscar's arm, less to stop him leaving than because his aged legs had lost balance, but Oscar gladly held him steady. "Olive Green. She's your wife? She's unbelievable."

Oscar smiled. "Yes, she is."

"You're a lucky boy. I hope you know that." The old man patted Oscar's arm with a chuckle.

"Believe me," Oscar looked down at his Playbill where Olive's face smiled back at him, "I know."

317

# Acknowledgements

My acknowledgements always seem to span more pages than my chapters do so I'll try my hardest to keep this brief . . .

Firstly, a book isn't the creation of one sole person. Lots of minds go into making an idea a reality, so a huge thank you to Hannah Ferguson, for deciding my writing was worth showing to publishers; Manpreet Grewal and Hannah Boursnell, for deciding my writing was worth publishing; Stephanie Melrose, for travelling across the country with me and having a million different coloured sharpies to hand, and Amy Donegan, Sara Talbot, Thalia Proctor, Viola Hayden and Marie Hrynczak for taking care of all the things about book publishing that I just don't understand! And Bekki Guyatt and Helen Crawford-White, for making all my books look so beautiful. I love you all and please never think that your work goes unseen or unappreciated. I honestly couldn't ask for a more brilliant team.

Secondly, to all at Curtis Brown who watch with fear in their eyes as I say yes to everything and are then there to feed me Colin the Caterpillar sweets whilst I lie haphazardly on a chaise longue, close to tears because

I'm about to die from exhaustion (true story). You're at every opening night, every closing night and most nights in between. You're there for the ups and the downs, the sweets and the gin, the love and the laughs. Alastair, Helen, Fran, Jess, Emma, Emily and Flo — I can safely say I wouldn't have got anywhere without each and every one of you. The official dream team.

Thirdly, to my mad family. Mum and Dad, Tom and I are the product of YOU. The books, the shows, the songs, none of it would exist if it weren't for you. I hope you realise that. Tom, Gi, Buzz, Buddy and Bump AKA The Incredibles: you're a constant font of support, wisdom, creativity and inspiration. I don't know how you do it. And, of course, Nan and Grandad. Always brilliant, always funny, always there. Love you forever. ♡

Fourthly, to my *other* family. The thespians, the luvvies, the darlings. This whole book is based around what I know the theatre to be: warm and dazzling, which it wouldn't be if it weren't for the incredible people I'm surrounded by every day. So to the cast of every show I've ever been a part of, thank you for all the memories that will undoubtedly last a lifetime. If I'm being specific (and in no particular order . . . ) Mollie Melia Redgrave, Celinde Schoenmaker, Alex Banks, Rob Houchen, Jonny Vickers, Anton Zetterholm, Natasha Veselinovic, Jo Goodwin, Sam Harrison, Matt Gillet, Emma Kingston, Darren Bell, Marc McBride, Alex Parker, Tom Barnes, James Knight and many, many more!

However, I must say a special thank you to Scott Paige and Oliver Ormson. Scott, I've never known friendship like yours. Even though each time you visit my loaf of bread goes missing, I wouldn't wish it any other way. Absolutely no one on this little planet makes me laugh as big as you. Oliver . . . I don't have the words. Nothing I could write would be enough to encompass how overwhelmingly much you mean to me. I love you both.

Finally, a HUGE thanks to *you*. If you've ever read a book of mine or come to see a show I'm in, thank you from the bottom my heart. ♡

*XXX*

**Other titles published by Ulverscroft:**

# ALL THAT SHE CAN SEE

## Carrie Hope Fletcher

Cherry has a hidden talent. She can see things other people can't, and she decided a long time ago to use this skill to help others. As far as the rest of the town is concerned, she's simply the kind-hearted young woman who runs the local bakery — but in private she uses her gift to add something special to her cakes so that after just one mouthful, the townspeople start to feel better about their lives. They don't know why they're drawn to Cherry's bakery — they just know that they're safe there, and that's how Cherry likes it. And then Chase turns up and threatens to undo all the good she has done. Because it turns out Cherry is not the only one who can see what she sees . . .

# ON THE OTHER SIDE

## Carrie Hope Fletcher

Evie Snow is eighty-two when she quietly passes away in her sleep, surrounded by her children and grandchildren. It's the way most people wish to leave the world. But when Evie reaches the door of her own private heaven, she finds that she's become her twenty-seven-year-old self, and the door won't open. Evie's soul must be light enough to pass through, so she needs to get rid of whatever is making her soul heavy. For Evie, this means unburdening herself of the three secrets that have weighed her down for over fifty years, so she must find a way to reveal them before it's too late. As Evie begins the journey of a lifetime, she learns more about life and love than she ever thought possible.

# THE BINDING

## Bridget Collins

Emmett Farmer is working in the fields when a letter arrives summoning him to begin an apprenticeship. He will work for a book binder, a vocation that arouses fear, superstition and prejudice — but one neither he nor his parents can afford to refuse. He will learn to hand-craft beautiful volumes, and within each he will capture something unique and extraordinary: a memory. If there's something you want to forget, he can help. Your past will be stored safely in a book and you will never remember your secret, however terrible. In a vault under his mentor's workshop, row upon row of books — and memories — are meticulously stored and recorded. Then one day Emmett makes an astonishing discovery: one of them has his name on it . . .

# A DISTANT VIEW OF EVERYTHING

## Alexander McCall Smith

Recently distracted by the arrival of her and Jamie's second son, Magnus, Isabel Dalhousie, editor of the *Review of Applied Ethics*, has a lot to worry about, including the delayed next issue. It is with some relief, therefore, that she returns to helping out at her niece Cat's delicatessen, where surely the most taxing duty is the preparation of sandwiches. But it's not long before she's drawn into customers' problems, specifically that of ambitious self-proclaimed matchmaker Bea Shandon. Bea has staged a potentially dangerous liaison involving enigmatic plastic surgeon Tony MacUspaig, who may not be quite what he claims. Intrigued, Isabel dives into the mystery. And when the truth finally reveals itself, she must conclude that no one, including herself, is immune to misunderstandings, or the neurotic fantasies that arise from keeping secrets . . .